Affairs at Hampden Ferrers

Affairs at Hampden Ferrers
An English Romance

Brian Aldiss

LITTLE, BROWN

A *Little, Brown* Book

First published in Great Britain in 2004
by Little, Brown

Copyright © Brian Aldiss 2004

The moral right of the author has been asserted.

The author gratefully acknowledges permission to quote from the
Stanley Kubrick film, *2001: A Space Odyssey*, 1968, courtesy of Time Warner.

A CIP catalogue record for this book
is available from the British Library.

ISBN 0 316 72581 1

Typeset by Palimpsest Book Production Limited,
Polmont, Stirlingshire
Printed and bound in Great Britain by Mackays

Little, Brown
An imprint of
Time Warner Books UK
Brettenham House
Lancaster Place
London WC2E 7EN

www.TimeWarnerBooks.co.uk

To my friends at Wolfson
especially
Jon and Jill
Martin and Nicola
Douglas and Barbara

AD *2003*

An Absolutely Average Village

Report from the *Oxford Despatch*, 23 May 2003

Oxfordshire sprang a surprise on the world yesterday. The tiny English village of Hampden Ferrers (population: 770) to the south of Oxford was rejoicing. The local church of St Clement was built 1500 years ago yesterday, and as our picture shows, at the heart of the celebrations was the Vicar, the Rev. Robert Jolliffe, together with his wife, Susan.

The Vicar organised a committee over a year ago. Thanks to a loan by a Chinese businessman, Mr Shoe, there was wine and food in the village street for everyone, while the church will be almost entirely rebuilt. Mr Shoe's daughter said she was in an unusual position, and the committee has taken advantage of it.

More than one wedding took place to honour the event. Music was played, there was morris dancing and a donkey race. The village public houses were open all day, and fireworks closed an event of intense jollity.

Some years back, the *Oxford Despatch* voted Hampden Ferrers an 'Absolutely Average Village'. For many of its inhabitants this description remains. They live ordinary lives, dying, being born, working. We can only say we now vote Hampden Ferrers an Absolutely Marvellous Average Village! And we give our patriotic congratulations to the ancient British church of St Clement's. Long may it rain.

AD 2002

I

A Better Day

A man was walking in St Clement's cemetery in his dressing-gown. The dressing-gown was of silk, gold in colour with dragons chasing themselves over the left shoulder. It flapped open, despite the chill of dawn, to reveal a portly figure clad in old-fashioned flannel pyjamas with vertical blue stripes. His slippers were brand new, and of leather.

The man was of dark complexion, aged about seventy, and wore a goatee beard. His hands in his pockets, he wended his way between the gravestones. He might have been out for a morning stroll, were it not that he continually cast sharp glances to left and right.

The dawn was gloomy. Visibility was poor: The sky was overcast and the day misty. The tops of the nearby tall conifers faded into the heavy sky. Moss on the gravestones gleamed with moisture. Every blade of grass held a bead of water. The leather slippers squelched on the damp ground but the pyjama-clad figure was undeterred.

From the church porch, out of which a dull light shone, another figure emerged, walking briskly. He gave a grunt of surprise as he almost collided with the man

1

in the dressing-gown. 'Oh, good morning. Excuse me. You startled me!' For all his politeness, he scrutinised the man before him rather closely.

'You thought perhaps I was a revenant?' said the other. He folded his arms across his chest defensively.

'The church has stood for one thousand five hundred years. As far as I know, my parishioners will wait for the Last Trump before they return.' This was said quite straightforwardly, while the speaker continued to regard the visitor quizzically, his grizzled head slightly to one side. He was clad in a pair of dark trousers and a black sweater, which had come out at one elbow.

'Mm. You seem to know something about it,' said the visitor, sounding not particularly friendly.

'I certainly should. I am the Vicar of St Clement's. I fear I do not recognise you.'

'My apologies. I am not trespassing? My name is John Greyling. I am renting the little house across the road, the Pink House.'

'You are evidently an early riser, like me. Welcome to Hampden Ferrers. I am Father Robin – Father Robin Jolliffe.' The Vicar held out his hand. Greyling shook it, and muttered that he was pleased to meet him.

'This is a quiet little village. We had an unfortunate incident yesterday, a scuffle, but by and large we are peaceable in Ferrers, and the Lord smiles upon our community.'

Greyling seemed to make nothing of this remark.

In his left hand, the Vicar was clutching a shallow plastic bowl. He held it out for Greyling's inspection. 'This is one reason why I'm out so early. It's the best time to catch these rather nasty creatures.'

With an exclamation of disgust Greyling backed away from the thing that was wriggling in the bowl. 'What have you got there? A big worm? A small snake?'

'It's a big worm – a flatworm. It eats our native small worms. These flatworms come from New Zealand, so I'm told, though how they got to Hampden Ferrers I couldn't say. They are most unwelcome.'

The worm glistened. It was almost half a metre long, and broad. It strove blindly to escape from the bowl but always fell back at the rim.

The Vicar continued, 'It's almost too dim as yet to see clearly, but all the grass in this graveyard has died. It's tragic. Everything looks so bare. Whether or not it's due to the activities of these invading worms, I have no idea. I'm going to get a scientist from Oxford to investigate the matter.'

Greyling took another look at the worm. 'You're going to kill the bloody thing?'

The Vicar shook his head. 'I let nature do that for me. I shall place it on my lawn in the bowl and the birds will eat it. I shan't let my wife see it.'

Greyling wrapped his robe about his body, dismissing the subject as of no further interest. 'Don't you have any fresh graves here? These are all from earlier centuries.' He gestured towards the ancient stones nearby.

The Vicar contemplated them with a proprietorial air. 'The latest headstone standing here is dated AD 1921, when a parishioner wounded on the Somme passed away, rest his soul. Newer graves lie on the stretch of land at the rear of the church. Are you looking for anyone in particular?'

Greyling replied evasively that he had arrived only during that week to take up his tenancy of the Pink House. He was simply looking round.

The Vicar, perhaps desiring a more precise answer, remarked that this was a chilly time to be out in one's pyjamas.

3

'I've still got a touch of jet lag,' Greyling said, 'and I will take up no more of your time.'

'Very well. May I hope to see you in church some time, Mr Greyling?'

Greyling did not answer. He had already turned away.

The encounter in the village churchyard was watched by a woman peering from behind the net curtain at her bedroom window. She occupied the upper floor of a house known simply as Number Twelve. Number Twelve stood opposite the Pink House. It was at least three centuries old: not particularly ancient by Hampden Ferrers standards.

After the two men had disappeared she remained at her window, peering out at the deserted scene. A street-light cast a yellow glow that smeared itself over the mist. Birds were singing. As she knew, they sang all night long, their circadian rhythm upset by the street-lighting. Marion Barnes could remember the days when there had been no street-lighting in the village.

At last she turned back into her room. The double bed, which until a year ago had accommodated both her and her husband, now dead, was occupied by a large black Labrador, Laurel by name.

'I'm going to get some tea, Laurel. Come on, girl.'

The dog's claws clicked on the bare floorboards as she followed her mistress out of the room to the rear landing, where a skeletal kitchen had been improvised. Marion peered from the little window across the garden to the rear road, Cotes Road, where the grander houses of the village stood. No one was about, and she was glad of that: the fight at the pub the previous evening had upset her and made her nervous.

She wore a light cotton dressing-gown over her old

4

nightdress. She was thin and growing bent. Her face was drawn; she had never been a cheerful woman and since Arnold's death her sense that life had cheated her had spilled into the open.

She switched on a twenty-watt light, set her kettle on the old-fashioned gas ring, then took down from a shelf an open tin of dog food and scooped the contents into the dog's bowl. She patted Laurel as the animal set to, jowls slapping against the side of the bowl. 'There's a good girl. You're a good girl, Laurel.' The dog did not respond but continued determinedly to eat.

The kettle began to sing.

A survey in the local Oxford paper, the *Oxford Despatch*, had declared Hampden Ferrers, referred to in the Domesday Book as Molesey, 'An Absolutely Average Village'. That had been five years ago. In that time, averages had ceased to apply. Nevertheless, the village bore a resemblance to many other villages in the area, not least in its antiquity.

Certainly it had remained the same in outline for centuries. It consisted of three streets. Highest on the gentle slope on which it was built was Cotes Road, named after the local farm. It connected at both ends to the high street, where the church and the better of the two public houses stood, amid many smaller houses, built mainly of local stone. Clement's Lane led off this main thoroughfare, to peter out in the cul-de-sacs of a small estate after it had passed the Bear, the pub humbler members of the community preferred.

The Molesey Hills rose above Cotes Road and the Hampden brook ran southwards from them. It passed under bridges on the high street and Clement's Lane on its way to join the river Ock near Marcham. A small river – 'hardly worth drowning in', as Jeremy Sumption, one of Ferrers's inhabitants, once remarked.

The day of the old kind of labourer, to accommodate whom the village had been largely built, was over. Most of the present inhabitants of Hampden Ferrers had academic connections in Oxford, only five miles away down what, within living memory, had been a country road. One of the most notable lived in a grand house at the west end of Cotes Road. He was an historian, Francis Martinson, a member of Wolfson College. He was in his late thirties, and had published several books on historical subjects, the best-known being *The Myth of Cities* and *Failed States in Medieval Times*. Now he had out a more popular volume entitled *Forgiveness*; in selling well, it added both to his bank balance and his self-esteem. Nevertheless, he was slightly nervous now, as he ate a strawberry yoghurt and drank coffee for breakfast. With him at the table was his brother, Fred. Fred said nothing: he suffered from Down's syndrome, and was already declining into middle age although he was only thirty-four – younger than his spruce brother who sat opposite him.

Frank addressed him while Fred tucked into a mountain of toast and patum peperium: 'Freddy, I'll be off in a few minutes. Nurse Ann will be here in a little while to look after you. I'm going to drive to Wolfson, so I won't be very far away.'

'Are you going to go abroad again?' Fred asked.

'No. Just to Wolfson. I must prepare for a meeting with a certain Maria Caperalli, Contessa of Medina Mirtelli.'

'Is she foreign?'

'Maria is from Italy. She will be in Oxford to give a lecture at Wolfson tomorrow.'

'Will I meet her?'

6

'I hope so, Freddy. She's very glamorous.'

'Oh. Will she like me?'

'Of course she will,' said Frank. 'I've met her only once, sixteen years ago, but I was much impressed by her then and we have intermittently kept in touch.'

'Did she come here?'

'No, Freddy. But I hope she will visit West End – and meet you – in the next day or two. I am planning a party for her. The catering has been arranged.'

He could not help asking himself if romance would bloom. Or would Maria turn out to be like Flora Finching in Dickens's novel? He could not but hope that she would more resemble the Marie of Dickens's youth, who had turned out to be 'a pocket Venus'.

As Frank rose from his table, he realised he had eaten without tasting the yoghurt. He patted his brother's shoulder and said goodbye.

Before he left he fed his goldfish in the ornamental garden pool. Sunlight glinted on their backs as they swam in leisurely shoals, heading first one way then another, unanimously, seemingly without intention. Some instinct, Frank Martinson reflected, must guide the little fish, yet who could say what without becoming a goldfish? And even then? He smiled at his thoughts. A similar sense of the inscrutable might well afflict anyone surveying the human beings working out their destinies between Ferrers and Oxford.

The fish accepted their crumbs without excitement: they were well fed. Then they wheeled and drifted in two different shoals across the expanse of the pool, swimming just below the surface, hardly disturbing it. Frank contemplated them for another minute, then turned, climbed into his Daimler and headed for Wolfson.

As he reached the gates, a cyclist approached. Nurse

7

Ann Longbridge waved cheerfully to him. He waved back. That reliable lady would look after Fred.

A line of houses of various sizes, with the pub, the Carpenter's Arms, ran along opposite the church to form the high street of Hampden Ferrers. Where the street curved, a close led up to the Manor, a well-set-up Georgian mansion. (The previous house on that spot had burnt down in a fire early in the nineteenth century.) It presented a four-square appearance, its pillared porch set in the middle of the façade, with two windows of good proportion on either side. It rose to three storeys in mellow red brick, cornered with stone, the size of the windows diminishing with each flight. The chimneys were grouped at either end of the roof, emphasizing the symmetry; they were merely decorative now, since the village had been declared a smokeless zone.

The Manor was a symbol of stability, but something of its grandeur had been stolen. Its first owners, the old Ferrers family, had fallen on hard times after the First World War, when Sir Austin Ferrers had died on the battleship *Irresistible* in the early days of the Gallipoli campaign, in 1915. Manorial land had been sold off and now the house was hedged in by a Hellespont of new housing. The manor was owned by Stephen and Sharon Boxbaum.

Mrs Andrea Ridley, who lived next door to it, let herself in at the back door with her key promptly at seven thirty that morning. She had brought with her a paper bag containing fresh croissants. The mist was clearing, the sun struggling to break through, although the day remained drab for early May. She switched on a light in the rear passage before going into the kitchen to prepare breakfast for the family. She switched on more lights and then the radio, which she tuned to BBC Radio Two. Sharon always tuned it to Radio Four.

A ginger cat appeared, stretching as it came.

'Hello, Bingo! Where have you been?'

The cat answered with a yawn, showing its spiky teeth. Andrea went to the fridge-freezer and brought out a slice of fish. As Bingo tucked into it, she bustled into the dining room and drew back the heavy velvet curtains. The newspaper boy, Sammy Aziz, was propping his bike against the pillars of the porch, about to deliver the Boxbaums' *Independent* and *Financial Times*. She waved to him. 'A nice polite boy,' she said to herself. He waved back. The papers landed in the hall. She collected them and placed them on the long table in the library.

When Sharon Boxbaum came downstairs, the breakfast table was already laid. 'Oh, you're wonderful, Andrea! Where you find the time I don't know. How's Duane?' Duane was Andrea's son.

'He's much better, thanks, Sharon, but I'm keeping the bandages on for a while. The queers stood on his arm. It was all ever so unfortunate. It was just a bit of a scrap, really. The demon drink, you know. Duane's really not a quarrelsome boy, like. And Rupert? How's he getting on?'

The two women had a common problem: their sons.

Duane Ridley had been in a slanging match outside the Carpenter's Arms, which had later developed into a fight with the two homosexuals living next to his parents' house. Rupert Boxbaum had declared that he was quitting university in favour of becoming a pop musician, to his father's distress.

While the women were still talking about the fight, Stephen Boxbaum entered the room, clutching his newspapers. A narrow shaft of sunlight had struck the room, slicing between the side of the Manor and the semi-detached next door. He gave his wife a nod, and apologized for not having shaved as he did most mornings. Stephen was a well-built man. He exercised every day, mainly by swimming in his pool. In his early sixties, he had taken to wearing steel-rimmed spectacles. He was dressed casually in a yellow and brown sweater.

'It's going to be a better day,' Sharon said. 'The fog is already clearing. But you look like it's disaster time. What's the matter with you?'

'It *is* disaster time.' He thumped the headlines of the *Independent*. 'Israeli disaster time. This madman, Ariel Sharon, is shelling Arafat's HQ in Ramallah. Can't he understand that violence just begets violence?'

'This time the Jews are fighting back, not just caving in.' Sharon spoke feelingly. Her grandfather had died in Auschwitz-Birkenau. 'Arafat has to get off Israeli territory, the way I see it.'

Stephen grunted to himself and took his chair at the head of the table. 'It's always a question of land. *Lebensraum*. As in Zimbabwe, come to that.'

Andrea was bringing in the teapot, and Stephen asked her what she made of the fighting in Israel.

'I don't know, sir. It's none of my business. Look at the way they carry on in Ireland. It's partly to do with religion, isn't it?'

'Partly,' he said, and opened the paper. 'Quite right.'

Sharon passed him the muesli.

They were a middle-aged couple, and both had been married before. Sharon inclined towards the skeletal. Her dyed fair hair was coiled upwards to resemble the frill on the side of a Cornish pastie; it was attended to regularly at the Salon Française, the local hairdresser. It framed a wide, doleful face, of which her clear grey eyes were the best feature. Stephen, twenty years his wife's senior, was a spare, dapper man, almost as slender as his wife. His high fore-head perhaps counterbalanced the bald patch developing towards the back of his head. He was a fellow of New College, and moderately well-known as a professor of law.

'There's no stability anywhere. How is it that no nation has ever managed to achieve just laws and wise foreign policies, with sufficient food production, equally distrib-uted, to sustain itself for – well, for a meagre five centuries, let's say? That means, of course, without slavery or other forms of oppression. It has never happened.'

'China?' Sharon hazarded.

'China's the best example of which one can think. Even then, women were oppressed, deliberately malformed to suit masculine taste.'

Sharon reached for the toast. 'I would say that the tides of human wickedness preclude Utopia.' She gave him a sick look.

'All of that, doubtless. Nevertheless, horrendous things, inexplicable and unaccountable, happen in history. Who can say why? Who can actually pinpoint the reason? Maybe the solar system periodically travels through poisonous interstellar gas . . .' He grimaced as he spoke.

Sharon laughed, uncomfortable with the memories stirred by the mere word 'gas'. 'So not the vengeance of Jahweh, then . . .'

'I think we can rule Jahweh out. Nasty but scarcely powerful enough.'

The Earth continued to rotate: the narrow strip of sunlight disappeared from the dining room as the shoulder of the next-door house intercepted it.

Opposite the neat houses of the Willetts Estate (built 1951–2) were two of more ancient vintage: the village shop and post office, and a cottage. The morning sun,

11

now gaining both strength and height, poured through the windows of the cottage, where Jeremy Sumption was taking a shower. Jeremy had a hangover. He stood under the spray of hot water, resting his head against the white tiling and breathing deeply.

He was not pleased when he heard the ring of his front-door bell.

'Perhaps it's FedEx,' he said, switched off the water and wrapped a towel about his waist. Hurrying downstairs, he left a trail of damp footsteps on the carpet. He unlocked and opened the front door.

'Your milk, sir!' announced the man – a stranger, not the milkman – standing outside, offering Jeremy his usual pint bottle.

Not pleased, Jeremy took the bottle, which the milkman had left on his doorstep. He asked the man what he wanted.

The caller was wearing a heavy tweed suit with a green shirt and matching tie. His neat goatee beard had strands of grey in it.

'Perhaps this is an awkward moment at which to call.' He looked the naked Jeremy up and down without approval. 'It is now ten past ten. I see you are a late riser.'

Taking this as a reproof, Jeremy repeated his question.

'I happen to be looking for a certain lady.'

'Oh, are you? Well, this is a lady-free zone, believe you me.' He attempted to close the door, but the man put his shoulder against it.

'You are Mr Sumption, aren't you?'

Jeremy admitted that this was the case.

'Excuse me. I am one of your readers.' He smiled.

'You'd better come in.' Jeremy was mollified. 'Hang about. I must get some trousers on.' He showed the stranger into the small front room, where the sunlight

12

illuminated the iMac computer and untidy stacks of papers, then rushed upstairs. He crammed himself into trousers and a sweater, frightened all the while that the stranger might steal something – although he didn't know of anything that might be worth stealing.

Going to put on his trainers, he found they were caked with mud. The previous night he had been up on the Molesey Hills on one of his 'amorous expeditions', as he called them.

'Well, what can I do for you?' He was downstairs now, running a comb though his lank dark hair as he spoke.

The stranger had seated himself in the only armchair. 'I should explain that I am newly arrived in the village. My name is Greyling, John Greyling. I seek someone I once knew before I spent some years abroad.'

'Can't help, I'm afraid. Do you want some coffee? I'm going to get myself some.'

'Thank you. May I smoke a cigarette?'

'Huh! If you give me one.'

When the cigarettes were lit, Jeremy retreated to the kitchenette at the rear of the cottage. Greyling followed.

'Bit of a mess here, I'm afraid. That's what comes of living alone. I don't really belong in Hampden Ferrers. As a matter of fact, I'm in the middle of a messy divorce. Which of my books have you read?'

Greyling drew heavily on his cigarette, then flicked ash into the sink. 'In your thriller *Piggy Bank*, you have a woman who gets shot whose name is Dickson.'

'I've forgotten. You make up names as you go along. Anyhow, I'm trying to give up writing thrillers. I'm on what you might call a Gogol kick – if you've heard of Gogol, Nicolai Gogol, which is more than anyone else in Hampden has. Everyone is so ill-educated, these days. Squalor and humour – that's my style.'

13

The kettle boiled. He switched it off. As he poured the hot water into two mugs containing instant coffee granules, he added, 'Gogol can be very funny. He talks somewhere of a chap sleeping well because he knows nothing of haemorrhoids, fleas or strongly developed intellectual faculties.'

Laughing, he flipped the top off the milk-bottle and added milk into the two mugs.

Greyling made nothing of Gogol. 'So you don't know any woman called Dickson? You never did?'

Jeremy passed him one of the mugs, handle forward. 'You could ask the Vicar, Father Robin Jolliffe. Very nice guy. I'm an atheist but he treats me as a valued parishoner. I really appreciate that.'

'I met Father Robin earlier this morning. He tells me that his church is one thousand five hundred years old. Can that be so?'

'Search me. I suppose so. What's it matter? I don't go to church.' He stubbed out his cigarette. 'I had a drink with Father Robin once.'

The doorbell rang again.

'Ah, could be FedEx with my proofs. Nice to have met you anyway.'

Greyling took the hint. He set down the mug, at which he had only sipped. 'Thank you for your hospitality. We shall maybe meet again.'

'Great!' exclaimed Jeremy, and headed for the door.

II

Hidden City

Stephen Boxbaum was driving his BMW back from Oxford. As Professor of the Science of Societies, and a legal historian, he had spent the morning working in the Bodleian Library, researching de Tocqueville's attitude to bourgeois life and legality for a paper he was preparing. As he crossed the bridge and entered the high street, he slowed and stopped. A number of carelessly parked cars was choking the main thoroughfare, centring on St Clement's Church, where a marriage ceremony had just taken place.

Stephen sat with his elbow on the steering-wheel, staring at the lively scene, smiling unconsciously. Bride and groom were standing before the porch, kissing each other with enthusiasm. Guests were cheering. One or two couples, carried away by the joy of the occasion, were also embracing. Everyone looked smart and cheerful.

How pleasant it would be to be madly in love again, was his thought. But 'madly', alas, he never had been . . .

It came to Stephen, in a sudden gush of emotion, how greatly he loved England, the country that had adopted

15

him. Other Boxbaums, distantly related, had gone on to America, often to great prosperity, but Stephen, brought here at the age of four by his parents fleeing Nazi Germany, had stayed.

His mind drifted to another church, distant in Macedonia. He had travelled in the previous year to the city of Veles, in the centre of that country, to enquire about legal handicaps experienced by Jews and other minorities during the disruptions of the twentieth century. There, he had visited the main church, Sveti Pantelimon, the centre of Orthodox worship in the region. The aged building badly needed funds for restoration. Stephen had gone to a collection box, preparing to stuff in a twenty-dollar bill, when his guide had stopped him, clutching his wrist. 'Thank you, sir, for your kind thought,' said the guide, 'but you are not a worshipper here. You do not believe, so you may not help. Pardon.'

Stephen had accepted this and did not complain.

From an outside vantage-point, overlooking a courtyard and a side entrance to the church, he had stood contemplating the tranquil scene, with its distant view of the valley of the river Vardar. A newly married couple, smartly dressed, had come gaily out of the side entrance, accompanied by friends and witnesses. Their laughter carried faintly to him. They had scarcely disappeared, rejoicing, when a second party arrived from the opposite direction. This was a sad group. Six people, five men and a woman, appeared, wearing black. Two of the men were carrying a stretcher, on which lay a corpse covered by a tarpaulin. They moved slowly, approaching the side entrance of the church, into which they disappeared. The episode might well have featured in an opera, such as *Cavalleria Rusticana*, so patly came the contrast between life and death.

16

Now an urgent hooting roused Stephen from his musing. In his rear-view mirror he saw a car close behind him. Rebuking himself, he drove on hastily. As he turned into Manor Close, he caught a glimpse of a woman at the wheel of the other car. She was a Mrs Penelope Hopkins but he did not know her personally.

It happened that he met Mrs Hopkins later that day, while Sharon was suffering one of her migraines. She lay on the chaise longue in the library with a damp cloth over her face. Bingo rested quietly on her lap. Stephen made her a cup of Lapsang Souchong. As she propped herself up and sipped it, she asked her husband to go to Hill's Stores and buy a loaf of bread.

He strolled along the high street in the afternoon sunshine. Hill's had once been owned by Frederick Hill, a grocer well known for molesting all the young ladies who worked for him. One of them, indeed, Alice Longbridge, had become his wife. Both Hills were now dead, and the shop was run by Mr and Mrs Aziz. Mr Aziz was behind his till now, counting out change for Penelope Hopkins. Sam Aziz had an unblemished reputation with young ladies, possibly because his wife kept a close eye on him.

Penelope Hopkins turned with her carrier-bag and saw Stephen Boxbaum. He stood, hesitating, in the doorway, smiling at her.

'Oh, Mr Boxbaum,' she said. 'I do apologise for hooting at you this morning. I'm afraid I was in a terrible rush to get home. I wasn't thinking.'

He nodded. 'Quite all right. I was in a daydream and blocking the traffic. As a matter of fact, I was looking at the wedding.'

'Yes, perfect for a May day like today. *A Village Wedding*. Isn't there an opera of that name?'

'If not, there certainly should be.'

He liked what he saw of this lady. Penelope Hopkins was of slight build, probably in her mid-fifties, with a wild shock of black hair and a winning expression. A proud nose and a high forehead made her face memorable. She was untidily dressed in a loose dark blue two-piece suit. On impulse, he asked her to have coffee with him to show there were no hard feelings.

She agreed. He bought a brown harvest loaf from Mr Aziz, and they adjourned to the little pâtisserie next to the shop. There, a good cup of coffee was to be had. A young couple seated at a table were arguing the merits or demerits of something as they drank Coke.

It was sunny enough now and warm enough to sit at a rather rickety table on the pavement. A foreign man, possibly Spanish, brought the coffee out on a tray.

'Do you mind if I smoke?' Penelope asked, as they made themselves comfortable. Stephen acquiesced. The cups were pale blue, with a gold band round the rim. The brown sugar came in lumps, in a blue bowl, not in narrow packets. 'I'm rather hard-pressed, to tell the truth,' she went on. 'I have an hour off and then I must get back to work. I was in a hurry to get home and pay my cleaner.'

'Oh, please stay a little longer. Can't your cleaner wait?'

'She's a foreign woman. I rarely see her. I feel ashamed . . . I generally leave her money on the kitchen table but I forgot this morning.' Penelope exhaled smoke and smiled at him rather questioningly.

'Why should you feel ashamed?'

'Well!' She laughed. 'Because I only give her money. She gives me service. Also, I feel bad about not seeing her and perhaps talking to her. I suppose it's too commercial an arrangement for my liking.'

18

'Unfortunately some arrangements are like that.'

Perhaps she felt that this was not a sufficient response. 'She's an immigrant, this cleaner of mine. I know she's poor – she must be to engage in such jobs as house-cleaning. Her name is Zadanka. I don't know her surname. She comes from Croatia, I believe. On the Aegean coast, I think.'

He had been watching her small gestures and thinking how elegant she was. 'Actually, the Adriatic coast. Croatia lies on the Adriatic.'

'I meant Adriatic.' Apparently not pleased to be corrected, she changed tack. 'You are a professor of law, I hear, Mr Boxbaum. It's odd we have not met before but, then, I'm always at work.' She sighed, then repeated, looking up at him from under her eyelashes, 'Always at work . . .'

'My wife and I have been at the Manor only two years. Two years and two months. I'm quite often abroad – my work. How long have you lived here, Mrs Hopkins?'

'Years and years.' She laughed again, rather curtly. She sipped her coffee and studied him over the rim of the cup. 'You're not as I imagined you.'

He regarded her good-humouredly over his spectacles. 'And what were you up to, imagining me?' he said, then realised the words might be construed as flirtatious.

Nimbly, she couched her reply in the abstract. 'One thinks that law historians are, in general, rather serious people. After all, study of the miseries and injustices of the past are enough to make anyone solemn.'

Stephen chose to change the subject. 'What do you do in life, Mrs Hopkins? What keeps you so busy?'

She said she worked at Brookes University in Headington. She was the overseas enrolments officer; many of their students came from abroad. The job kept her well occupied. 'In fact, it keeps me busy right now.' She rose. 'I must get back to Brookes. Excuse me. Thanks for the coffee, Mr Boxbaum, and for forgiving me the toot at your car. It was nice meeting you.' She picked up her carrier-bag, then paused, as if waiting for something more.

'You may toot at me at any time,' he said, then took her hand, saying that they must meet again.

'Yes, I'd like that,' she said, with unthinking enthusiasm. She turned away abruptly.

'I'd like it too,' he said, in a whisper to himself.

He stood in the sun, clutching his loaf, and watched Penelope's departure. She wore a pair of elegant calf-length boots, and her garments flapped about her. He admired her confident walk. She turned right, down Clement's Lane, the little road that wound behind the church with views down the hill.

'So that's where she lives,' he said to himself. 'If only I deserved someone like that . . .'

In the afternoon, Marion Barnes was walking Laurel. She had taken her through Knoleberry Park, keeping her on the lead so that she could not run off. She pulled the dog close when she saw two boys approaching. There was always the fear of a mugging. Young men had been fighting only recently, as she knew . . .

The boys passed her without a sideways glance, deeply involved in conversation about a dealer they knew. It came to Marion immediately that they must have been talking about a drug dealer.

Only when she drew near the church did she say to herself, 'It might have been a car dealer.'

Feeling lonely, Marion called on the vicar.

Father Robin Jolliffe, his wife and two sons lived in a small stone house close to the church. Robin was sitting in his parlour in his favourite chair, his stockinged feet lodged on the edge of the table, his hands behind his head, thinking comfortably about precious little.

A hand-delivered note lay on the table beside him. It was addressed to him and read,

> 'We have had nothing but snubs since we came to Hampden. We were married in the Netherlands legally. We keep ourselves to ourselves. Now we have been attacked by a thug who lives next to us and another young yob who calls himself Starman. Both should be arrested. Who knows what will happen next? We accuse you of also being homophobic. A bad influence on the village. We hate this village. Oxford is much better.
>
> Eric Horbridge and Teddy Caird.

Father Robin had sighed when he read it. He had shown it to Sonia, his wife. He had no prejudice against gays, although the idea of two men marrying each other seemed ludicrous to him. He understood they had been in a drunken brawl on the previous evening and had got the worst of it. And nothing could be done.

His small room was decorated with a framed Hokusai print of *The Wave*, and photographs of his wife and their two boys in various stages of growth. When his front-door bell rang, he rose and opened the door. He asked Mrs Barnes, affably, what he could do for her.

'I came to see how you were, Father. Are you well? I thought you were looking a bit peaky on Sunday,' she said, as the Labrador snuffled and whined by her side.

21

He pretended puzzlement. 'I didn't see you in church on Sunday, Marion.'

She clucked. 'Oh, Father, now, you know what I mean. You know I never visit your church. I'm not a believer.'

He asked her dutifully if she would like a cup of tea. 'Sorry about my stockinged feet.'

She tied Laurel to the boot-scraper by the front door and almost skipped over the threshold into the Vicar's dark little hall.

'Sonia not at home?'

'She teaches down the road, Marion, as you well know. A parson's stipend is meagre – and rightly so. It keeps a man humble, and in touch with his God. But his poor wife is driven to supplement the family income. It's a case of squeezing from Caesar what is Caesar's.' His intonation was flat, with an element of self-mockery, as was often the case.

'I hope you don't gamble,' she said, with downturned mouth.

'Not unless you count a quid each way on a filly in the two-thirty as gambling.'

Marion said disapprovingly that he should not joke about such matters.

'Oh, but I should, Mrs Barnes. One need not take the material world seriously. Render unto Caesar and all that, but don't be afraid to pull Caesar's leg.'

'What an idea! I suppose you approve of the government's intention to open casinos everywhere.'

The Vicar pretended to look worried, and cast glances to all corners of his little hall. 'Everywhere? You don't mean they're going to open a casino in Hampden Ferrers, do you?'

She clucked again, then said he knew perfectly well what she meant.

Robin led the way to the bright chintzy kitchen. He made the tea with Ty-Phoo teabags, and slipped a plain wholemeal biscuit onto Marion's saucer.

She told him it was ever so kind of him, and ate the biscuit immediately.

Robin replied that it was his duty to look after all parishioners, whether or not they were believers. If he kept them well enough nourished, he said, they might one day find their faith in Jesus. 'The disciples were always eating and drinking, Marion, according to the New Testament, Wine, loaves and fishes . . . Goodness me, happily the Gospels pass over the next-to-Last Supper.'

Marion seemed not to enjoy his way of being half in jest. 'How do you expect me to believe in God when he took my Arnold away from me? And after what was inflicted on me in my childhood, shut in that awful cupboard? Ask yourself that, Father,' she snapped.

'I do, and I reply to myself that God always gives us the opportunity to live our lives anew, to set us on another path, whether we think we like it or not.'

'I'm too old to be set on another path, as you call it, Father. Where would I find another path to be set on? Not here in Hampden Ferrers, that's for sure.'

'But, Marion, my dear, we always retain the power – do we not? – to choose the happiness that is next to godliness, however much we may feel ourselves sinned against.'

'I am not able to forgive them as harmed me. That is my nature now.' She spoke rather proudly. 'I am too old, too heartbroken, to change anything.'

The Vicar sat with his hands folded in his lap, watching her intently, not without a gleam of sympathetic humour in his eyes. He leaned forward.

'But you bought yourself a new computer, didn't you?

23

That sounds to me, an ignorant man, very much like a new start in life, if on a modest scale. But every journey starts with the first step. How are you getting on with it? Do you know which buttons to press?'

Marion Barnes brightened. Her brow cleared momentarily, and he saw in her worn countenance something of the young woman she had once been. She said that the computer was different. It gave her something to do. She was proud to say she was getting on well and had even mastered email.

'Well, there you are, Marion! It's a new path for you. Congratulations.'

'I did it without God's help. God knows nothing about email.'

'You must cling to your disbelief, Marion, as long as you enjoy the discomfort it brings you.'

She took another sip of tea, and essayed a grin at him. The vicar declared that he would come over to her house some time and get her to send an email to his bishop, asking for better pay.

'Who was it you was talking to early this morning, Vicar? I happened to glance out my window and there you was, talking to some funny chap.'

'That was no "funny chap", that was John Greyling. He's renting the Pink House, he tells me. He was looking at gravestones. An odd hobby, some might think.'

'You shouldn't be up at that early hour, Vicar. It's bad for your health.'

'I'm nearer to my God at that hour, Marion. There are no parishioners to distract me, to come between me and Him.'

'Oh, you . . .' She let the sentence dangle. She did not smile, although he was beaming benevolently at her. She thought that perhaps he meant what he said.

24

She endeavoured to believe that what he said was true. Or not true. He was a bit of a joker, was the Vicar. It was nothing to do with her.

She drank the last of her tea, then set down the cup gently in its saucer. 'Very nice, thank you, Vicar.'

As they got to the door, he advised her not to be lonely. 'God is always with you. Or, failing that, you can always come and see me. Regard me as His wicket-keeper.'

The Vicar closed the door on Marion's back and returned to his parlour, where he resumed his previous position, ignoring the note on the table.

He must remind Sonia to get some more digestive biscuits from Hill's.

Then there was the Sunday sermon to be thought about. Robin groaned. He put on his slippers and walked outside through the kitchen door, picking up a biscuit on the way. Ideas were easier to come by in the garden, once he had banished the thought that he should mow the lawn. The confounded moles were throwing up their earthworks again.

The vicarage garden was rather overgrown. A football lay in long grass. Unable to afford a gardener, Robin and Sonia managed it themselves, with occasional grudging assistance from one of their sons. Three old apple trees, planted in the days of the young Queen Victoria, inter-locked branches in vegetable friendship, perhaps in memory of Old Times.

All the gardens round about, long established, supported mature trees. As Robin often said, they might have been living in a forest. He liked the idea: it increased the sense of life's mystery.

A squirrel had ventured precariously out on to an apple branch. Robin stopped and stared at it. The squirrel stared

25

back. Thought processes were working in both mammals. Cautiously, Robin broke off a piece of his biscuit and offered it upwards. Eventually, the squirrel decided there was nothing to be gained by hanging about. It turned and was away like lightning up the tree.

Ah, thought Robin, all things work towards God . . . The grey squirrel regards the man. An opportunity for communication opens. The man intends no harm to the little creature, yet it turns away and is lost. So we turn away from God. We are too busy, or we fear His majesty . . .

He hurried back into the house, to his study and his old typewriter.

The Pink House had become a paler and paler pink as year succeeded year. A rose that once had flourished over the porch had died. Ivy had climbed to the roof to entangle itself with the guttering. Rainwater, spilling from the guttering, had soaked down to one of the upper windows, whose frame was rotting. Curtains had been drawn across the panes. The house gave the sardonic wink of an old *roué*.

Inside, the theme of desolation continued: it was chilly and damp. A framed oleograph of a plump woman disguised as Cleopatra hung in the hall. Such furniture as there was had been selected arbitrarily, bought here and there from junk shops. Only in the kitchen was there some comfort to be had. A rug, patterned and thread-bare, lay on the floor. A small oil-fired Rayburn had been installed within recent years.

Enjoying some of the warmth from this oven, John Greyling sat at the kitchen table. He was working at a laptop and smoking a Marlboro, whose ash he shook into a saucer by his right elbow.

26

The warmth had permitted him to remove his heavy jacket, which hung on the back of his chair. He sat in his shirtsleeves.

From a small portable radio came strains of Wagner.

Through the window above the sink, he could see the sun shining fitfully on a nettle-crowned bank, and on the tiled roofs and chimneys of houses beyond. The houses appeared, to a casual eye, to be half buried by the bank in the foreground.

Greyling had received an email, which read:

My dear darling Peter – Why you do not answer? I hope you receive this. Will you be in Berlin as you hope? Things in Buenos Aires are even worse since you are left. The country is in a collapse with its finances. I must to escape. People sometimes are hammering at my door. I had fear they shall break in. So I rent the apartment for very little to some person and now am I in Montevideo, where I stay with my sister Isobel in her flat. It is so terrible what happens. I have no money. I lose touch with Juan. Please return soon. Then we will be happy again. With love, Natalie

Greyling finished his cigarette, looking out at the weed-choked back garden. He typed in a reply to his wife.

Natalie – Please remain calm. I am happy to hear you have moved to Montevideo. You will be safer there, with your sister. Uruguay is a good country. I hope you got a lawyer to draw up a contract for the rental of the BA apartment. I am in London, busy but I hope successful. Excuse brevity. Management meeting about to take place. Do not email me again. Danger of censorship. Kisses, Peter

He arose and walked up and down the passage, thinking, trying to plan. Soon he must go out to eat. As he paraded, a slim magazine was pushed through his letterbox. He went to the front door and picked it up. It was the *Parish Pump*, the monthly magazine of St Clement's Church. Greyling tossed it irritably aside.

Towards evening, Hampden Ferrers people who worked in Oxford returned to their homes. The main road was at its busiest. Lights came on in windows. Trade picked up in the pubs. Sam Aziz called his wife, Rima, into the shop to help serve and look out for thieves pocketing the goods.

Among those returning were the two homosexuals who lived at number twenty-two, driving back from the science labs of Oxford University, and Dorothy Ridley, commonly known as Dotty. Dotty drove her Renault Clio into the parking space in front of the Ridleys' house, number twenty on the Willetts Estate. Her mother, Andrea, was at home, and gave her a quick hug, saying she would put the kettle on and get out the Battenburg cake.

Both mother and daughter were all smiles as they went into the well-ordered kitchen-diner. A small television set was burning bright in one corner of the room: two funny animals were knocking the stuffing out of each other. Duane was sitting on a stool at the counter, his left arm still bandaged, reading a trucking magazine. He turned it over, open but face down on the counter, as he greeted his sister.

'Hi! Made your fortune yet?'

'Not yet. Tomorrow, most likely.'

As Andrea was pouring water on to the instant coffee

in their mugs, a cat appeared at the window, pressing its face against the pane and mewing.

'Oh, it's that Bingo from next door! You'd think they never fed it.'

'Let the poor thing in, Ma,' said Dotty.

'No, don't,' said Duane. He accepted a steaming mug with a half-grin, saying, 'If you haven't got anything stronger than this . . .'

Dotty asked how her step-father was. Andrea said he was not too good. Arthur Ridley lay upstairs in the final stages of cancer. He had been a college servant at St John's, and had served in the Falklands War, twenty years ago, and been wounded. He had never entirely recovered, readily slipping into a valetudinarian helplessness from which he was now highly unlikely to recover.

Andrea had almost forgotten why she had married Arthur. Her first husband, Douglas, had left after beating her up. She had turned for support to Arthur. He had seemed a nice enough man. And well enough. Now she was supporting him.

Dotty kicked her shoes off and perched on the stool next to her brother, elbowing him gently until he made more room.

'No fighting, you two,' said Andrea automatically, as she had been doing for the last sixteen years. She leant her bottom against the oven, in which a large pizza was heating for their supper. In better years, Andrea had been a seedswoman in the Oxford Botanical Gardens; she had been forced to give it up in order to look after Arthur.

'So, what's been happening in the big world today, Dotty? Give us the news.'

Dotty worked in Debenham's. She told them about a funny customer who had come in over lunchtime, and left behind a nice pair of gloves. Some assistants had made puppets out of them. She loved working in the store. Debenham's new branch in the centre of Oxford was very nice. The girls on her floor had a very nice floor-controller. She had very nice manners and was very nice to all the staff. 'Thanks,' she said, accepting the slice of Battenburg Andrea offered her on the end of a knife. From then on, her report was given with a full mouth.

The nicest time of day was early in the morning, when the store had just opened. When all the lights went on, it was ever so nice – really like a scene in a movie. Posh. Everything was nice and quiet that early. Dotty chatted to the other girls and they had a bit of a giggle. Maeve had changed her hairstyle and it didn't suit her one bit. The odd customer came in, but they didn't give any trouble. Often they were quite nice.

The men customers were nicer than the women customers but, of course, there were more women customers than men, worse luck. She giggled. Besides, you didn't get many men in the china department. Men didn't seem to buy much china.

'Don't blame 'em,' commented Duane.

Having finished the cake, Dotty took a chocolate biscuit out of an open tin. 'I'm famished,' she said, and bit into the biscuit with her sharp white teeth. 'Better go up and say hello to Pop.' She sighed.

'Oh, yes, do, there's a love. Ask him if he wants anything.'

'What's actually wrong with the poor old sod?' Duane asked. 'Apart from him dying of cancer, like, I mean.'

'You are not to speak about your step-dad like that. How many times have I told you? Have a bit of respect, will you? Some chap at the Radcliffe said he'd got progressive nuclear decay.'

'You got that wrong, ma,' said Dotty. 'The consultant

said it was progressive supranuclear palsy. Like what Dudley Moore died of. Then this gink up at the John Radcliffe said it wasn't that at all.' Dotty looked quite pleased to have got the matter in perspective.

'Still, Arthur was never as funny as Dudley Moore, was he?'

The women ignored Duane's remark. 'I think I'll just let the bloody cat in,' Andrea said.

Bingo came swiftly through the open door, mewing. Duane aimed a kick at him. 'I'm off out, Ma, if there's nothing on telly.'

'Arsenal's playing Charlton. Don't you want to watch the game?'

''S a foregone conclusion, innit? 'Sides, the match will be on down the Carpenter's. Why can't we have digital like next door? The poofters are on digital.'

'Oh, don't go getting into any more fights, Duane. Learn your lesson, for God's sake.'

Dotty went up the narrow staircase and into the front bedroom where her step-father was lying. Although the window was slightly open, the room was stuffy and smelt unpleasant. The walls had been painted green, and seemed to cast their reflection on the dying man's face. The only decoration was a framed photograph of Montmartre, souvenir of a trip to Paris that Arthur and Andrea had taken in more palmy days.

'It's a bit dark in here, Pop. Can't I put the bedside light on?'

The old man responded weakly, saying that, yes, she could if she really wanted. 'I've got the wireless on. I was listening to the news. There's fighting all over the place. I don't know what the world's coming to.'

'But not here, Pop, not in England or Europe. We don't have to worry. We're a bit more civilised.'

31

She went over and drew the curtain across the window.

He wiped his pale mouth on an old handkerchief he was clutching. 'They've got this euro there now. I hear they've got it in Ireland, too, but that don't stop 'em fighting each other, do it?'

She did not answer. After a pause, she said, 'Next door's cat's downstairs. Bingo, the ginger tom from the Manor. Do you want to see it?' She had a vague idea that invalids responded well to pets.

'I don't want no cats up here, Dot, thank you. They only climb all over you.' His voice was frail and distant. She stood over him, sympathetically, not touching him.

'Bingo is quite affectionate, remember.'

'That's as may be. I couldn't stand him climbing all over me.'

'Supper's coming up soon, Pop.'

'You know I can't hardly eat.'

'I'll help you.'

'Best to leave me be. I'm not long for this world, Dot, my girl.'

'Nonsense, Pop. You'll be fine. I'll bring you up a cup of coffee, if you like.'

'I'd rather have tea, thanks.'

'Okey-dokey. I'll bring you up a cup of tea, then. Aziz's best!'

'I don't want none of that foreign stuff, Dot.'

She laughed. 'This tea was grown just down the road, in Kidlington. They got acres of the stuff there – next to the paddy-fields.'

She made her way downstairs, grinning at her own wit. The smell of pizza, almost cooked, greeted her as she descended.

Her brother had disappeared. Andrea was sitting on a kitchen stool, reading a brochure. She looked up at Dotty, studied her for a moment, then said, 'Look, don't tell Duane, but I think I'm going to take up one of these Open University courses.'

'You going to get a diploma, Mum?'

'We'll have to see about that. Switch that telly off, will you? It gives me a headache.'

'Are we going to get rich or summat, Mum?'

Her mother rested her elbow on the counter and her head on her fist. 'I just want to feel a bit better about myself, that's all.'

The sun was low in the sky, wreathing itself in long flat clouds, as Penelope Hopkins returned to Hampden Ferrers for the second time that day. She had been kept busy at Brookes University, checking in the first of a new intake of overseas students.

Among the new arrivals were two young women from Hong Kong, Hetty Anne Zhou and Judy Chung. Both girls were suffering because they had been stopped at Customs in Heathrow airport: when their luggage was examined, it was found to contain the bulbs of a hybrid lily. Under the new security arrangements, the bulbs had at first been regarded as suspicious. The girls, eighteen and nineteen years old, training to be computer technicians, had been taken to a remote office in the airport building and interviewed for an hour before being released. Their lily bulbs had been confiscated.

The girls had arrived at Brookes in tears. Penelope had comforted them, and taken them under her wing.

They had soon become articulate. 'They are bulbs of the lily called Yellow Dragon. We grow them in our gardens on Victoria Island. They smell so beautiful of their perfume.'

Judy Chung added to Hetty Zhou's explanation: 'We

think they would stop us being homesick. Now they are taken away.'

'Didn't you know it was illegal to bring agricultural products into Britain?'

'We did not think anyone would suspect us.' More tears.

'The Customs men had to confiscate them,' Penelope said. 'A red lily beetle has become prevalent in the south of England, which must be prevented from spreading. Perhaps your bulbs were infected with the beetle's eggs.'

More crying, and Hetty Zhou, the more articulate of the two, kept saying, 'We never heard of this beetle. We don't have such things in Hong Kong. We wish we had never come to Britain.'

Penelope had put on a pair of reading-glasses and told them that the authorities suspected that the red lily beetle came from China and Hong Kong. And that, in any case, they had come to study English and transistor technology, not to plant flowers. She had offered them a box of man-size Kleenex.

Now the women were sitting in the back of Penelope's car as she turned down Clement's Lane and into her short drive. They had cheered up during the ride, making remarks like, 'Ooh, look, there's a red pillar-box! How splendid!'

Penelope led them into her sitting room and sat them down before an electric fire. She had to master the impulse to treat them like children, little knowing what the morrow would bring.

'Oh, you are so kind,' they said in unison. Just a final trickle of tears.

Penelope went to her fridge and produced a bottle of Chasse du Pape. When she had uncorked the bottle Hetty said, 'Mrs Hopkins, we do not drink. Very sorry for that.'

Penelope was a determined woman. 'This will do you good, after the upset you have had.' She poured three glasses of the white wine and stood holding out two of them until Hetty rose and collected them from her, with thanks. Penelope lit a cigarette and drank from her glass. 'I don't suppose either of you smoke?'

They retorted firmly that they regarded smoking as a disgusting habit.

'I smoke in times of stress,' Penelope said tartly. 'Now I am going to cook you some pasta for supper. It's about all I have in the house. Then you can both sleep in my bedroom. And when you wake in the morning, you will find that all will be well. The sun will shine. We will drive back through the village – have a little walk if you wish – and go back to Brookes where I shall check you in. Where everyone will be friendly and utterly charming. Except Mr Boucher, of course, who is terribly fierce and has red hair.'

The young ladies laughed and sipped cautiously at their wine. Their spirits were rising. Judy cadged a cigarette from Penelope. 'Since I have also been under stress.'

Before Penelope went into the kitchen to cook, she refilled her glass and put a Beach Boys album on the record player.

In the kitchen, she picked up her cordless phone and dialled her lodger, Bettina Squire, who lived upstairs with her daughter. 'Bettina, I urgently need some pasta. Have you got some you could lend me? . . . Oh, good! . . . Yes, please . . . Right now, in fact . . . An emergency! . . . Thanks a lot.'

The Bear was a reasonably comfortable little pub. True, it had two gambling machines, while a TV set burned in the public bar – the Arsenal–Charlton match was in progress – but there were no horse brasses and no imported photographs of bygone people, defunct railways or antique agricultural processes. A framed reproduction oil of a gigantic rectangular cow hung on one wall, and of a record fat pig on another.

The food, though unambitious, was reasonably tasty. At half past seven, John Greyling sat down to a plate of two sausages, baked beans and mash. A pint of Old Speckled Hen stood to the right of his plate.

It happened that a fat, red-faced man arrived at a nearby table and ordered the same dish. Soon he was even drinking the same beer as Greyling. His brown eyes were barricaded behind solid little bags of flesh; every now and again they shot inquisitive glances towards his neighbour.

The companionable remark he tossed at Greyling was to the effect that you could never get food such as they were eating in foreign parts.

Greyling uttered a surly agreement but went no further.

After a while, the fat man tried again, observing that he had not seen Greyling in the pub previously. Greyling admitted it was so.

'Do you live in the village?' was the next question.

Always guarded, Greyling said that he did, in a manner of speaking.

Silence fell. The fat man's face grew more rubicund as he ate. At length, he remarked that he had just returned from Sweden.

Greyling said he had never been to Sweden.

'Good people, the Swedes. Decent people to deal with. I sell them sanitary equipment and make a decent living out of it. My name's Langdon, by the way, Geoff Langdon.' He reached out a hand to Greyling.

Greyling became more interested at the mention of the name Langdon. He shook the proffered hand.

36

'I'm just back from South America myself,' he said.

'Are you really? My company is thinking of expanding to Brazil and Argentina and so on: Unfortunately, business is bad there just now. What's your job, may I ask?'

'I'm in railways.' It was not an informative answer and Greyling hastened to change the subject. 'Sausages are good.' He was mopping up his plate with the remains of his bread roll. He then ventured, 'It happens I am trying to get in touch with a lady by the name of Langdon. Joy Langdon. Maiden name Dickson. I feared she might be dead. I was looking among the gravestones in the churchyard, but I found no Langdons there. Name mean anything to you?'

'Joyce Langdon? No.'

'No – Joy. Joy Langdon. Ring any bells?'

The fat man shook his head. 'It's rather a common name, is Langdon. There used to be a cartoonist in *Punch* called Langdon.'

Greyling had lost interest. He drained his glass, nodded to the other and stood up to go.

Stephen and Sharon Boxbaum had invited two guests to dine that evening. Henry Wiverspoon had just arrived. He was a professor of English, a bachelor, who lived in one of the large houses in Cotes Road. He was getting on in years and had become completely bald; his shoulders, which in his youth had proved a formidable asset to the university rugger fifteen were now somewhat stooped. He retained the caustic tongue that had terrified several generations of students – since, in fact, the days when they had been known as 'undergraduates'. His large moustache, white now, was another source of awe for students who could only raise a whisker or two every few days.

Stephen and Henry had wandered into the garden, where the last rays of sunshine lingered, discussing whether it was the spirit of the enlightenment or of romanticism which now prevailed in Europe, or whether both had given way to greed.

At the western end of the garden, Stephen had created a small hill – or, rather, had ordered his gardener to create it. Two hundred tonnes of topsoil had been brought in; when the extension of the M40 was being built to connect Birmingham with London, topsoil was comparatively cheap. The hill was now verdant; primroses and bluebells currently flowered on it. At the top, a white gazebo had been installed. It was in there that the two gentlemen had established themselves to enjoy the sunset.

'I would say that the French in general have always espoused the enlightenment,' said Stephen. 'Were not the major figures French?'

'Undeniably so. However,' said Wiverspoon, with an emphatic pause to lend weight to his words, 'I observed when I was in Paris earlier last month that the bust of Voltaire, which stands not too far from the River Loire, had been mutilated. So there are dissenting voices. Or possibly one should say dissenting hooligans.'

Stephen made no reply. His wife was approaching.

Sharon had already greeted Wiverspoon. She was smiling, and giving a characteristic little writhe of the hips to show her pleasure, as she said that she had come simply to see that they were both comfortable.

'We are perfectly comfortable, thank you, Sharon.' Stephen gave no answering smile.

'Do you see how lovely my hyacinths are, Henry?' she asked. 'Past their best but still an absolute delight.'

'We did not notice your hyacinths, Sharon,' Stephen

said. A look of hatred passed between the couple. 'We were in conversation.'

'I shall call you when dinner is ready.' She turned on her heel.

Stephen regarded her receding figure as if, in the midway of this our mortal life, he found himself in a gloomy wood astray, gone from the path direct.

Silence fell between the two friends. Stephen stared down at the grass at his neatly shod feet.

He broke the silence by saying that Jeremy Sumption would be joining them for the meal. 'He's a writer.'

'Sumption? Don't know his name.'

'He's not in your line, Henry. He writes thrillers.'

Wiverspoon gave what passed for a chuckle. 'Bless my cotton socks, a writer of thrillers in Ferrers! What are we coming to? Perhaps he will regale us with some of his plots over dinner.'

'I understand that his title *Piggy Bank* might be made into a film.'

'If they make a film of the title only, as you suggest, we can rest easy.'

Sometimes Stephen found his guest a little trying, but he merely smiled.

Jeremy arrived. At first, he was subdued by the forbidding presence of Professor Wiverspoon, but a glass of wine revived his spirits.

It was comfortable in the Manor of an evening. The men talked. Sharon said nothing. In the garden, only birdsong broke the calm and silence. The encroaching dark came like a gentler breath; it brought snugness inside the old house, as night fell over the domestic hill and Sharon's hyacinths.

John Leach hunting prints in the hall gave way to something more interesting in the spacious dining room.

The tall candles in their silver candlesticks, which Andrea had placed on the dinner table, barely illuminated the paintings on the walls: a Vlaminck, a dusty gold Redon and a glowing village street scene by an ancestor of Stephen's, Max Pechstein, the expressionist. They testified to Stephen's love of colour and his eclecticism. In a far corner of the room hung Sharon's opposing choice, an Ingram steel engraving of the Radcliffe Camera, Oxford, in a Hogarth frame.

Sharon, Stephen, Henry and Jeremy sat talking in comfortable high-backed chairs with glasses of port to hand. Jeremy had become friendly with the Boxbaums and frequently called on them to beg a meal, which the Boxbaums readily supplied.

Dinner was over, yet they lingered at the table in relaxed fashion, without anything important to say. Sharon was smoking a cigarette.

'I am grateful to you for feeding me,' said Jeremy, helping himself to a belated sliver of cheese, the St Agur. 'I cook for myself but hate the results. My second wife, the same Polly Armitage who is currently trying to grind me down, was an equally dreadful cook. She could make beef taste like spinach.' He pulled a face to show its adverse effects on his digestive system.

'What did her spinach taste like?' Stephen enquired.

'Duckweed.'

Sharon asked about Jeremy's first wife.

'Oh, Joy Langdon — Joy Sumption, I should say — was brilliant. If I had not been so silly when I was young, not that I'm much more sensible now, I should have stuck with Joy. As a writer of thrillers, I thought somehow that it was up to me to behave recklessly. Well, badly, in fact. Now you can see where it's got me.'

'Yes, to Hampden Ferrers. What a terrible fate!'

As they laughed, Henry Wiverspoon leant forward and asked Jeremy why he wrote thrillers.

'I don't know . . . It pays. Well, it pays a bit. And I suppose I like vicarious excitement.'

'Bless my cotton socks, who needs excitement of any kind? Not at my age. Why not be like Alan Sillitoe and write about the working class?'

'Why? Huh, because I am working class.'

'One had gathered that.'

Jeremy looked down at his plate to conceal his annoyance at the jibe. 'So you did some detective work, eh? You assumed that since I married the ladies I was shagging I must be lower class because the middle class don't get married any more . . .'

'How very conventional of you,' Wiverspoon said. 'But the working class always set us a good example in that respect.'

'Respectable and gallant,' said Sharon, moving to Jeremy's defence.

'Respectable and galling, you mean,' Henry snapped at her.

Jeremy decided to light a cigarette.

'But you are generalising, Jeremy,' said Stephen, gently. 'Everyone is still getting married – and, of course, divorced – all the while. Why, there was a wedding in St Clement's this very morning.'

'Of course everyone looks pretty middle class when they get married, all dressed up, and in toppers and everything.' Then Jeremy could not resist asking Henry, 'Are you an expert on marriage, Professor? Have you been married yourself?'

'Alas, no. Who would possibly have me? Pass the port, would you? There's a dear man.'

Jeremy considered it his duty to repay his hosts with

41

some form of amusement. After helping himself again to the port before passing it on, he was soon giving an impersonation of an imaginary paedophile Roman Catholic priest. A priest featured prominently in the papers at present, having been caught in the act.

'Oh, paedophilia is disgusting, absolutely disgusting,' he said, in a high creaky voice. 'I'm always ashamed when I do it. I always have a good wash or a shower afterwards. But the boys enjoy it. It teaches them to fear God. Besides, I can't resist them. They look such darlings in their choir robes.'

Stephen and Sharon were laughing politely.

'I like to get to the bottom of their religion,' creaked the 'priest'. 'I prefer the term "fundamentalist" to paedophile.'

'Oh, Jeremy dear, that's too bad,' said Sharon, admiringly.

'It is too bad,' said Henry, whose face suggested that he was blessing his cotton socks inwardly.

'At least it doesn't apply to our Father Robin.' Jeremy dropped back into his own character. 'He's a really good sort, at least in my view.'

'I agree.' Stephen nodded. 'A fine example of a Christian.'

'I learnt the other day,' said Jeremy, 'that his church is one thousand five hundred years old. Pretty good going.'

'Is that so?' Stephen leant forward. 'Well, there's an example of stability for you . . . One thousand five hundred . . . Are there going to be any celebrations of the event?'

'I don't suppose so. Should there be?'

'We ought to do something about it, surely?'

'The Church is too poor.' Jeremy looked perplexed at Stephen's interest.

'And too ridiculous,' interposed Henry.

'We ought to do *something*.' Stephen punched the open palm of his left hand. 'Such things – such occasions, should I say? – are important and should not go without being acknowledged.'

'I'm afraid I'm an atheist.' Jeremy shook his head.

'And I'm a Jew. Still, we should do something about it. We must do something about it.'

And that was how the idea for the celebrations occurred.

At ten o'clock, the south of England was sinking into a light darkness, mitigated by a tentative moon over Knoleberry Park and a vague, unpunctual star. Penelope Hopkins had seen the Chinese women into her bedroom and was enjoying a drink and a smoke outside her back door. With her was her lodger, Bettina Squire, being rewarded by a drink for her rescue with timely pasta.

Penelope had called in Bettina's aunt, Nurse Ann, to have a look at the two young women to ensure that they were not in need of either counselling or medicine. Both Hetty and Judy had appeared alarmed by the portly, big-bosomed woman, then relieved when they were passed fit and Ann went off on her bike.

Penelope and Bettina were not always on the best of terms, but had sunk their differences on this occasion. Bettina was small and dark of hair, with an anxious manner. She dressed in rather poor taste in Oxfam clothing, which in this instance was a long beige dress. As a lone parent, she had her difficulties. In fits of generosity, she gave Penelope a free coiffeure in the Salon Française, where she worked part-time, often in recompense for being late with her rent money.

Penelope was telling Bettina about the problems of the two Chinese when the front-door bell rang. 'Who could that be at this hour?' Penelope asked, as she headed for the door. It always stuck so she wrenched it open.

A smartly dressed woman in her late thirties stood there, looking vaguely amazed at something, possibly her own audacity. 'Please excuse me. I know it gets late. I have been foolish. That is, foolish and romantic. It's not advisable. Could I please call for a taxi from your phone?'

Penelope was immediately sympathetic and invited the woman in. 'You may have to wait a while. Taxis have to come from Oxford.'

'If I could sit down I would be glad. I am so sorry to disturb you.'

'No problem. My friend and I are outside. Perhaps you would like to join us.'

'Very kind of you.' They enjoyed a few polite exchanges, in which the newcomer said that she was Italian. Another foreigner . . . thought Penelope. What was going on today?

The taxi company said there would be a half-hour wait. 'It's run by Sikhs,' Penelope explained. 'They're reliable but always busy.'

The two women went out into the tiny garden, where a scented candle burned on a table. The newcomer was introduced to Bettina. 'Please address me as Maria,' she said.

'What are you doing in Hampden Ferrers, may I ask?'

Maria smiled. 'I am on what might be called a secret mission. I just wanted a private look at a house called West End. Earlier today I had to visit the hospital, then I came here by taxi. An old friend lives in West End. He was not at home. It was naughty of me, but I shall meet with him tomorrow.' She gave a laugh. 'I am a little nervous, as you can see.'

Penelope went to the kitchen cupboard and returned with a plate of lemon-curd tarts. Inside their dimpled crusts lay hearts of honeyed yellow. 'I made them yesterday, to cheer myself up,' she said.

With some caution, Maria approached them. To her and Penelope's relief, she found them delicious.

Penelope poured her a glass of the Chardonnay. Maria took a sip and produced a packet of cigarettes. They all began to smoke and chat.

A little moth known as a shoulder-stripe fluttered in and flew about their heads. As it swooped towards the candle, Bettina clapped it between her hands. The body fell on the table. She blew it off into the dark. Maria winced with pain but made no remark. Bettina had already been drinking.

Penelope told Maria of her two remarkable Chinese women, and of her job at Brookes.

'So you are not married?'

'No. My husband died some years ago.'

'I am sorry.'

'But just today – oh, how silly I am to say this – I met a man who made a deep impression . . . too deep, perhaps . . . You are married? I see you have a ring.'

'Mmm. And I have a child.' She inhaled the smoke of her cigarette and made a forbidding expression that prohibited questioning. 'In Rome,' she added, after a long pause. She took a second tart.

Bettina felt she had been silent for too long and asked if Maria did not find Ferrers a curious place.

'Well, no. I don't know. How can I judge? It seems to me – I have been here only an hour or maybe two – an average English village. And so many trees! I saw a squirrel in one.'

'People may think that it's average,' said Bettina,

mysteriously. She poured herself more wine, then embarked on one of her pet subjects.

She said that the outlines of the village, not counting the park and not counting the line of new houses at the end of the main road, copied exactly the outline of a city of the dead buried beneath the upper village. The owner of the Carpenter's Arms had found this map in an old chest in his cellar, in a part that had been walled up because of damp. Bettina took a pencil and drew on the back of a shopping list an oval to represent the underground city. The upper curve represented Cotes Road, the lower Clement's Lane; the line through the middle represented the main road and the high street; the diagram bore a resemblance to a closed mouth.

'It will eat us all up in time.' She bit into her tart.

'You're being morbid, Bettina,' said Penelope, warningly.

'This city of the dead is an exact duplicate of the village above.'

'How strange,' said Maria, doubtfully. 'How deep below the ground is this "city of the dead", as you call it?'

'Only a few steps. Once, there were ways down to it.'

'And so *from* it,' said Penelope.

'For instance, there were steps down from the cellar in the Carpenter's. They were blocked off in the nineteenth century as being unsafe.'

'I should think so!' exclaimed Maria. 'We don't much want to deal with the dead. How very curious.' She looked at Penelope.

Penelope pulled a face. 'We have enough to do, dealing with the dead in our lives,' she said. 'They certainly haunt us.' She raised her glass and stared at it as if she had never seen it before, then sipped from it.

'It is true that they do,' Maria agreed. 'Yet it is the future that should concern us most.'

46

They sat there, gazing into the deepening night, enjoying their cigarettes. An owl called nearby. Sweet scents greeted them from a philadelphus bush. It was going over: discarded petals patterned the flagstones like designer blobs of white paint.

'What I think,' said Bettina, 'is that it's nice to make the transformation from life to death as gradual as possible, so the city underground was built as much like the one above ground as they could make it.' She sprawled across the table as if to embrace it. Penelope snatched up the wine bottle so that it was not upset. 'The great difference being that below, below, all the rooms of the houses and the streets and everywhere are full of earth and clay. Because the dead people don't have to breathe, of course. There's earth up to the ceilings.'

'This is very creepy,' said Maria. 'This idea is not within Christian thinking, is it?'

'Of course not,' said Penelope. She felt protective towards her foreign guest. 'It's just Bettina's morbid idea. She's been drinking.'

'No, it's true!' Bettina protested. 'This very garden is duplicated down below. Dead people are sitting there now. Dead people have a kind of sex life and can—'

'Oh, stop it!' exclaimed Penelope. Fiercely she stubbed out her cigarette. 'That's a load of nonsense, Bettina. I don't know where you got it from.'

'You can't accept it because it frightens you!' She wagged a finger at Penelope.

'But how could it possibly be?'

They started to argue in a rather tipsy way. A thin cry from upstairs interrupted them.

'That's my darling Ishtar! I must go!' With that, Bettina drained her glass and rushed into the house, her beige dress flapping round her legs.

Penelope and Maria sat in silence. 'We're not all mad,' said Penelope. 'Please don't go away with that idea. Bettina's had too much to drink.'

'Many religious ideas are mad. Or seem designed to drive us mad. Curiously, I remember a clever book by an Italian author, Italo Calvino, called in Italian *Le città invisibilie*, in which he talks about cities of the dead. But he is making a joke of a kind. I am sure there are eccentric British writers who also write books as learned jokes, serious jokes.'

'As far as I know, Bettina never reads books. Certainly not in Italian.' She laughed at the thought. 'Do have another tart, Maria.'

'Perhaps we should sometimes regard our lived lives as serious jokes. I regard myself as absurd, coming secretly like a ghost from the past to reassure myself, to see this house of my English friend. He has never been my lover. Our bodies have been too distant. I say that with some regret. And yet . . . we have been so spiritually close at times. Almost soul-mates. Is that not some kind of joke of fate?

'I am quite a sensible and successful person. Yet why did he fall in love with me so long ago – and I with him? This English man, this Italian girl. It is a metaphysical question. I could not be without it in my life. It is part of the meaning of both our lives. Is that a frivolous thought?' She gazed at Penelope through her rimless glasses, hardly expecting an answer.

'How I wish I had a lover.' The words were breathed out into the stillness of the night.

Maria touched her hand. 'It is the beginning of love that is so sweet, and so painful.'

Penelope did answer: 'Perhaps Bettina's idea of a hidden city exactly duplicating this village is not so daft. Not if taken as a metaphor. I told you I met someone this morning, a man . . . Very – I suppose – very suave. I have realised since then that, under the life I have been living for some years, another life has been lived, almost unknown to me.

'I have always worked so hard. Being industrious . . . Perhaps in order to shut off the steps downward to that other life. Do have another tart.'

Maria nodded. 'And what was this other life, if I may ask?'

'*Ohhh.*' She lit another cigarette, and gave one to Maria without being asked. 'My husband dying. All that kind of thing. Being a young widow – dreadful label . . . My attempts to be an artist.'

Companionable silence.

Maria spoke again: 'It is not very unusual, is it, to have a whole vein of life of which others know nothing? Which we cannot articulate? My cities have been in the air. *Castles* in the air. Not at all underground. Not recently. Once it was different, when I was young. It's strange, because I am always afraid of dying. It's a morbid fear.' She cast a glance over her shoulder. The air was growing chillier.

'So you meet this remote lover tomorrow. You came a day early, secretly, to look at his house, to see where he lives? You must be suspicious of him,' Penelope mused.

'No, I came secretly a day early because I wanted to consult a doctor at the hospital in Headington. An Italian doctor, old friend of our family. To silence old fears. The fear of cancer.' She gave a small laugh. 'How can I love my dear Englishman for ever if I am destined to die tomorrow?'

'Were you afraid you might find he had a woman living with him?'

Maria answered only indirectly: 'I saw only a rather fat old nurse.'

Penelope stroked Maria's bare arm. 'But you are well? You certainly look well. Your skin is so clear. You are so beautiful . . .'

'This doctor, he says I am healthy. We must always trust someone.'

A horn sounded from the front of the house.

'There's your taxi.' Both women stood up, reluctant to part.

'I must go, Penny. Thank you for your hospitality. If there's a secret we share, it is that no life is entirely happy – and that's common knowledge . . . I know you for a wonderful warm-hearted woman and I'm glad we met.'

'You are wonderful, too, dearest Maria. Perhaps we will meet again.'

'I truly hope so.'

They embraced and kissed each other, and Maria left.

The quadrangles of Wolfson were deliciously, academically silent when Maria entered them. The absence of scholars reinforced the solemnity of the place. Maria went quietly to her room, where she undressed, washed, and slipped into bed, to lie naked between sheet and duvet as was her custom at home. From a little gold casket by her bedside she extracted a white pill, swallowed it with a gulp of water and switched out the light. She curled up on her right side, tucked her hand between her thighs, and was asleep in no time.

She became aware of watching her little pale feet descending stairs, daintily tripping from stone slab to stone slab. Every one of the slabs had its own story. Laid down in the ocean in warm Triassic centuries when no intellect existed, the stone contained the fossils of extinct shrimp-like creatures, hardly larger than a toenail, which even now strove to escape their imprisonment.

The more deeply she descended, the less impenetrable became the night about her. As she gained level ground, the cathedral-like limits of her surroundings faded into visibility. Her spirit was enclosed within an ambiance extraordinarily ornate, every metre of walls and ceiling being decorated, or rather morphosed in some way. Straight lines were abhorred: it was as if she glided through the belly of a vast organism whose entrails had solidified into an arcane architecture without precedent.

She believed she recognised the halls of the pre-Adamite sultans, as described in Primo Levi's translation of the writings of the obsessive Englishman, William Beckford who, from a scandalous seclusion, had composed *Recollections of an Excursion to the Monastries of Alcobaca and Batalha*, and the more famous novel, *Vathek*. And now she could hear the oppressive music of the place, played on a concealed organ, reinforcing the sense of solitude and frustrated desire.

As she moved, motifs of the decor moved with her, their writhings recalling the drugged lethargic movements of an oriental dancer. The melancholy grandeur of her surroundings was not distasteful to her, even when she had to walk though dark water where gloomy things glided underfoot, seeking food or consolation or extinction.

Maria turned her head to look back. Following her was a skinny thing, all white, resembling something as yet not quite born, not quite human; she recognised it as a form of her earlier self, an imago that never was. Not wishing to be accompanied by this manifestation, Maria quickened her pace.

Now those pale feet were walking over elaborately

51

patterned tiles. No other part of her had such pertinent existence as those dainty extremities. Regularity of movement was theirs, even though a heaviness, a gloom was now gathering about her, as fog into a desolate glade. The ground seemed to slope ever downward, the murk to become ever more oppressive. Now there was nothing remaining, only the two pale feet, progressing nowhere. Then they too were gone, absorbed into the enigmas of sleep.

Midnight. One in the morning. Two. An hour when, as doctors and soldiers agree, human resistance is at its lowest.

As the man calling himself Greyling was about to leave his kitchen, he went to close the window he had opened only an hour earlier. A movement in the neglected garden caught his eye.

A large fox stood on the bank outside, amid the cow parsley and nettles. Its gaze met Greyling's: its eyes were brown and golden. Greyling could not look away. He became aware of the brilliant consciousness of the animal, its sprung immobility, as it summed him up. He was aware of his own hunted life of pretence, whereas – the thought entered his head – this creature outside was ferociously pure.

Having decided that the man, that poor thing trapped in houses, was of no moment, the fox moved on, picking its way daintily with furred footprint. It was there; then it had vanished.

Greyling closed the window and went slowly up to bed, still worried by the feral encounter.

Now he was asleep. The village was as if dead. The Pink House, being ancient, creaked by day and night. These new creaks were different. They seemed to be made

52

by a slow-moving person or a wounded animal inching its way upstairs. Greyling, waking, had a different interpretation: he believed the creaks were made by a deceased person climbing slowly up to his room.

Creak. Pause. Creak. The bedroom door was ajar. It opened with a different creaking note. A figure appeared, dimly visible, almost luminescent. It made its lethargic way to Greyling's bedside. It was a woman in a grey shift or shroud. Its eyes gleamed as it looked down on the cowering man.

'Joy!' said the man. 'Please, go away! . . . Please, Joy!' He could hardly speak for terror.

The figure made no answer. Its throat had been cut. Congealed blood ran from its neck down the length of its garment.

Greyling lay transfixed, eyes bulging as he stared at the apparition, which began to fade. He believed his eyesight was going. Soon only a stain remained, hanging before him. Then it, too, was gone, seeming to flicker out of existence.

All that remained was a nauseating smell.

Greyling climbed cautiously out of bed. He was wearing only a T-shirt. Shaking with terror, he crept barefoot down the very stairs the apparition had recently ascended. His steps were clumsy: he felt as if he had hoofs rather than feet.

Once in the kitchen, he switched on the light over the gas cooker and looked about him fearfully. The room seemed unnatural, unkind, uninhabitable. He looked out into the darkness. No fox, of course.

'Bloody house is haunted,' he said, half aloud.

From the drawer in the kitchen table he removed a folded cloth and took out of it a paper package, unwrapped it and tipped some of white powder into the palm of his left hand, which he snorted up both nostrils.

53

A glow pervaded his body. He shook his head. He felt better.

On his way back to bed, he checked the front door. It was properly bolted.

The church clock gave a solitary chime, to announce to the Christian world that it was now quarter past two of a Thursday morning and all was well, at least where the pure of heart were concerned.

III

Spiritual Life

The day dawned much like any other. Sam Aziz was woken by his alarm. He sat up. His wife groaned luxuriously beside him and tried to go on sleeping. Sam climbed out of bed, for he had to get down to the shop and unlock the door to receive the morning newspapers.

He pulled on his dressing-gown and tugged back a curtain to peer out past the fire escape at the scruffy garden behind his shop. The world, as far as he could see, was white.

Over the low roof of the Bear, a fat red sun was attempting to rise.

'Oh, my God, there is a heavy frost! Rima, wake up! Do you think that dratted boy has covered up our runner beans? Otherwise, all will be killed dead.'

In her doze Rima knew that her son, Sammy Junior, that dratted boy, could not possibly have remembered to cover up the tender runner-bean shoots, which were just poking their heads, like little green cobras, above the soil. It was too late to do anything and she might as well sleep. She had sat up until after midnight, watching a movie on Channel Five. She enjoyed Channel Five movies: they had lots of explosions in them. Rima liked explosions.

Although Sam was in a hurry to unlock the shop, he burst into the room where his son slept – scarcely a room, more a large cupboard – and roused him. He demanded anxiously to know if the lad had remembered to cover the little bean plants with newspaper.

'Of course, Father,' said Sammy Junior, drowsily. 'What do you think I am?'

'Wonderful, wonderful boy!' He bent and kissed the boy's cheek. 'Enjoy a further hour's sleep.'

He got downstairs just as the WH Smith van drew up outside. The usual black driver entered, smiling, and dumped the stack of papers on the counter. 'Make your fortune today, eh, Sam?' he said, and he was gone. Always in a hurry.

Sam stood out on the pavement to watch the van disappear in the direction of Nuneham Courtenay. The morning smelt good and fresh, full of promise, despite the litter on the pavement. Since all was still at this early hour, he could hear a faint cry, not repeated, coming from Rodney and Judith's house across the road.

'A new life,' Sam Aziz said to himself, under his breath. 'That's what we all need. That's what Hampden Ferrers needs. A new life.'

An old woman was coming slowly along the street. Sam watched the effort she had to make to get along. She was a shapeless bundle, rigged out in dark and ancient clothing. The bundle was balanced on two fat pillars of legs that she moved only with a great effort. Her gaze was fixed sternly on the pavement.

As she came level with Sam, she raised her head, with its sparse grey hair, and said wheezily, 'Morning, Mr Aziz.'

'Good morning, Mrs Stone,' he said.

She passed on in her laboured way. Sam felt a great happiness in his heart. He could not say why. The street was empty again, apart from a man going by on a bike. He regarded the trees that lined the pavement, with their fresh foliage. How beautiful it all was. There were trees everywhere. It was almost like living in a forest, to be in Hampden Ferrers. This view was given to him as a beatitude.

Sam entered his shop, locked the door behind him and began to sort the papers into the news rack. *Daily Telegraph. Times. Mirror. Daily Mail. Independent.* Mr Wiverspoon's *Financial Times.*

He looked over the headlines. Everywhere else in the world there seemed to be war or trouble: in Kashmir, Pakistan, Afghanistan, Iraq, Indonesia, Argentina, Colombia . . . almost everywhere. But on the front pages the English papers mainly talked about the injury to the footballer Beckham's foot. Sam clicked his tongue, though whether in admiration or disapproval even he could not have said.

When that was done, he looked at his watch and retreated into the room that served both as kitchen and store. There he made himself a mug of Cadbury's Original Drinking Chocolate, ate a mango, then enjoyed a bowl of Shredded Wheat.

While he was looking over the pages of the *Daily Mail*, Rima came down, swathed in several dressing-gowns. 'Sam, how you can sit here in such cold? Put on the electric fire.'

'I am not cold. Soon the day will be warmer. Sit down, woman, stop complaining and I will make a mug of Cadbury's for you.'

She did as she was told, as she always did. Smiling, as she always did.

* * *

So another miraculous version of Everyday began. The weakling light grew steadily stronger, prompting the street-lamps to switch themselves off. Gradually other people and their vehicles appeared.

Despite the semi-rural nature of Hampden Ferrers, no cocks were ever heard to crow above its rooftops. A village committee had met five years earlier to ban fox-hunting, but had decided instead to ban cockerels from crowing.

The cockerel on Cotes Farm had had its neck duly wrung, despite the protestations of Yvonne Cotes. Without it Cotes had become – as Yvonne said – less of a farm, and the onslaught of BSE had further reduced its animal stock. Now the old widower Jack Cotes was attempting to sell North Pasture to a local contractor for twenty-four houses to be built on it against the opposition of the village community, but with the cordial support of his sons and daughters.

The sons and daughters were a clannish, amiable lot, Rog being the eldest, followed by Dave and Sophie, who was now seventeen. Rog had a partner, Jean Parrinder, a buxom lady with a ready laugh. Jack's sister, Yvonne, who had never married, lived in the farmhouse too, with a dog called Duke, full of fleas. Also on the premises, aged now, was Joe Cotes, a distant cousin of Jack, who had served in the army in the Second World War. Joe had leg problems from an old wound and did not get about much. His considerable dependence on the NHS meant he was often taken into hospital, which he portrayed on a scale of comfort as akin to army barracks.

These seven people all fitted into the worn old home, using goodwill and a generation-long habit of endurance to make the arrangement work. The livestock had been reduced to goats, chickens and ducks, with one Jersey cow, Mildred.

The Cotes family survived by selling vegetables, jam, marmalade, cheese, cakes and bread on a Saturday, under the general heading of Yvonne's Homemades, from a little wooden stall facing Cotes Road. The women ran the stall, with assistance from Bettina Squire. Dave and Rog also dealt in bicycles and bicycle repairs, as well as car maintenance and the mending of just about anything. This they did with an appearance of good cheer. Their chief hope was that Jack would make a packet from the sale of North Pasture.

When she was not baking, Yvonne Cotes generally kept to her room in the attic, which she called 'cosy' – more on account of its size than any particular warmth. She was wont to compare it to Captain Cook's cramped cabin on the *Endeavour*. Yvonne was an intelligent woman who had educated herself over the years. She was short, ruddy-complexioned, and studied the world through thick, dilapidated glasses.

On this morning she woke early, pulled a rug about her thin shoulders and sat up. As usual, she felt unwell first thing. She hooked her spectacles over her ears and stared out of her narrow window. There had been a slight frost overnight. North Pasture was patched with white.

Despite the chill, Dave was about, dressed only in jeans and T-shirt. He was feeding the free-range hens. I know where Dave's been. Up on the hill with that nurse, Yvonne thought. But even the all-knowing Yvonne did not know everything.

Close to the house deserted farm machinery stood about. The fat bulk of the liquid manure container looked particularly bleak. She thought of dead animals, extinct animals. From there, it was but a step to more personal extinctions . . . Yvonne tried to recall one unusual thing she had done in her life. There was that time in childhood her father had driven her – why? how? – to Tintern Abbey, where a woman who had taken a fancy to her had given her a small book she still kept, a selection of William Wordsworth's poetry.

She sighed, misting one of the small window panes. 'I never became famous,' she whispered. 'I never became anyone important.' Yvonne's Homemades did not really count, if one were honest, as Yvonne always strove to be. She removed the spectacles and rested her eyes.

Yvonne kept a journal. She turned to it now for consolation. It had become more elaborate as her leisure time increased and her sight blurred. Her grandmother, Annie Cotes, had talked to her about the origins of the Cotes farm. Yvonne had since written this fragment of local history into her journal, along with such items as the milk yield of the goat, and the record crop of broad beans.

Towards the end of the eighteenth century, naughty Harrison Ferrers, lord of the manor, had seduced a country maid, the daughter of a farm labourer named Ron Cotes. This young lady, Pat or Patricia Cotes, was, said Granny Cotes, 'too pretty for her own good'. In due course, as a result of her liaison, she had given birth to twins.

Illegitimacy was a commonplace of country living although, in this case, it seemed that Harrison had behaved reasonably; perhaps he had liked Pat. He had taken some considerable interest in the two boys, who turned out to be good-looking and high-spirited. He had christened them Tarquin and Edward, after two of his favourite thoroughbreds.

Upon the boys' attaining their majority, Harrison had seen to it that Tarquin took holy orders and became Vicar of the parish, while Edward was given a few acres of farmland, which became known as Cotes Farm. On falling from his horse, Tarquin, when drunk, Harrison had broken his neck and died. The Reverend Tarquin's first official duty as a priest had been to preside over the funeral of his father and benefactor.

This story Yvonne, peering through her misty lenses, wrote down at length, together with an account of Tarquin's later behaviour, when he deserted his pulpit to travel widely abroad, in particular to Africa. The story went that while in Ethiopia he had accumulated some valuable treasure of a religious kind, which had brought with it a curse. Whether or not there was any truth in this, the treasure had never been found.

The Reverend Tarquin had also died in horrible circumstances. June of the year 1814 had been subject to freak weather conditions: a sudden whirlwind had snatched up the travelling Vicar and carried him to the top of the church tower. Then it had cast him down among the gravestones where, badly injured, he had lain helpless until a pack of wild dogs, descending from Molesey Hill, had set up on him and torn him to pieces.

One day, in the Oxford library, Yvonne had come across a magazine that offered advice to novice writers on how to have a book published. Accordingly, she had bundled up her handwritten journal and sent it off to a small publisher with offices in Old Burlingham Street, London.

Four months had gone by and she had heard nothing. Now, in the early morning, Yvonne commenced writing again. She had no intention of getting up until the day became warmer and the coat of white faded from the pasture. No cocks crowed. Nothing disturbed her, although she could hear distant murmurs about the house below her, much as Captain Cook must have heard the crew of the *Endeavour* going barefoot about their duties.

61

It was cosy under the blankets. She fell asleep over her old fountain pen.

Some other denizens of Hampden Ferrers also left their beds, but less nimbly than had Sam Aziz. Near the pâtis-serie lived a widower, now in his eighty-fifth year, by the name of Valentine Leppard, a professor. He had woken and dozed off again. Now he lay awake, unmoving in his bed, trying to remember which day of the week it was. Certainly if yesterday had been Wednesday, today must be Thursday, when he would have coffee with Henry Wiverspoon; but evidence to confirm that yesterday had been Wednesday was singularly lacking. Indeed, one day was much like another.

Without his glasses, Valentine could not see clearly. He watched the flicker of reflected light on his ceiling. It moved as early traffic passed along the road outside. He was always comforted by the sight. He always thought that if he had a cine-camera – whatever they were called nowadays – he would like to record that play of light.

Nothing was as beautiful as light. He mustrusted and hated almost everyone he met, but light, ah, how he concurred with the dying words of the painter, Turner: 'The Sun is God!' Moistening his lips, dry from sleep, he said aloud, 'They are all gone into the world of light.' He wondered where the words had come from, but it was of no great moment.

He mused and snoozed, and would do so until Nurse Ann Longbridge came to help him get up.

Not too far from where Valentine Leppard lay, in a house on the edge of the village where the road led on to Marcham and Bishops Linctus, 'Starman' Barrie Bayfield, Duane Ridley's friend, was also in bed. He opened an eye to view daylight, found it painful, closed it again, tacky upper lid joining tacky underlid. He attempted to sleep – in essence, to 'sleep it off'. The throbbing headache kept him conscious while rendering consciousness obnoxious,

'Mum!' he called feebly. No answer. He could hear the bloody dog barking in the yard. 'Mum! Tea! Help! Oh, God, I'm fucking dying,' he told himself. Still, it had been a bit of a laugh in the Carpenter's the previous evening, with his mate, Duane. You had to expect to suffer later. You never got owt for nowt. 'Mum, bring us some tea, will you?'

No response from below.

The Starman heaved himself out of bed and staggered downstairs, bollock-naked, to see what was going on.

His sister, Kyle, was eating Weetabix. She glared at him in disgust. 'That ghastly thing will drop off like a slug if you don't quit flashing it, kidder!'

'Get lost!' he replied. 'Dreadful slimy alien creatures from Jupiter are on their way to eat you alive.'

'Sugar Ray' Willmot trundled along the streets in his electric milk float, planting sturdy white bottles of milk on various doorsteps. Sammy Aziz Junior came out, muffled in sweater and scarf, to deliver newspapers through various front doors. As he cycled along, he passed Nurse Ann Longbridge going to work on her bike. They exchanged a word of greeting.

A little later, along came Bob Norris, pushing his bicycle and dropping junk mail and bills through various letter slots. On this day of days, Bob had an additional load; he was delivering letters written by Stephen Boxbaum only the previous afternoon, inviting people here and there to participate in the celebrations of the local church's one and a half millennia and to offer their services to the committee in whatever way they could.

These letters were opened, by thumbs or knives, over the village's breakfast tables, to be read either with excitement or indifference.

Marion Barnes had a brother living in the village. Brother and sister did not agree with each other. Nevertheless, Rodney Williams was a pleasant enough man, a solicitor with an Oxford firm, not particularly communicative, and given to wearing bow-ties to work. It was over this indicator of pretentiousness that he and Marion had quarrelled.

However, this morning, Rodney was not going to work and was not wearing a tie at all. His partner, Judith Mayes, was about to give birth to their first child.

Judith lay on the double bed in the front room upstairs, groaning. The contractions were coming ever more rapidly. There was every sign of crisis in the house, quite apart from Rodney's failure to put on a tie. The central heating was at full blast. Radio Three was pouring out Chopin piano concertos. The midwife, Miss Stadway, who was only twenty-three to Judith's thirty-nine, was standing by, red in the face. A mug of cooling tea and a biscuit crumb were on a table by the bedside. A bowl of hot water stood on the chest-of-drawers, while the floor was covered with a blanket and a Mars bar wrapper. 'Get that bloody dog out of here!' Judith cried.

The young spaniel, called Tony after the Prime Minister, was kicked out and the door shut on him. At that moment, Judith gave an extra heave and the head of the new baby appeared between her legs.

Penelope Hopkins was walking with the two young Chinese ladies on a brief tour of the village street. They were admiring. They found everything very pretty, especially as seasonal trees were still in blossom in various front gardens. Having finished his paper round, Sam Aziz's son was setting off to school on his bicycle. He gave them a smile and a wave as he went by.

As they passed Rodney and Judith's house, the cry of a newborn child reached their ears.

'Oh, that is lucky!' said Hetty Zhou. 'How beautiful. Could we go to see the baby?'

'I think we had better not,' said Penelope, smiling. She was charmed by the idea that the girls should wish to see the infant. She herself disliked anything newborn, preferring to wait until it was eighteen years old before she saw it.

Dotty was leaving number twenty and driving off to Debenham's in her Renault. Later, further down the street, Sonia, the Vicar's wife, emerged and went on foot towards the primary school, where she taught.

As the young ladies sauntered along, a removals van came down the street and stopped at the door of number twenty-two. Men in aprons climbed out and went into the house.

'Someone's leaving,' said Penelope. She regarded the semi-detached with some amusement. It stood out from all the other houses in the street, most of which showed evidence of wear and tear. But number twenty-two had been painted a bright pink ('Much pinker than the Pink House,' she said to herself), with the window-frames, gutters and downpipes picked out in white.

'Will the house be empty?' Judy Chung asked.

'I suppose so.'

'What is the situation with regard to it, Mrs Hopkins?' Judy persisted.

'It may be for sale, I suppose. Or it may be sold. There's no board up.'

'Let us go and ask,' said Hetty. Without waiting, she marched through the front gate and up the path. Two men, carrying a table between them, stopped to let her pass. Judy followed, while Penelope stood rather helplessly on the pavement, beyond the wooden fence, wondering amusedly at what sort of girls these were, who had yesterday appeared so submissive and had since proved so determined.

She saw them briefly in the bay window of the front room, talking to two young men, who looked flabbergasted. Next, she saw them through the upper window. Now the two young men were nodding and smiling. The group disappeared. Some minutes later, narrowly missing a collision with the removals men, Hetty appeared at the front door, beckoning to Penelope.

There was nothing for it: in went Penelope. Men stopped rolling up a strip of floor carpet to let her by as Hetty led the way into a small rear kitchen. Clearly it had once been clean and orderly; now a man was wrapping and packing kitchen utensils into a cardboard crate.

Two young men, one fair and thin with hair dyed copper, the other rather plumper, dark and with a small moustache, both plainly in a state of excitement, had rescued some cups and were pouring coffee for everyone.

They introduced themselves as Eric, the fair one, and Teddy, the dark one; both shook hands politely with Penelope.

'Oh, Mrs Hopkins, delighted to meet you! We're about to leave house and home. This village really doesn't suit us – such unpleasant neighbours. Neighbours from Hell! Ooh, shouldn't say that!' Eric put his fingers to his mouth.

Teddy, who seemed the more masterful of the two, said, 'The fact is that these charming Hong Kong ladies—'

66

'We wish to buy this house,' said Hetty. 'We can redecorate it and it will suit us very well.'

'And we will have our very own garden,' said Judy.

Eric was gazing intensely at Judy, his hands clasped together. 'Ooh, your dress . . . That colour mauve. I almost faint when I see it. The mere word . . .'

'Please do not faint when we are talking business,' replied Judy, in a kindly tone. 'Could you have a glass of water instead?'

'And you can come to tea with us,' said Hetty. 'We would welcome you when we are settled.'

'We're frightfully bucked,' said Teddy. 'We've agreed to the deal on the spot, Mrs Hopkins.'

Penelope was bewildered. 'But . . . well, the price . . .'

'Oh, we'll pay whatever they ask,' said Hetty.

'But when we didn't know you I think we asked too much,' said Eric. 'Don't you, Teddy? Weren't we just a tiny bit greedy?'

Teddy hesitated only momentarily before he agreed. 'We'd take less, really we would.'

'We couldn't possibly let you!' shrilled Judy. 'It's ever so cheap!'

'But – but, my dear girls,' said Penelope, 'you know nothing about English house prices.'

'Please, Mrs Hopkins, allow us. We think it is a bargain. It's so convenient. And it would be so amusing to live in an English village. Our relations would come and visit us.'

'Excuse me,' said the man with the crate. He pushed carefully past them. He winked at Penelope – she was the only other normal person present.

'We would ever so much rather not overcharge you,' said Eric, 'particularly since you are Chinese. Otherwise, you would have a terribly poor opinion of we English people. Isn't that so, Mrs Hopkins?'

'Oh, do please call me Penelope.'

'No, we insist on taking less.' This was Teddy, holding up both hands in protest. 'You pay us four hundred thousand pounds and we shall be terribly happy.'

'Let's say three hundred and fifty thousand,' said Eric. 'I mean, we're not greedy people, are we, Teddy?'

Teddy nudged his friend. 'Not at all.'

'We do not wish to pay you so little,' said Hetty. 'It would be crooked.'

'Shouldn't you give this matter a little thought?' Penelope looked severe. 'How *are* you going to pay these gentlemen?'

'We have lots of money in the HSBC,' Judy said airily.

'And how do you imagine you will get to Brookes from here?'

Hetty stared at Penelope as if she was making a new and possibly adverse judgement on her. 'We are going to buy a car, of course. What did you think?'

'A Daihatsu.' That was Judy.

'Or something better. A BMW.' Hetty again.

'Buy a Bentley,' suggested Eric. 'I was in the back of a Bentley once. They're ever so snug.'

'So,' said Teddy, anxious in case his friend went still lower with the price, 'we are agreed on three hundred and fifty thousand, are we?'

'I think we should pay you the full four hundred thousand,' said Judy.

'There's no garage for our car.' Hetty sounded a cautionary note.

'You'll have to get a solicitor to draw up a contract,' said Penelope. 'Luckily, there is one in the village. Rodney Williams.'

Again she received a curious stare from Hetty. 'We shall get our private solicitor to fly over from Hong Kong.

Our fathers are completely rich, you know, Penelope.' The 'Penelope' was definitely a polite put-down.

Eventually addresses were exchanged, coffee was drunk, hands were shaken all round, then Penelope and two triumphant girls left the removal men to their labours. Eric and Teddy came to the gate to wave them goodbye.

Judy was ecstatic. 'What a dear little house! And isn't Teddy sweet! I could marry him.'

'You silly girl,' said her friend. 'Do you not understand that he will only marry another man? Did you not notice the mirror attached to the ceiling above their double bed?'

The previous night, Penelope had had an unsettling dream. She had slept downstairs on a couch in her little back room, under a decorative print of a garden on the Cornish coast. In her room, the two young Chinese slept.

Shortly after three in the morning, she dreamed she was entering a house she seemed to know. However, on opening a door she found herself in an open space occupied by many men. They walked about and talked with each other, appearing busy but achieving nothing. The sun shone. She became trapped in a conversation with two of them. All the time, she was feeling in her pockets for something she had lost, it was never clear what. One of the men said something that reminded her of someone she loved who had died. In the dream, she was crying. She walked alone in a garden. A feral thing, too large to be a cat, followed her. She feared it greatly, yet it was blazingly beautiful.

She had awoken. The blanket had slipped off her. She rose stiffly, feeling bad, and went to the lavatory. She sat there for a while after she had relieved herself, head in hands. The dream tormented her. She could not think what she was living for. She thought about Bettina's city of the dead.

Henry Wiverspoon walked slowly towards the pâtisserie in the high street. There, every Thursday, he met a fragile old man for coffee. Henry had no great liking for people, but he relished the company of Professor Valentine Leppard, who also had no great liking for people. They had argued once that the exercise of dislike was one of the privileges of old age; one was free to hate. Valentine was already seated inside the little shop, by the window, dressed in coat and scarf, enjoying the warmth of the sun through the pane of glass. He left it to Henry to order the coffee.

Valentine was a distinguished paleontologist who had had his finger in many intellectual pies and controversies. He was also an authority on the arts, and had written monographs on Walter Sickert and other painters. Now long retired, he was writing a philosophical autobiography under the title, *City Utterly Fallen*, a quotation from Seneca's tragedy, *Oedipus*.

Valentine Leppard lived alone, attended daily by his hired nurse – the same Ann Longbridge who washed and dressed Henry every morning.

'Well, what news have we from the wider world?' he asked Henry, scrutinising his friend through misty spectacles. Such was generally his opening gambit. It amused him to treat Henry as if he were a mere youth, although Henry was in his mid-sixties.

'There's a morsel of news from the narrower world, Val. Stephen Boxbaum has decided that the village should celebrate the church's one thousand five hundredth year.'

Valentine formed his wrinkled face into an expression of astonishment.

70

'I received his circular this morning. Couldn't believe it. Thought it was some kind of a joke. Boxbaum is a Jew. Why should he wish to celebrate the longevity of a C of E hideout?'

'You know well that the motives of others are inscrutable, including the motives of those who are Jewish.'

A young waitress was delivering their coffee. It came with a foil-wrapped morsel of biscuit. Without lowering his voice, Valentine said, 'I do wish people would not say "Jewish". It's like saying people are "leftish". Either he's a Jew or he's not. Either you are left wing or not.'

'I'm certainly not,' said Henry, his moustache bristling at the thought.

'Might this idea of his to celebrate the longevity of our beloved church be construed as slightly impertinent? Or a *touch impertinent*, as I gather people say nowadays, the gods only know why.' As he spoke, Valentine gave the ghost of a smile for the world's foibles.

'Once Stephen gets something into his head . . . He's a determined man. What he is enthusiastic about is not the religious aspect of the thing but the stability of English life, of which he sees the church as a symbol.'

'A symbol of all that is reactionary, in fact.'

The waitress, with little else to do, leant against the nearby counter and listened, with dull interest, to the conversation. Valentine shot her an angry look and told her to mind her own business.

'You are so impolite,' said Henry, parenthetically. 'I understand how Boxbaum feels if you don't. His family has undergone terrible upheavals – not only in the Nazi period but before that.' He stared at the professor over the rim of his cup.

'I suppose so, but who knows? I've nothing against

71

him. What's he want to celebrate St Clement's for? What's *his hidden agenda*, as politicians like to say? I struggle daily, to tell the truth. I mean, when I'm writing my damned autobiography. I have nothing to lose by telling the truth, not at my age, yet I become puzzled by what the truth is, or was, about many early episodes in my life.

'I am troubled by the thought that if I set down that such-and-such happened, when nobody can verify it or contradict me, then it *becomes* what happened, irrespective of whether it happened like that or maybe did not happen at all. I can't even remember whether I was happy or miserable at certain times in life.'

'You've been miserable ever since I've known you. I thought you had nearly finished the book.'

'So I had. Then I decided to go back and revise it. I'm afraid I may have got some things wrong . . . Some rather large things. It's all a matter of perception.' He stared down at his cup. 'I can remember when this place was a tea-shop.'

'No, it was a vet's place. I brought a dog here to be put down.'

'Also, you should understand, I have a superstitious fear that if I finish my damned book I shall die. Life's mission accomplished, as the media put it nowadays . . .'

Henry stirred his coffee slowly, as if he were dealing with a cup full of treacle. 'I was thinking. Steve is planning to put together a *festschrift* for these episcopal celebrations. You are the village's most distinguished inhabitant. Why not let him have a few pages to print in his pamphlet?'

Valentine showed a flicker of impatience. 'You know how I hate the damned church and all it stands for. Don't expect me to make any contribution of any sort to it, or to its survival. If I put anything in the collecting box, it'll be anthrax.

'In our generation, Henry, we have enjoyed the inestimable privilege of piecing together the long history of the Earth. It has needed much patient enquiry from all manner of men and women. Dedication! Intellectual curiosity! New panoramas have opened up.' His husky voice grew stronger. He spoke faster. 'We now have a clear idea of the turmoil of the early Earth, under cometary bombardment, a bombardment that was intense for a million years. Can you grasp how long that period is?

'Imagine those raging oceans, dumped by comets, according to one theory – which I find persuasive. Imagine the mighty thunderstorms, year after year . . . Bacterial life eventually emerging. For that to happen, it was necessary that there was no oxygen present in the atmosphere. Earth was an alien world. Millions of years passed before anything like multi-cellular life emerged.

'Where do you think God came into all this? Why did Jesus Christ turn up so late in the day? He didn't arrive when the place was being bombarded by comets. We have no record that he preached to the bacteria. Why didn't he team up with Socrates? How does his death save us all? Why didn't he hold on until there were television cameras to record his crucifixion?'

Henry rattled with his kind of laughter. 'I hope those questions go into your book.' Still listening, the waitress went red with shame.

There were indications that just posing the questions had made the professor irritable. His aged hands twitched as if he yearned to take the offending Saviour by the throat. 'The man was a complete loser. All that stuff the Church preaches – it's well enough as a fairy story but it's all so *tiny* compared with true cosmic history as to be laughable. Laughable!'

73

He had worked himself up so much that his hand shook, rattling the teaspoon against his cup.

'Of course you're right, Val, but the Gospel story does no harm.'

'You vex me. Of course it does harm. Lies always do harm. We must love truth more than anything. Otherwise, we are sunk!'

Henry gave a chuckle. 'You're right, Val, but Steve doesn't see it that way.'

Valentine had calmed himself. He said quietly, 'Well, then, he ought to. Doesn't he remember how the Church persecuted the Jews? Why should Boxbaum care about the village church? I say, "Keep your hands off it!"'

'He's determined to go ahead. You can be an amused bystander like me, Val.'

'Amused? Horrified, you mean.' He began to laugh, but it turned into a coughing fit.

St Clement's Church had been built almost entirely of local stone. A foundation stone had been excavated bearing a date that had been read as 503. It was on this that Father Robin Jolliffe based his claim that the church was fifteen hundred years old, although there was evidence that a wooden building had occupied the site in pre-Saxon times – traces of posts had been discovered.

The stone bearing the date had been used to form the base of a romanesque chancel arch, built in the twelfth century. Since then the church had never ceased to change: it had been added to, renovated, restored, repainted. Through the centuries, both attention and neglect had been lavished on it. In 1814, it had been closed and boarded up for a while, the minister in residence declaring it the site of 'an unholy atmosphere', according to papers held in Christ Church, Oxford. Now

74

it presented a squat and rather unprepossessing appearance, relieved only by its unusually tall, square tower, which dated from the late fourteenth century.

Despite its somewhat unattractive aspect, the Reverend Robin Jolliffe loved his church and, by various campaigns, had raised enough money to install modern heating and lighting. In consequence the interior was welcoming, giving a visitor the feeling that he would be comfortable there.

Robin was now kneeling by the altar, the church being otherwise empty. His hands were clasped, his head bowed in prayer. 'O Lord, forgive Thy humble servant yet another failure of his ministry. I come before Thee burdened with guilt to ask pardon because I have not cared enough for my flock, as Thou hast charged me to do. Two young men who came to live here were cruelly victimised, O Lord. They were homosexual, and who should know better than I, Thy fallible servant, that Thou desirest not the death of a sinner, but rather that he should turn from his wickedness and live?

'I did not find it easy. Nor should I expect to find life easy. But these young men appealed to me and I vouchsafed them no response. Now they are gone from Thy parish, Lord, and I have two souls less to worship Thee.'

His attention wandered. A butterfly had found its way into the chancel. He watched with compassion as the insect fluttered about helplessly, sailing up to one stained-glass window after another, sometimes touching the glass, sometimes swooping away as if in disappointment.

'O Lord, hear my prayer and make me a better man and vicar to serve Thy ends. I pray now for those two poor queers, driven away by the bigotry of this Thy parish . . . All this I pray in the name of God the Father, God the Son and God the Holy Spirit. Amen.'

He rose rather hastily, opened the door and endeavoured to drive out the butterfly before it exhausted itself. His efforts were rewarded: the butterfly, like a departing human soul, found its way from the dimness of the church into the bright cold light of the other world.

As Robin stood in the porch, he saw Judith Mayes walking slowly through the graveyard towards him, carrying her new baby. He gave her a cheerful greeting. She held the sleeping babe for his inspection. Robin had had much practice in speaking admiringly of the newborn, and did not disappoint her.

'So, Judy, have you come to pray for your child's soul?'

She explained that she wanted Robin to christen the baby. It had been so long since she had been in church – well, she had come to the carol-singing at Christmas, but that was different, and the church had been crowded. She just wished to soak up the atmosphere.

Robin welcomed her in. He remained on the porch, waiting to lock the door. He was perfectly patient. As he stood there, gazing among the gravestones, watching for signs of the hated flatworms, worry clouded the horizons of his mind.

Once Judith had departed, he went back into the church. He took the torch he kept in the locker of the pulpit and went down on his knees at the base of the chancel arch. He blew away dust from the worn inscription on the stone. The date had been incised in roman numerals. It had been chipped, possibly in its removal to serve as the base of the arch. Even by the light of the torch, it was difficult to make out the lettering. Many years had passed since an elderly church historian had examined the stone and pronounced the date to be 503. His judgement had never been questioned.

'Gracious me!' exclaimed Robin. 'It's not 503 at all.

It's 602! I can't believe it! I just can't believe it. Oh, hell!'
He gasped. 'Sorry, Lord! Didn't mean to say that.'

He struck his forehead.

The surface of the stone was uneven. Chips and cracks
made it difficult to decipher. The second letter in particular was hard to read, but the spacing seemed to make
it clear that the figure was DCII and not DIII.

Robin's church history was somewhat vague. St
Augustine had written *The City of God* in 411 – that was
easy to remember – after Rome had been sacked by
someone. Attila? No, Alaric. In the fifth century, Honorius
had withdrawn the last Roman legion from Britain, after
which the situation was rather confused, not least in
Father Robin's mind. He had always believed that the
Romans, as well as building good straight roads, had introduced the class system to Britain. The uppers enjoyed
baths, the lowers cleaned lavatories. The arrangements had
proved so popular that they had continued ever since.

In 503, a Celtic church would probably have been
standing on this ground. And before that a pagan altar.
But by the seventh century, St Augustine had arrived in
England. Christianity was spreading. On the face of it,
602 was the far more likely date.

It followed that the one and a half millennial celebrations should by rights be postponed for another
century . . .

Oh, no! Robin looked in anguish at the dimly glowing
interior of his church. Expensive repairs were needed:
the tower was unstable; the bells were about to fall down.

And, of course, he would not be here in another
century.

He switched off the torch and went to kneel in front
of the altar. Fervently, he prayed for enlightenment. Would
the Lord instruct him to make the correct date known

immediately in the parish? Or, conversely, would the Lord like to see His House restored pretty promptly? Perhaps a buttress to support the tower, O Lord. After all, it was not the Lord's present vicar who had made the perfectly understandable mistake about the date, was it? Thy humble servant was not the cause of the misunderstanding, not to be blamed. Lead us not into temptation, O Lord. But . . .

Would he not be better to keep quiet about his discovery?

His eyes were bad. Could he possibly have been mistaken?

He ceased. Eyes closed, hands together in prayer, lips pursed.

Silence in the church, grave, deep and righteously ruminative . . .

The Lord pronounced to his vicar a favourable verdict.

Nothing was to be said.

Celebrations were to go ahead.

Father Robin rose from his knees, crossed himself and went out serenely into the open air. Some things were meant to be.

At ten thirty, Penelope Hopkins got off a bus in Oxford High Street and walked along to the Café Regale. The Café Regale was rather imposing, with Corinthian pillars framing its entrance. No matter that they were rather too tall for the width of the frontage.

You took three steps up to enter by a glass door into an elegant interior. Here, dark shining wood panelling was punctuated by long mirrors in which customers could contemplate themselves or their companions.

Stephen Boxbaum was already seated at a round table that commanded a view of the doorway. When Penelope appeared he rose to his feet, smiling in welcome. He was casually dressed, in a dark maroon shirt, a fawn jacket and brown trousers. His hair was slicked back. He had tucked away his spectacles in his breast pocket.

Penelope had chosen – not without misgivings, fearing it might be out of fashion – a blue dress with a high neck, and a pair of amethyst earrings which had belonged to a favourite aunt.

She had not visited the Regale before, and commented on its pleasant ambience.

'I doubt whether royalty have visited it at any time, Regale or not,' he said. 'Or is the name a pun on "regale" as in "feast"?'

She hoped he was not going to be clever.

They regarded one another, he with a degree of satisfaction that prompted him to speak with a certain deference. 'It was good of you to come, Mrs Hopkins, particularly when I did not specify what favour it was I hoped to ask of you.'

'I was happy to be invited. It happens I have a free period this morning, with no more overseas events to attend to.'

She told him briefly about her Chinese girls.

A waiter appeared and took their order for coffee and a particularly luxuriant cream bun with which Stephen was familiar. They talked of this and that before he took the opportunity to announce that he was forming a committee to celebrate the long existence of St Clement's Church, which stood as a monument to England's stability and relative peace. He hoped very much that Mrs Hopkins would care to serve on the committee.

'I received your announcement this morning, thank you.'

'Was it suitable? Did it suit you?'

'A fine idea although, as I told you, I am a non-believer. And you will be the chairman?'

'Until we find someone better able to manage it, yes.'

She sat silent for a minute, looking down at the table, until, flashing a glance at him, she asked him why he should be interested in celebrating the longevity of an Anglican church.

He caught the inference. 'As you cannot fail to realise, Mrs Hopkins, the Jewish people have perforce led unstable lives, not least through the persecutions of the twentieth century. I have in consequence a profound preference for stability. Here we have a fine example of that quality, which we can only hope will continue. It's not that St Clement's is an architectural masterpiece. I lend my support because I find I am established happily in Hampden Ferrers.' He spread his hands to show the openness of his reply.

'In Hampden Ferrers, where harmless young homosexuals get beaten up and feel impelled to leave?' she all but murmured.

'Maybe homosexuals – but not Jews.'

She could not resist joining in his laughter. 'I suppose that Ferrers itself is not a bad place. It's near to Oxford.'

'But that's another reason to celebrate, Mrs Hopkins. By the way, may I say how much I admire your earrings? I mean, the church helps sustain village life. Rather like the post office, I suppose. Without the church and its congregation, the village would probably have disappeared long ago, being so close to thriving Oxford.'

'My name is Penelope,' she said. 'Call me Penny. Everyone does. Please abandon "Mrs Hopkins". I, too, have a confession to make, if that is what we are into.

'I am no churchgoer. As a child, I was taken to church regularly. Once I became adult I lost interest, or I was

80

too busy for many years. Well, I suppose I'm too busy now. Also, I don't really care for the idea of begging favours from an invisible entity. Is it perhaps what you might call undemocratic? And, to be honest, I believe that in this world it is a case of every woman or man for her- or himself. We may want to help others, but to be able to do so we must first look after ourselves. Without begging.

'Sorry, that's a long speech. I suppose I remain confused on the subject. I guess I'm a doubter, an agnostic.'

Their coffee was brought on an ebony tray.

'But you lead a spiritual life.'

'Oh, I don't know about that. I don't even know what it means.'

'You're too beautiful not to lead a spiritual life.'

Before the words were out of his mouth, Penelope saw, with a perfect and undeniable understanding, what was in his mind, what had been in his mind as she entered the café, even what had been in his mind when they had met in Hill's Stores over a brown loaf. Perhaps it had always been inherent in his body language, which she had interpreted without realising until this very minute. Because their gaze met as he spoke, she revealed to him with her eyes that she had perceived his underlying intention. Regret that she had inadvertently done so filled her; at the same time, she appreciated that she did not regret his desiring her. She had been approached not infrequently over the years, but had deflected such advances; inasmuch as she had male friends, they were men who accepted the invisible line she drew, which told them, So far and no further. Yet this smooth man, whom she judged to be in his mid-fifties – much, in other words, her own age – might be the one who would slip past her defences, provided he conducted his campaign correctly . . .

She was surprised to find how elated she was at the prospect. And even sexually aroused.

Stephen, seeing that his approach had been premature, beat a retreat. He told her it had been impertinent of him to enquire into her spiritual life. He covered his retreat by venturing into description. 'What does one imply by "spiritual life"? In my case, it simply means worrying about my deficiences and all those deficiencies that seem inseparable from the – well, let's say from the human condition, if there is such a thing . . .'

'Oh, I'm sure there is, Stephen.' By using his first name, she showed him that his retreat need not be permanent. 'Mmm, there certainly is such a thing. I suffer from the human condition most of the time.' She smiled.

He sipped his coffee. 'I wish I could alleviate your suffering.' He paused, smiling boldly at her, then added, 'Instead of adding to it by conscripting you on to my committee.'

To escape the tone of the conversation, she asked him what he wanted her to do.

'There is much we must do. For one thing, we need to talk first to the Vicar. We must have Father Robin's approval. I wrote him a special letter. We must let everyone in the village know what we intend, to generate sympathy and, if at all possible, enthusiasm. Get everyone involved. We need to raise money, of course, invite more people to join the committee – a maximum of six, perhaps – and decide how we should celebrate. Perhaps engage a symphony orchestra for the day. Are you musical?'

'I listen to Shostakovich. And Wagner. I like some of Wagner's music very much.'

'What in particular?'

Penelope wondered if Wagner was a sore point with him. 'I find the Prelude to *Lohengrin* sublime. Its exquisite

82

lyricism . . . But never mind that. Go on. Where will these festivities be held?'

'Some in the church, some in the primary school, perhaps. And I thought we might be able to close off the village street for the day, if we get permission from the council. Have a street party, ending with fireworks. We must pick a fine day, if possible.'

'And the finances for all this?'

'Ah, the finances. I think we might pass round a begging bowl.'

'You've thought it all out already. You *are* decisive.'

He regarded her unhappily. 'Sadly, no − in this perhaps, but otherwise, oh, far from decisive. My weakness. One of them.'

She nodded, pleased that he confided, but in the first flush of her excitement she did not pay enough attention to what he was actually telling her.

There and then, they began a discussion that even the cream buns could not entirely disrupt.

He put his hand over hers, beaming, saying that he knew he could count on her involvement. She did not withdraw her hand as she asked: 'What part will your wife play in all this?'

'Sharon is not interested in the question.'

But what, she asked herself − not without some inward excitement − *was* the question exactly?

Humming to herself, Andrea Ridley finished cleaning the kitchen and prepared to take a tray of Earl Grey tea to Sharon Boxbaum. She worked at the Manor only until eleven o'clock, when she let herself out of the back door and went home to see to her husband, lying in bed.

Before taking the tray through, she carried a mug of coffee up the back stairs and tapped on Rupert Boxbaum's door. He called her in, smiling and welcoming her. Rupert was a small, wiry version of his father. He grew his hair long and wore a T-shirt that said, 'SAME OLD SHIT', above a tattered pair of jeans. Rupert went barefoot about the house. He was currently composing on an electronic keyboard.

'You are so kind, Andrea,' he said. 'My only friend . . .'

She regarded him with a saucy look. 'I heard you had another friend.'

He coloured immediately. 'I don't know what you mean.'

'Same one my son Duane has been known to visit.'

'Sorry, Andrea, still don't know what you're on about.' His expression contradicted his words.

'A trip up the hill at midnight . . .'

'It's good exercise.' Then, realising his excuse carried a double meaning, he burst into laughter. 'Oh, shit! Well, don't tell Dad!'

'What — me?' She dismissed the subject. 'I just thought you'd like a cup of coffee before I go.' She smiled affectionately at the lad. He was always polite — and his rebellion against his parents was of a more courteous variety than Duane's, she reflected with regret.

'A cup of cuffee! How nice! I'm thinking of composing a song called "Andrea and Dreams". How'd you like that?'

'I should be delighted, provided you don't ask me to sing it.'

They chatted for a while longer, until she went downstairs to take the tea tray through to the reading room. There sat Sharon with her feet up on the sofa and Bingo sleeping on her lap. She was reading a paperback and smoking a cigarette. She had put on no makeup and her hair was untidy. 'Very kind, Andrea. I'll have it in a minute. This is such a silly book. I'm really quite bored with it.' She waved it as if to throw it across the room.

'You don't have to read it, Sharon.'

'I've nothing else to do. It's too chilly to garden. I know I look the absolute pits. Would you like to borrow this book after me? It's called *Sarah and Society*. Quite funny, really, I suppose.'

'I don't ever find time for reading, I'm afraid.'

'Let me read you this bit. This is what it's like.'

She began to read, while Andrea stood by politely, waiting to leave.

'Derek was just perfect for her. They took a walk from the villa. A giant tree that had shaded the house from the Tuscan heat had recently been sawn down. Its wood was probably made into nasty little pepper mills and wooden salad bowls for the middle classes.

Beyond lay the valley, misty with promise, and covered with the bright yellow glare of celandines. Sarah clutched Derek's hand, speechless with happiness.

'"Fresh figs and goat's cheese for breakfast," he told her.

'"Marvellous!" Sarah breathed.'

Sharon uttered a sound like a laugh. 'If only life were that perfect, eh, Andrea? "Misty with promise . . ." But I can see I'm boring you. I think I bore Stephen. I certainly bore Rupert.'

'No, no, don't think that. It's just that I must get back to Arthur.'

'How is he?'

'About done for, to be honest. Progressive nuclear decay, they say it is.' She bade goodbye to the unhappy woman on the sofa. As Andrea entered her house Sharon

85

was still on her mind. Duane was there, in ragged jeans and T-shirt. She had not been expecting him. His back was turned to her, and he was standing by the stove, pouring himself orange juice from a carton. 'Duane! Did you get the job?'

'No.' He said no more and did not turn round.

His mother stood looking at his back. 'You mustn't give up.'

He turned then, grinning his mocking grin. Opening his mouth, he waggled his tongue at her. He had had a bead inserted in it, a white one resembling a pearl.

She could not hide her distress.

Duane laughed. 'It's all right, Ma. It's cool. The girls will dig it.'

'It'll ruin your teeth.'

'Balls. 'Sides, what have I got to live for?'

'This despair of yours, it's a pose. I know you want to upset me, but you have everything to live for, dear. You're not like that poor melancholy woman in the Manor next door.'

He lumbered over, hugging his glass in both hands. 'That miserable old bitch Sharon? What's she got to do with it?'

'Well, nothing, I suppose. But she's genuinely miserable, unlike you. You—'

'How do you know I'm not genuinely miserable? My life's a dead loss.'

'You're inventing it! Just because your dad did a runner, don't take it out on me. Doug was no fucking earthly good, but you don't have to be like that. Dotty's doing something with her life. She's—'

'What?' He set the glass down on the kitchen table in order to be more expressive. 'You're always slagging off my dad. Well, I liked Doug and I reckon you drove him

86

away, you with your constant nagging. He was a bloody good footballer, and you didn't like that either, did you? Played for Oxford United.

'As for Dotty doing something with her life! Working in bloody Debenham's? You call that something? She might as well be banged up in the nick! If you think I'm going after rubbish jobs of that sort, Ma, you've got another think coming!'

She was frightened by his vehemence, but would not give in. 'Duane, please! Look, you and that Barrie Bayfield—'

'Starman, if you please.'

'Whatever daft thing he calls himself. You and him beating up those two poor gays. Can't you see you're turning into a right yob?'

'Them queers annoyed us in the pub, didn't they? Anyhow, they're gone now, so forget it.'

She gave a sigh. 'You look so ugly when you're angry, Duane. I hardly recognize you.' As she turned away, she added, 'You must always have it all your own way.'

'I bloody *will* have it all my own way.'

'I'm going up to see Arthur.'

'That'll be fun!'

Left to himself in the kitchen, Duane perched himself on a stool. He rested his elbows on the counter and his head in his hands. So he remained, with his undrunk orange juice beside him.

Sir Sydney Barraclough, president of Wolfson, his wife Caroline, vice president John Westall, the poet, and Francis Martinson stood in the entrance hall, awaiting their visiting lecturer, Maria Coperalli, Contessa di Medina Mirtelli.

Maria had phoned Frank in his office to tell him she

was on her way. She had said, 'Better be warned, Frank, I've changed since we last met, so long ago.'

'We've both changed. The world's changed.' He spoke lightheartedly but now, as he stood in the entrance hall, he was remembering their one and only meeting, when he was already well known and Maria still a student. They had been in San Marino. Frank had been in the little mountain republic to research its recent history; in 1940, San Marino had declared war on the Allies, together with Mussolini's Italy, but in 1943 it had asserted its neutrality before Italy surrendered. This quasi-independence was to be the subject of a paper Frank was writing.

Maria had asked him questions about his career and about archaeology. An affinity had arisen between them. Although he had had a friend with him, the charming Lady Annette Biggs, he had invited Maria to lunch. They had talked compulsively, looking at each other with aroused interior eyes, as if some elusive mutual understanding had always existed between them. Annette had not been pleased.

After the lunch, when they both smoked cigarettes, a boy had come to collect Maria and off she had gone, with a farewell wave. Francis had thought then, Why should she care? But the parting had caused him an intense pain of loss, regret and love. He had stood on the balcony and watched her go, hoping she might glance back. She did.

So she had changed. Of course she had changed over the intervening sixteen years. Perhaps she had become fat. Or ugly? No, she could never be that . . .

A shiny black limousine drew up in the courtyard outside Wolfson. A chauffeur climbed out and opened a rear door.

Maria stepped out. Frank breathed more rapidly.

The president and his wife moved forward to greet her, talking animatedly. Frank hung back, taking in her physical presence. Maria was far from being fat: her slender figure was elegantly clad in dark trousers, with a fawn blouse under a light brown jacket. A white wool sweater was draped over one arm. Her calfskin shoes were sharply pointed and matched the fawn of her blouse. She was blond, her hair cut fairly short. She had on plenty of jewellery, he saw: multiple bracelets on the right wrist, a diamond watch on the left. And a sapphire ring on the index finger of her left hand.

She appeared to wear no makeup. Her eyes were brown; they evidently required a pair of small rimless glasses. Her mouth was small. She was, thought Frank, just amazingly, cunningly, confidentially beautiful.

It was a shock to find that this was the woman with whom he had been corresponding intermittently, listening to her troubles and triumphs, for some sixteen years. Through his bemusement, he was amused to hear the president, a rabid socialist, addressing Maria repeatedly as 'Contessa'.

'I am sorry to arrive so early,' she was saying to John Westall.

'Never early enough, Contessa,' the poet replied gallantly.

There goes the Contessa again, he thought. Then she was shaking his hand and smiling. 'So, Frank, we're a little older!'

'But no wiser, I hope.'

They looked at each other without speaking, half smiling. Again he felt that unbidden mutual understanding, that empathy he was sure she also was experiencing.

Sydney Barraclough was summoning a porter for Maria's considerable luggage, and saying, 'Frank, would you like to show the Contessa to her suite?'

When they were in her room, and the luggage stacked on a side-table, Maria prowled around as if curious about everything. She looked out of the window at the lake, where two swans sailed, and the river Cherwell and countryside beyond. Then she turned to him. Although her look was not unmixed with shyness, she was perfectly direct.

'I owe you more than you can know, Frank, my dear.' She spoke in a soft voice he had not really remembered. Her English was practically without accent.

'You have been a part of my life all these years,' he said, almost bewildered by her presence. 'All these years, although we have never managed to meet.'

'And you of mine, despite my marriage. I can say it. As you know, I have a child, a daughter, who is eight now.'

'Yes. How is she? You are still married to the Count, then?'

'Yes, yes, I am still married to Alfredo. And how is Lady Annette?'

'Oh, she got married to someone. A magazine editor, George de la Touche. He has just won a libel case in the High Court. Why did you marry Alfredo? Can I ask?'

'I ask myself that.' For a moment, she looked down at the carpet. He took in the parting of her hair. 'Alfredo wasn't threatening. Then there was his title, admittedly. His palazzo. It offered some security. All that time I thought I would die.'

'The breast cancer?'

'Oh, stop it! So is Wolfson College pleasant for you, my dear Frank?'

As they talked Frank was conscious that a phantom of

90

himself stood on the very spot that he now occupied, a Frank Martinson who had lived with this extraordinary woman for many years past, had lived in her native city of Rome, had had a daughter by her. This phantom's life felt more real to him than his lived life had been.

And as they talked together in the room – they were holding hands now – they were not listening to what they were saying. They seemed to be moving still closer to each other when a knock sounded at the door. When they called, 'Come in,' there was John Westall, smiling, immaculate, deeply unwelcome, announcing that drinks were being served in the Senior Common Room, if the Contessa would care to join them.

They made polite conversation with senior members of the college, and admired a bust of the founder, Sir Isaiah Berlin. After half an hour, Maria suggested to Frank that she would like to take a look at Oxford. She was not due to give her talk until eight o'clock that evening.

'Perhaps you would like me to come too, Frank?' suggested John. 'I know Oxford like both sides of my hand.'

Frank caught the naughty twinkle in the poet's eye. 'I think we'll manage. Christ Church, New College, Magdalen. We can't go wrong, really, John, thanks all the same.'

Half an hour later, Maria and Frank found themselves entering the portals of the Café Regale for a cappuccino. They stood back to allow a man and a woman to leave.

'How funny!' Frank said, as they sat down at a table for two. 'That chap lives in Hampden Ferrers. His name's Boxbaum.'

When they had ordered the coffee, Maria started to

tell him about the discovery of Otzi the Iceman, as they called the mummified body discovered in recent years frozen in the Italian Alps. Twelve thousand feet up on the Similaun peak, the body had been preserved by cold for 5300 years. 'Otzi is the perfect link with our Stone Age ancestors,' she said.

Sixteen years ago in San Marino, her meeting with Frank had moved her to become an archaeologist. As he recalled, she had studied and taken her degree. She had gone on a dig in Tuscany but had found it boring and, by luck, had been invited by a television crew to act as commentator on the excavation and its frustrations. She moved on to television, and from then her life had been prosperous as a star presence on RAI TV. 'But I still see Otzi. There he lies in the Bolzano lab, dead for so long, yet still a formidable presence. I always think about death.' Frank held her delicate hand. 'I fear death so much. It's my shadow. And there is this poor human creature, still without a grave after so many centuries . . .'

She shivered. He felt the movement. Their knees were touching.

'It was this horrible cancer. I still fear it will return.'

She put a hand over his. Looking directly at him, she said, 'Let's go back to my room. We don't have to talk to anyone.'

So it was in her Wolfson room that, after fifteen years of waiting, they first embraced and kissed. They went directly to each other, held each other, stood there mouth to mouth, exaltation sweeping over them.

It was a great mystery, a miracle. They had always loved each other. It was magic.

It was one minute past noon.

And everything changed.

★   ★   ★

92

The coach was painted a deep Oxford blue and labelled, in flamboyant lettering along its flanks, 'Oxford Express'. It shone in the sunlight, having been through the auto-wash that morning.

Penelope fell into deep thought on the coach going home from the Café Regale. As she stared vaguely out of the window at the undistinguished countryside, she tried to put together a coherent anatomy of her feelings for Stephen and his feelings for her. She was in no doubt that something significant had happened between them, something that paddled timidly in the tiniest shallows of that great stormy ocean she thought of as love.

Or that spread like the branches of a great oak.

Or that reached deep underground like the veins of a volcano.

Or that stretched across the world like her overseas enrolments.

Or that was the essence of everything like the air she breathed.

She smiled to herself as she gave up the hunt for appropriate similes . . .

But why? And why now? She had armoured herself against such things. Many years ago, almost fifteen of them, she and her husband – that young, distant Gregory, her beloved Greg – had been walking along the top of a steep Dorset cliff, enjoying the day, the view, each other's company.

Greg had fallen silent. Suddenly he had looked at her, face pale, stopped and clutched her arm. Had that been from affection or dizziness? 'I'm not well . . .'

She had been alarmed: not alarmed enough, as she had realised since. 'We can sit down,' she said. There was an oak bench nearby. Greg reached it with her assistance. He sat down on it and died.

She directed her thoughts back to the present, away from the pain that never faded. She thought instead of Stephen and how he might see her. Perhaps she was the cup that held the drink, but was she only the cup, and what did he think he would drink?

A car was running parallel with the Oxford Express coach. She collected herself enough to notice that the driver's hand was waving across the empty passenger seat – at her? Then the car accelerated and was gone, bearing the hand with it. If it had been a Citroën, the question arose as to whether Stephen drove one – *that* Citroën . . . She did not know the external circumstances of his life, never mind the interior ones. And yet, she had to acknowledge it: she was already afloat, like an impulsive adolescent girl, in that great perilous ocean she thought of as love.

The coach called in at Hampden Ferrers on its way through Nuneham Courtenay and Bishops Linctus to its depot in Witney. Several people got off at the high-street stop. She saw the Citroën parked, waiting, nearby. She alighted last. She had delayed, in a cocktail of delight and apprehension.

'Thank you,' she said to the driver. She stepped down on to the pavement. The coach door closed. The vehicle drew away.

Stephen Boxbaum was standing on the other side of the street in the sunshine, relaxed, smiling. 'I raced you home,' he said.

Penelope almost heard the words. She was crossing the road towards him. She realised that her face had lit in a smile in a most ridiculous way. Not only did he look wonderful but she knew he was thinking exactly the same about her, ordinary Penelope Hopkins.

Stephen clutched her upper arm. He told her he

94

wanted her to come with him. He knew he was doing something irredeemable, something terrible, something that would change the world. He would have dragged her into the nearby church porch, had she not come tripping by his side, almost pulling him along as if she understood perfectly the decisive step they were about to take.

Both were saying something utterly trivial, and laughing, not hearing, hardly thinking.

They passed quickly among the memorials to the local dead, who were lying under the bare earth, not complaining, not criticising, indeed regretting only that they had not lived enough when they had had the chance.

Penelope and Stephen gained the semi-privacy of the porch. He wrapped his arms about her. She wrapped hers about him. They became engulfed in each other's warmth, as if the accelerated circulation of their blood had become one stream. They stared into each other's faces. She thought – though barely thought – that she was the cup from which he must drink.

It was one minute past noon.

Their lips met.

They kissed each other.

And – as they might have anticipated – everything changed.

Grass sprang up tall and green among the graves.

The sun hastened its tardy climb past its low spring zenith and whizzed up to the highest point of the heavens.

A sudden wind sprang up, whirling petals from blossoming trees about them for all the world like confetti.

Rodney and Judith's baby stopped shrieking, sprouted two tiny wings, fluttered out of the bedroom window and flew above Hampden Ferrers, swooping and dipping in its delight. The dog, Tony, ran below, barking in excitement.

Bettina Squire's dark child, Ishtar, zoomed up like a rocket and was off in the direction of Jupiter and the Medician moons.

Jeremy Sumption, waking late, opened an envelope and found a cheque from his American publisher for a hundred thousand dollars. He rushed out into the street to buy a drink to celebrate, at the same time as Greyling heaved his considerable bulk out of the Pink House to go and get some more cigarettes.

Old Joe Cotes's leg miraculously healed. He danced about the farmhouse while Duke barked his head off.

Duane Ridley resolved on the spot to temper his lifestyle of despair, ran out of the house, bumped into his mate the Starman's sister, Kyle Bayfield — whom he had hitherto regarded as a stuck-up little monster — and embraced her. She proved not stuck up at all, and walked with him up Molesey Hill. Later, in a golden glow, they ate fish and chips together.

Starman Barrie was flabbergasted to find among his Terry Pratchett collection a Discworld novel of which he had never heard, *The Sign of the Crossword Puzzle*.

Rupert Boxbaum found the perfect lyric for his song 'Andrea and Dreams'.

Fowels and Bowles, contractors, managed to bribe a county-council chap to permit them to buy North Pasture off Jack Cotes for a considerable sum.

Andrea Ridley, going upstairs to see Arthur, found him — to her astonishment — standing gaunt and sepulchral at the top. 'Andrea,' he croaked, 'I was determined to die standing up!' He did so, and not another word said he.

'That's the second one gone,' said Andrea, collapsing, not without a certain cowardly relief, on the bottom stair.

Bob Norris, doggedly pushing his bike, stuck a substantial package through the side door of Cotes Farmhouse.

Later, when Yvonne Cotes opened it, she found it came from Old Burlingham Street, and contained the page proofs of her journal, which the copy-editor had entitled *Cockerels over Cotes*. A letter had been sent earlier, but evidently the goat had eaten it. 'Congratulations on becoming Queen of the Village Chronicle,' wrote the copy-editor this time.

'I'm famous! I'm someone! At last!' shrieked Yvonne, and danced with old Joe Cotes.

In the Manor, Sharon Boxbaum turned the final page of her novel. 'Brilliant!' said she, and lit another cigarette.

Father Robin received a holy visitation. The entire church filled with sweet-smelling mist. An angel came down in a soiled T-shirt, on which was printed the legend, 'King Kong Also Died For Our Sins'. Robin was transfixed and went down on the knees from which he had only just risen.

The angel told him to look behind a false panel in the old worm-eaten cupboard in the vestry, then vanished in a cloud twice as bright as a magnesium flare, leaving no ash behind.

'I swear he was real, a real angel,' he told his wife. 'He floated.'

In Wolfson College, the loving kiss between Maria and Frank also wrought miracles. A gentle, cleansing light, more like music than illumination, filled the building. Many a learned essay blanked out on many a screen, many a learned paper floated to the floor, many a learned library book was dropped in astonishment.

The learned company, too, was transformed. The poet John Westall fell silent in mid-verse; the president, Sydney Barraclough, fell silent in mid-lecture; Caroline Barraclough, his wife, fell silent in mid-song; all scholars and tutors fell silent in mid-something.

As well they might! For, lo and behold, they were all suddenly clad in flowing golden robes, such as Athens had never seen in its golden age! All eyed each other with amazement and something approaching reverence. Rivalries were forgotten in the bliss of a common under-standing.

Nor was that all.

A turbulent commotion had seized the normally placid lake. There was now no longer a lake but a roaring torren-tial sea, stretching beyond the Cherwell as far as vision went. Great sea monsters sported in the flood, sported and spouted and spurted and splashed, like buxom babies in a tub.

And from those overwhelming waters a gigantic figure arose, accompanied by *Götterdämmerung*-like chords, garbed in seaweed, with a crown on its head and a trident in its hand. It was, recognisably, a reincarnation of the founding president of the college, Sir Isaiah Berlin, while behind him, mistier and mistier, like all the birds in Oxfordshire and Gloucestershire, rose another Berlin, singing in a bird-sweet tone, his words distorted by ampli-fication: 'gum on a log, gum on a log, like the Tate Rubens is ham . . .' It was not that it made sense but that it made music.

His pretty voice was drowned by a stentorian Isaiah, who addressed the glittering Wolfsonians in a mighty voice: 'O all ye students of remote sciences and arcane humanities, know that there is one wisdom above all others, and that is the wisdom which comes closest to folly, the wisdom of faith, the wisdom of pulses and impulses, the wisdom of extravagance, the wisdom of genes and gonads, the wisdom of well-tested testosterone, the wisdom of astonishment, the wisdom – what do I mean, folks? – the wisdom of—'

And all the senior members, male and female and those in between, cried out the answer in one voice: **'LOVE!'**

'Excellent,' said the gigantic figure. 'But louder next time.' And it sank beneath the waves, to be seen no more.

Then all concerned began to debate what had happened – all, that is, except Frank and Maria, who held each other tightly and tenderly in her little suite, among her still-packed baggage.

Adam Hamilton-Douglas argued that perception was almost everything. Certainly there was a structure, although many of its elements were hypothetical, which we called 'the real world', but the dominant reality was our perception of it. He claimed that it was useless to deny that they had witnessed the apotheosis of Sir Isaiah Berlin although, statistically speaking, less than one per cent of the population of Oxford had.

Hamilton-Douglas would go so far as to say that they had all shared a perception of it. Although there were but eighty-one of them present, that did not invalidate the experience. Moreover, he continued, the experience, or the perception of the experience, would have been just as valid had only eight people been present. Had there, however, been but one person perceiving it, then doubt might have been cast on what he liked to call the external reality since there would have been no available corroboration.

Howard Azdabji, a gentle Parsi *savant*, said that he was loath to disagree with Dr Hamilton-Douglas, but it occurred to him that in everyone of sensibility there is not only the Doer but also the Watcher, who witnesses all in a state of calm, who looks on tempests and is unmoved, much as it says in the Bhagavadgita. The Watcher is in a sense ineffectual, but on occasion may influence events, particularly if the Watcher is emotionally disturbed. Equally, the Doer may have its effect on the Watcher. Continuing, Azdabji said they should all consider that there was in everyone the need for love, while in the minds of those who had known Isaiah Berlin in life there was a special love for that great man: so great that it engendered an unwitting – he might even say *unconscious* – longing for him to return. Possibly they had all suffered a mass hallucination, projected by the Watcher in all of them.

Caroline Barraclough said she, too, tended to favour an inward explanation for what she termed a visitation. Whether one could say, or not, that Isaiah had manifested himself, he certainly prompted them to look more closely into themselves. Indeed, the prompting to love more – and here she cast an affectionate glance at Sydney, which did not go unobserved – was necessary in this alarming time of national and religious hatred, against which Wolfson had always made a stand.

She said she would like to remind them, if she might, of the words of Socrates: 'The unexamined life is not worth living.'

'Excuse me, dear,' said her husband, 'but I believe that the Greek has it that "An unexamined life is hardly a life."'

'Children all lead unexamined lives,' said Irene Muntberg. 'That's why they are so damned unpredictable.' She had four and was ignored.

'Socrates' phrase was coined ahead of time for androids,' said John Westall. 'We assume that androids, when they exist, will not be able to examine their so-called lives. That will always be an important distinction between android and human. An unexamined life's a total loss. An unexamined life's not worth a toss.'

A line of philosophers quickly formed on the shore:

Dame Rita Diamond, Jerry Hooja, Azdabji and
Hamilton-Douglas among them, dancing with linked
arms and singing joyously:

'See me dance the polka,
See me singing this song.
We think the unthinkable.
That's where we all belong.

An unexamined life is just no good
Or you've stood under what's not understood.
So brood in silence well before you speak –
Be like the wise old owl, the wily Greek,
And peep deep down into your very being:
It's cloudy there and doubtless full of doubt.
Though you may not savour what you're seeing
That's what examination's all about!
Yippee! That's what examination –
Without procrastination –
Get on your knees for Socrates –
That's what examination's all about!'

IV

Connections with the Neolithic

It is an uncomfortable fact that good things are often accompanied by bad things. Philosophers sometimes prefer to make the statement the other way round: bad things are often accompanied by good things. While the man in the street may say that nothing is ever as good or bad as it seems, the truth of the matter is that the glass is half full and half empty at one and the same time.

The kiss threw both Stephen and Penelope into confusion. Still clinging to him, Penelope said, 'Oh, but Sharon . . . There's Sharon . . . There's Sharon to deal with. You must be kind. As kind as you can.'

'Oh, her . . .' he murmured. 'I know, I know.'

'I should never have kissed you!' She broke away and rushed into the church – to take shelter, stifle her emotion, calm her heart.

Stephen made to follow her. He paused with his hand on the worn oak door. Hesitation was deeply embedded in his nature. At that moment, he decided to let dearest Penny remain alone to regain her poise. He, too, was choked with emotion, predominantly delight but also

102

fear: he knew he must either deceive Sharon or face her with the truth. It was a decision too far.

He turned away. And, facing into the high street, Stephen Boxbaum witnessed an accident.

Enfolded within the silence and shadow of St Clement's, Penelope allowed herself to sob. It was a luxurious, deep, dry sob, as she breathed in the atmosphere of the church. Oh, a man had kissed her and the world could never be the same again! The figures in the stained-glass windows seemed to dance around her. She had to go and seat herself in a nearby pew to recover from the emotional effect.

She hardly took note of the hymn book before her, or the hassock hanging from its hook, richly embroidered in purple and red, contrasting with the shining darkness of the wooden pews.

Gently, a voice said, 'You do well to come here for solace. Would you care to talk to me?'

She looked up, not in startlement but almost as if she had expected the voice, although she had heard no step. There stood Father Robin in his patched grey sweater, his black trousers and his grey trainers, with a half-smile on his face. An ordinary comfortable man. He was holding a chisel and mallet, which he now placed carefully on the nearest pew in order to attend unencumbered to Penelope.

On seeing her glance at the tools, he explained, 'I have had a vision – the first ever, I may say. I haven't been terribly good at visions. I was told to break into the back of an old cupboard. Which I am rather reluctant to do since it probably sailed with Noah on his Ark.'

She smiled vaguely, none too sure what he was talking about. 'Oh, Father, excuse me! I didn't mean to be here. I mean, that is, I didn't come to pray.' Unthinkingly, she brushed back a lock of hair that had fallen over her forehead. 'Why are women so feeble? The truth is . . . Oh, I have fallen violently in love with someone.' She tried to stop herself trembling.

The Vicar nodded. 'I thought I felt the church shake.'

'I'm fifty-five, Father, soon to be fifty-six.'

'You are not implying, are you, that a shutter comes down at fifty? That we cease to feel deeply at fifty or at any age?'

'To be honest, I don't know what I'm saying . . .'

'The virus of love can strike at any time. Just like the virus of religion – the hope of the world. We know of no penicillin that will cure it. Fortunately it is a benevolent virus. Although that rather depends on whom we catch it from.'

'That's easy to say, Father. But you don't understand.' She buried her face in her hands, feeling she could not continue this or any other kind of conversation.

'I catch the religious virus every day of my life,' said Robin. 'And the virus of love that goes with it. Perhaps I am more used to it than you are.'

She started up, facing him. 'Oh, I'm not used to it, certainly not. I thought I was safe. I really thought my door was locked against it. And now I have fallen for a married man.'

'That does raise a few questions, I must admit,' Robin said, in his casual way. 'But the question that immediately occurs to me is, does this married man love you in return?'

She looked quite wild. 'Oh, he does, I'm sure he does! Yes, yes, I know he does. I'd die if he didn't . . . But why am I telling you all this?'

He looked about him. 'Because there's no one better here to whom you could tell it. Besides, it's nice and quiet, the very place for confidences. The church is deserted but for me – and One Other.'

'We do well to remember that this poor church, greatly in need of repair, stands like a metaphor for our life. But up above us, in splendour, stands the City of God, which needs no repair.'

The remark subdued her. She had risen from the pew and now stood silently, regarding him. She thought, He's a good man: he won't tell anyone. But she did not know that. 'I'm sorry, Vicar. I'm all right now. I must go. I am glad to have spoken to you.'

'But you haven't told me about the third person in this triangle.' He spoke gently, almost apologetically, as was his habit.

'Oh. I don't know much about her, only what I have heard. That she is a distressed kind of person.'

'I see. And do you think that knowing, or finding out, that her husband loves someone else will make her less distressed?'

She shook her head. 'That's what upsets me. He's not free. It's him I think of.'

'And yourself . . .'

Penelope felt tears welling up. 'Yes, it's true, I do think of myself. Don't blame me for that, don't reproach me. I know it's against religion . . .'

'Religion certainly speaks out against adultery, if we are talking about that. You may know the cynical rhyme, "Do not adultery commit, Advantage rarely comes of it". But I'd say it is not religion speaking but something in human nature that leads us as an imperative to think of ourselves. I am always suspicious when I hear that someone has performed a selfless act. I ask myself, What's he or she up to?'

A little pridefully, Penelope replied that she always tried to be honest with herself.

'It's a start. Good. If you are troubled, come and see

105

me again. I can generally be found hanging about here.'

'You are very kind. I appreciate what you have said.'

He took her hand, without shaking it, then let it go. 'You are a serious person, I can see. Of course you take this matter seriously.'

She managed a small laugh. 'Oh, God, yes!'

'And so does He.'

He escorted her to the door, and closed it softly behind her.

It was almost noon. The high street was busier than usual. Some small boys were trotting home for lunch, endeavouring to push each other off the pavement as they went. Duane and Kyle were heading for the fish-and-chip shop, which was run by Cypriots. Greyling was taking the air, and Jeremy Sumption had just emerged from the Carpenter's. Stephen Boxbaum had left the cemetery and was heading slowly for the Manor.

Cars were passing. From the direction of the primary school, young Sammy Aziz was heading on his bike for his father's shop. At that moment, the two Chinese girls, Hetty Zhou and Judy Chung, emerged in their sky-blue dresses from the gate of number twenty-two.

Young Sammy was amazed at the sight. His eyes went wide, his bike went wobbly. A car heading in the direction of Oxford struck him, knocking him down and running over the bike.

The Chinese ladies and the others screamed. People ran forward to help. Henry Wiverspoon climbed out of the driving seat of the offending vehicle. He knelt by the body of the boy. On seeing the pool of blood spreading by his front tyre, he collapsed, weeping, against the side of his vehicle.

Stephen ran forward to help his old friend to his feet, while others dragged Sammy from under the car.

Looking on from the opposite pavement, close by Jeremy, Greyling remarked, 'Well, now, there are plenty more of them where he came from.'

Jeremy hit him in the stomach, and Greyling went down on his knees, gasping, open-mouthed, his heavy face contorted with pain. He fell forward on to his hands, to remain there, head hanging, grunting.

Bettina Squire propelled Ishtar in her pushchair across the road and went into Hill's Stores to break the news as gently as she could to Sam Senior and Rima. She asked herself if this was another person to descend into the city of the dead below Ferrers, but wisely kept the question to herself.

Someone called an ambulance. Duane and Kyle, meanwhile, helped to lay Sammy tenderly on the pavement as a small crowd gathered.

Starman Barrie Bayfield sat in his little bedroom, surrounded by books and videos of Discworld by Terry Pratchett, his favourite author, and various science-fiction magazines. He was watching an episode of *Star Trek* he had recorded earlier. For once he was paying the screen little attention: he was trying to puzzle out why his mate Duane should wish to go with his sister, Kyle. It was not as if she was pretty or clever or interesting. Besides, she was only a girl – and eighteen at that. At the age of twenty Starman was a real man.

'"Men are from Jupiter, girls are from Mars", he misquoted to himself. He felt bored and lonely. He planned to get to Mars one day, and would build a temple called Discworld on the Syrtis Major Planum.

Orbits of Earth and Mars featured on a large chart on

his wall, close to a poster of Terry Pratchett in a black stetson.

On his bedroom door notices said 'Danger: Demolition' and 'Parents and Aliens Keep Out'. The house was silent. Barrie's mother and father were out at work. They would return after six in the evening, quarrel and shout at each other and, almost certainly, yell at Barrie – he would yell back because they refused to call him Starman – and then they would disappear to meet up with friends at the pub. Barrie would be alone again. Or he would meet up with Duane.

This he decided to do. He snatched up a bag of crisps, and went out, slamming the door behind him. His parents refused to provide him with a latch-key in case he lost it, but Barrie had thoughtfully left a rear window ajar, through which he could climb in when necessary.

He knocked on the Ridleys' door.

Andrea let him in, all smiles. 'How are you, Mr Starman?'

'Just got in from Mercury, ma'am.' Barrie saluted smartly. 'How are things on Earth?'

'I'm so glad you're here. The world needs you. We're coming under attack by androids from Galaxy B.'

'I'll get my men. Leave it to me.'

Both were cheered by this conversation. Andrea lapsed into her normal self, put an arm round Barrie's shoulders and invited him into the kitchen for a mug of tea. Barrie was fond of Andrea: she was the one adult he knew who was fun.

In the kitchen, lolling about or sitting at the table, were Dotty, Duane and Kyle. Duane and Kyle were close together.

'What are you doing here?' Starman asked his sister.

'I come to see Duane, if you must know,' Kyle said.

'No, I come to see Duane. Me and him are going to the Carpenter's.'

Duane leant back nonchalantly in his chair. 'Sorry, chum, but that's what we aren't doing. Me and Kyle are going out together, on our ownio. Right, Kyle?'

'Too right,' said Kyle, smiling in a superior way at her brother. 'Go home, Starman.'

'Look,' said Barrie, 'I met an old guy today. He's got the name of an animal, a tiger or a leopard, and when I chucked an empty fag packet away, what do you think?'

'Who was he?' asked Andrea. 'What did he look like?'

'I dunno who he was, do I? Face like damp news-paper. This guy tells me to pick it up! I didn't do nothing at the time. There was a lot of people about. But I know where he lives – just past the coffee shop. I thought as we could call on him.'

'Forget it,' said Duane.

'Starman, dear, you mustn't cause trouble,' said Andrea. 'Not when an alien being was knocked down just outside here this morning. Besides, that old man you mention is very distinguished, a credit to the village. Maybe he secretly rules the universe. Concentrate on the war on Mars. Why don't you take our Dotty out instead?'

'Maaa-mm!' Dotty was instantly up in arms. 'I don't want to go out at all, and I don't want to go out with one of this village's well-known bovver boys. So forget it. No offence, Barrie!'

'So why don't you just fuck off?' Duane asked, pointing a finger at his friend and grinning fiercely.

'You fuck off yourself! A fine mate you turned out to be!'

And with that parting shot, Starman left the house, slamming the door behind him.

★ ★ ★

109

'You shouldn't play him up, you know,' said Andrea. 'He's really in a bad way. Fancy even thinking of attacking Professor Leppard – he's well into his eighties.'

'He's a regular pest, Mrs Ridley,' said Kyle. 'Mum can't do nothink with him.'

'He'd do well to attack his bloody awful dad!' said Dotty. 'The way that man looks at you! Gives you the creeps . . .'

Barrie climbed in through the back window and latched it behind him. Soon he was ensconced in his room. 'It don't bother me if I'm alone,' he said aloud. 'I shall overcome the forces of evil. I like being alone. Lonelier the better.'

He switched on his laptop with DVD facility, and was soon watching one of his favourite moments in all his collection. He spoke in a zombie-like voice in time with the computer on the spaceship.

'"Just what do you think you're doing, Dave? Dave. I really think I'm entitled to an answer. I know everything hasn't been quite right with me . . . But I can assure you now . . . I feel much better now, I really do. I can see you're really upset about this . . . I know I've made some poor decisions lately . . .

'"Dave, stop. Stop. Will you stop, Dave? Will you stop, Dave? Stop, Dave. I'm afraid. I'm afraid, Dave. Dave. My mind is going. I can feel it. I can feel it. My mind is going . . . There is no question about it. I can feel. I can feel it . . .

'"I'm afraid . . ."'

The afternoon had lapsed into somnolence. As Frank drove Maria to his house, the countryside seemed to doze. He switched on the car radio. A woman was talking about

110

the Crisis in Education. It was so far from their current preoccupations that he switched it off again.

Maria sat in the passenger seat, looking about her. 'I believe I'm supposed to take an interest in the country-side. Is that so? It's not something we learn to do in Rome.'

He flashed an amused glance at her. 'It's not compulsory here. It depends if you find fields at all appealing. Ahead, you can see the outline of the Molesey Hills. It's a bit hazy. It's quite a spooky lonely place.'

'Maybe we can go up there one day.'

'Certainly, if you'd like. There are good views from the top. As long as we don't encounter the phantom dogs supposed to haunt the place.'

Maria's talk at Wolfson had been a great success, as the presence of John Westall and the president of Wolfson at the party afterwards had testified. She had lectured with slides, emphasizing the unique connection between Otzi's mummified body and the Neolithic age. There was always a frisson, she suggested, about contact with something from the remote past.

She had talked about the surprise when an arrow-head was discovered, buried in Otzi's shoulder, while her TV documentary was being made. He had been killed while fleeing from a foe. Analysis of the Ice Man's teeth had enabled the scientists to pinpoint the exact region where he had spent his boyhood. It was a small trumph for modern science.

At the dinner afterwards Maria — now hailed as the Divine Contessa — sat next to President Sydney Barraclough, who had been charmed, sufficiently charmed to irritate his wife. Indeed, thought Frank, who would not be charmed by this delightful, modest woman whom he adored?

111

The car pulled into the drive of West End. Another car, a BMW, was carelessly parked ahead. As Maria and Frank were getting out, its owner, Stephen Boxbaum, approached. Frank and Stephen had only a nodding acquaintance. They shook hands and Frank introduced Maria.

Stephen made a gallant attempt not to look too interested. 'This is your first visit to Hampden Ferrers, Contessa?' When she said it was, he became quite eloquent about its beauties and invited them both to join his committee for the celebration of the local church's longevity.

While they made their excuses, Frank put a hand on Stephen's back and guided him towards the house, suggesting he had a cup of tea with them.

Stephen assented cheerfully, then said that he had come to see if he could talk to Frank's gardener, Alec Bingham.

'What do you want to speak to him for? He's a good gardener. You mustn't try to pinch him! Besides, he's tidying up the place for our party.'

'It's a bit embarrassing, really.' They entered the house. Maria looked about her with great interest. She immediately recognized the framed engravings of Piranesi's *Vedute*, with their glorified visions of Rome. 'Does Frank have a glorified vision of me?' she asked herself. And there were other questions in her head, such as the one about divorcing her husband, and the one about where Frank and she would live. Could she pursue her career in England or he his in Italy?

They settled themselves in a pleasant room overlooking the goldfish pond, where water-lilies were already showing fat buds. Frank had asked his housekeeper to bring them tea and cakes. And Stephen was explaining his problem. He wished to speak to the gardener on his own, because Alec Bingham was married to Violet, who worked for his friend Henry Wiverspoon, and they let a couple of rooms in their house on the Willetts Estate to the old retired nurse, Ann Longbridge.

'Yes, I know Nurse Longbridge. She looks after my brother. What of her?' asked Frank.

Stephen looked embarrassed. 'Well, you see . . . This is hard to explain. To be honest, I think she's a bit of a, well, a whore. Am I correct in thinking that a prostitute does it for money and a whore for pleasure?'

Frank laughed. 'And if it is so? But the nurse, she must be – what? In her fifties anyway.'

'Oh, age makes little difference,' said Maria. 'Believe me, I have known many women in their fifties more eager than ever for sex. Some, of course, are glad to be done with the entire business after the menopause, but many others feel freer to enjoy themselves. My mother is a good example there.'

'My son Rupert consorts with this nurse. I don't know how often. I found out only last night.'

'Did you catch them at it?' asked Frank.

Stephen explained the situation. He could not sleep and had been walking about the house in the dark. He had climbed up to the attic. When he glimpsed a light in the garden, he had assumed it was a marauder. However, he took up a pair of binoculars he kept for bird-watching and saw it was Rupert, heading away from the house with a torch. He was mystified.

He kept watch. The light became more distant. He soon realized that his son was going up on to the Molesey hills. He asked himself why he should be doing that, and could think of only one answer: sex.

An hour later, Rupert was coming down again. This time, Stephen was certain someone else was with him.

When they reached the bottom of the hill, he saw two lit cigarettes, confirming his suspicions.

He continued to watch. The pair parted. He could make out his son returning to the Manor. The other figure was less easy to follow because of obscuring houses, until he saw it pass under one of the street-lights in the Cotes Road. He was sure it was Nurse Longbridge, riding her familiar bike.

'Did you speak to Rupert when he entered the house?' Marie asked.

'No. I was ashamed to have kept watch on him for so long. I could have told Sharon, but we're not on the best of terms.'

The housekeeper came in with a tray, and they fell silent. She took a good look at Maria before she retreated.

Frank asked Stephen again what he wanted to speak to Alec about.

'I thought he might understand. I can't lock Rupert in. I thought Alec might be persuaded to lock up his house properly at night.'

'You mean lock this nurse in her house?' asked Maria. 'Oh, Mr Boxbaum, these two people are both adults. You may not find this liaison very desirable but—'

'I certainly don't find it desirable,' Stephen said. 'I can't let it continue. A boy of eighteen with a woman in her fifties?'

'I'd say it was quite romantic, up on that hill after midnight.' She laughed.

Frank supported her. 'Maybe this was a one-off. Honestly, Steve, I don't think you could expect Alec's co-operation in your scheme. He's a stubborn old chap, not liable to change his ways.'

'I was dreading speaking to him,' Stephen admitted, 'but I have to protect my son.'

114

A silence fell. Then Maria spoke, slowly and seemingly reluctantly. 'I have some experience in these matters, so forgive me if I say that you may feel unhappy about your son's activities, not only for his sake but for reasons involving yourself. Your poor Rupert no doubt needs a woman. Be kind to him, introduce him to young ladies you think are more suitable. The desire for sex, the desire to be loved, is so strong in all of us . . .'

Frank looked alarmed by her readiness to speak out. Stephen, however, lowered his head into his hand. The words had struck home.

As if embarrassed by the effect they had had, Maria rose and went to stare out of the window. She could see an old bent figure, which she supposed must be Alec, moving slowly across the front lawn, trundling a barrow full of compost. What pleasures has he had in his life? she wondered. It was always more difficult for the poor. Was he content? She thought of Stephen Boxbaum as a sad man, and could not quite make him out.

Frank joined her at the window. 'He's Alec Bingham. My dear old aunt used to call him Wheelbarrow Bingham. You can find the names of two Binghams on the local war memorial. His grandfather and his grandfather's brother. They were both in the Ox and Bucks in the First World War. The Binghams have been here, or hereabouts, for donkey's years.'

Stephen spoke from where he sat: 'I'd better be going.'

'Don't go, Steve. Stay and have a slice of that excellent sponge cake.'

'Do stay, Steve. I should not have said what I did. It was impolite.'

'But apposite. I thank you for speaking out. I will perhaps have a word with Rupert.'

'Be careful which word you choose,' said Frank cheerfully.

To change the subject, Maria asked after Frank's handicapped brother, Fred, of whom he had often spoken in his letters.

'He'd be too shy to appear,' said Frank. 'He's probably in the blue breakfast room, where he keeps his guinea pig. Go and say hello, if you like.'

She entered the breakfast room cautiously. Fred was sitting on a straight-back chair, looking at his pet, which was sitting, unmoving, in its cage, watching him.

Maria introduced herself. Fred was clearly overwhelmed by her presence, and could only stammer. She asked him the name of his guinea pig.

'Fred,' said Fred.

'But that's your name!'

'It's Fred's name too.'

When she returned to Frank and Stephen, she was looking sorrowful. Frank assured her that his brother was perfectly happy, and enjoyed the company of his pet. He remarked that a good many people in Hampden Ferrers had pets. Pet food and equipment was a thriving industry in Britain.

Maria gazed out at the grounds, where Wheelbarrow Bingham was still working. 'How did this village get its name?' she asked.

Frank said the Hampden bit was easily explained: John Hampden was a seventeenth-century parliamentarian who had defied Charles I. He had been educated at Magdalen College, but later attacked Oxford. 'No wonder!' he said, with a grin.

Stephen joined in: 'Yes, there was a skirmish, I believe, up on the hill. Hampden was seriously wounded by Prince Rupert – another Rupert! He died, I believe, in

Thame. There are Hampden villages all round here. Hampden Poyle, Hampden Gay, Clifton Hampden . . .'

'The Ferrers bit got tacked on later,' said Frank. 'You may have heard of the naughty Harrison Ferrers and the almost equally naughty Tarquin Ferrers, who became the Vicar of the parish.'

Maria nodded. 'It's always the rich and powerful who give their names to places, then.'

'Of course. Never the Binghams of this world.'

V

The Happiest Years

Stephen Boxbaum was floating on his back in his large, elegant pool, lined with Portuguese marble tiles – he always mentioned the tiles when speaking of the pool – and filled with pure heated water. He paddled himself lazily from one end of the pool to the other.

The afternoon was dozing. Only swallows were active. Heedless of the man, they swooped down from the eaves of the house to scoop up a drop of moisture in their beaks, then rose again to wheel back to their nests. They were continually active.

Stephen had much to think about. It was a week since he had kissed Penelope in the church porch, and still he had not brought himself to speak to Sharon about the situation. This evening, his first committee meeting was to be held, and he would see Penelope again. And she would be bound to enquire . . .

As he heaved himself out of the water, the swallows veered away, only to return again, twittering with annoyance as they flew.

Stephen saw that Sharon was sitting with her friend Bettina Squire, watching television. She had recently bought one of Bettina's rather amateur watercolours depicting St Clement's Church. It was newly framed and hung in Sharon's boudoir. The two ladies had been upstairs to admire it.

Entering the house through the side door, Stephen heard them talking about a strange underground city. Ishtar, Bettina's baby, lay on the floor, arms spread wide, as if in a gesture of welcome. Heaven knew what she was thinking about.

It was none of his business, Stephen decided. He showered and put on a suit to mark the solemnity of the first committee meeting. First, he wanted to see Henry Wiverspoon, to coax his friend out of the depression into which he had fallen since running over Sammy Aziz in the high street.

He went through the back gate, crossed Cotes Road, and walked up the drive to ring the Wiverspoon doorbell. After some delay, the housekeeper let him in.

Violet Edith Bingham was a big, solid woman. Her mother had been a farm worker. Her husband, Alec, was gardener to Frank Martinson. Violet still held herself upright, although her hair was grey and thinning.

'He's in a bad way, sir. I made him an omelette for his lunch − cheese omelette, the way he likes it. Would he eat it? No way! I tried to pursuade him. He's an awful handful at times. What did he do, the old rogue? Slung the whole caboodle into the fireplace, plate and all, sir. One of them nice gold-rimmed plates. I said to him, I said, "You're in a fine old mood," and he told me to mind my own business. I said to him, I said it *was* my business, I was only trying to look after him. He told me to clear off. What do you think to that? I mean, it is a bit upsetting, wouldn't you say, sir?'

Stephen looked grave. 'Yes, it is. You will have to derive

119

some consolation from the fact that, after all, the smashed plate was his and not yours.'

'He flung it with such force.'

'I dare say he did. But look, Violet, you mustn't be upset. Mr Wiverspoon is upset, as we might expect and—'

'Upset! I'll say he is.'

'He's an old man, and please don't take it to heart. The loss of the plate – and the omelette – is entirely his, and he will soon recover and be his old self. I've spoken to the doctor about him.'

Violet was about to say something more when Stephen edged past her and entered the blue drawing room, where Henry was sitting. He had a shawl over his knees and was reading the *Financial Times*, his spectacles perched on the end of his sharp nose.

As Stephen came in, he looked up, smiled, and set aside the newspaper.

'Well, Steve . . .'

'Well, Henry, how is it?'

'I heard Violet complaining about me. She's annoyed about the plate, I know. Dash it, I've got a whole damned dinner service to get through yet.'

'She was vexed at the waste.'

'Not only the waist. The stomach as well.'

When they had exchanged a few desultory remarks designed to accustom themselves again to the sound of the other's voice, Henry announced that he was too old to drive a car, and should never have been at the wheel the previous week. 'I'd better face it, I'm in my dotage.'

'Henry, it was not your fault. I was a witness. I saw young Aziz wobble in front of you, quite unexpectedly. You were not to blame.'

'You see, this is not the first time something like this

has happened to me. Get us out the whisky decanter from the cupboard there, Steve, be a good chap. Bring us a couple of glasses . . . I was in Punta Arenas in Chile. I ran over a young girl, about Sammy Aziz's age. Terrible. The poor girl died on the way to hospital. Of course, I had been drinking then, I remember.'

'What were you doing in Punta Arenas?'

'As a young man I had a hotel in Argentina. It had belonged to a friend who had owned a pub down in Cornwall. He persuaded me to go out and help him run this hotel in Buenos Aires. Which I did. Going to South America was a big step in those days. But Charlie got ill. I took over the management and eventually I bought the hotel from him. Got it cheap. Poor old Charlie came back to England to die. Died down in Bovey Tracey, of all places.'

Stephen had poured whisky into two glasses, just an inch in each. Henry sipped reflectively. 'It's Tobermory, a fine malt, I think you'll agree. All the best malts come from the east coast.' Without pausing, he continued his tale: 'I did up the hotel. Got rid of the cockroaches. It prospered. Then I met this Chilean chappie, Ricardo, who had been on the wrong side when Allende took over. He had a chain of hotels and wanted me to buy them. That was what I was doing in Punta Arenas. A woman was involved, needless to say. She belonged to this Ricardo. I can see his face now.'

He took a meditative sip of the malt.

'Ricardo wanted this floozy to seduce me. I wanted to be seduced by her, oh yes. Lovely, high-spirited woman. But I didn't want to buy Ricardo's hotels — or not till I'd had a good look round them. Three of them there were.

'Well, anyhow, this floozy and I got on well. Too well,

you might say. It turned out that while I was mixed up with her – she took me out to see one of the hotels and we spent the night there – Ricardo got himself mixed up with a girl in a bar. He was a bit of a fool. He got himself knifed.

'You may think South America was like that. It wasn't at all. Everything was fine, as a rule. Very quiet. It was just Ricardo. I bought those hotels of his. Got them cheap, while he went down to the coast to recover from his wound. It's a wonderful country – or it was. Lovely people, lovely climate. The people there, they make the best of life.'

'So I've heard,' said Stephen, rather impatiently. 'What happened to the floozy, as you call her?'

'Oh, vanished into the woodwork, the way they all do. Funny lot, women.'

'Funnier than men?'

'You should go there. You'd see it's true what I say. The way they sing! At night there's music everywhere. They can make a song of the most trivial incident, sing it so that it tears your heart. You realize then that opera is like life, life is like opera, that there's something magnificent about everything that happens. That was where I made my money—'

'Henry, look, I want you to be on my committee. You have to show your face. Everyone is sympathetic about how bad you feel. We're going to meet at my house in a hour. Fifty minutes. Please come. I'll send my car for you.'

Henry's friend, Professor Valentine Leppard was propped up with velvet cushions in a wheelback chair in his little front room overlooking the street. Slowly and painfully, using one skeletal finger of each hand, he was tapping

122

out a paragraph of his autobiographical study, *City Utterly Fallen*: 'One major cause of misery, especially for a youth, is the desire to be a great man. Once the desire seizes him, it may not burn itself out until life itself is extinguished.'

Valentine stared through his glasses at these words. He shook his head, muttered to himself, then pressed the delete button on his iMac. Swiftly, silently, the two sentences disappeared.

He lay back and closed his eyes, but could not rest.

He started the paragraph again: 'While the quest for perfection is a torment, a major cause of misery is the desire to be a great man and have one's name known. Once this desire catches fire in a man's breast, he knows no peace; the fire will burn until life itself is extinguished.'

'Too damned long,' he whispered to himself. Again the delete button, and again his sentences were eaten away from tail to head.

He pulled off his spectacles. There had to be a best way of saying anything. Sighing, he tried again: 'The desire to be regarded as great is a great misery. One cannot rest. Only the grave brings a cure.'

'Better.' He stroked his curly white moustache, thinking.

He remembered one of Bertrand Russell's letters, in which Russell talked about the forgotten painter, Benjamin Robert Haydon, who had made himself miserable by comparing himself with those who had achieved real greatness. There was, on Valentine's shelves, an edition of Haydon's autobiography. He could check the reference and possibly quote it, but that would entail getting up out of the chair in which he was comfortably ensconced and tottering about in front of his bookcase.

He took a longer rest, then tapped out another

sentence: 'The grave is also the only known cure for old age, another great misery.' But he did not want his possible hated and feared readership, that abstraction, to feel pity for him. Down went the delete key again. Away went the new sentence. By accident, he erased the previous one too.

Someone tapped gingerly with the iron knocker on the front door.

'Who is it?' he shouted angrily. 'And don't say "me"! "Me" is not only unilluminating, it is grammatically incorrect.'

Answer came faintly: 'It is I, Maria Caperalli, Contessa of Medina Mirtelli, on a visit. May I enter?'

'No, you can't. Wait!'

He screwed up several pieces of rough paper and threw them into his wicker wastepaper basket, following them with a half-eaten cheese sandwich: his lunch.

Painfully, he got himself out of the chair and hobbled to the door. When he opened it, a radiant vision confronted him. On his doorstep stood Maria Caperalli in her youth and beauty, clad in a linen trouser suit, white with scarlet slashes, wearing a neat pair of scarlet shoes, and clutching a striped package. 'Hello! You are Professor Leppard, aren't you? My name is Maria. Do you wish to let me in? I promise I shall not stay.'

Valentine dithered somewhat. 'The house is only meant for one. It's untidy. My cleaning woman left. She says I was rude to her. Stupid woman! Well, you'd better come in for a moment, since you're here.'

All of this Maria treated lightly. She stepped into the little front room, sparsely furnished, except for the books. Very few signs of comfort. She regarded the bent old man with curiosity. 'Do you manage for yourself, Professor?'

124

'Nurse Longbridge comes every morning. Do you always ask personal questions?'

'I can see you are busy.'

'I'm always busy. Busy writing. It keeps me alive. Half alive.'

'I'm interested to meet you, Professor.' She held out her hand.

He took it and showed no inclination to release it. 'You are Italian? You don't sound very Italian. You're Maria – who did you say?'

She told him. He looked blank.

'Are you thinking of offering me a chair?'

'Oh, of course. There's not a great selection.'

Maria drew up an old wheelback, the only other chair in the room, removed a reference book from it and sat down, resting her striped package on the floor by her side. Valentine sat down in his own chair, shedding a cushion as he did so.

'I should offer you something to drink, I suppose. Bovril, tea, instant coffee? I don't drink alcohol these days.'

'Thank you, nothing for me. When were you last in Italy, Professor?' A certain tension was evident in her manner.

He sighed deeply. 'Years ago. Another life.'

'Professor, do you remember Andriena Sagati? She asked me to call on you when I was in Oxford.'

Maria watched the old man's face change. The dark flesh beneath his eyes lightened. The eyes themselves became brighter and more focused. He raised his hands in an almost Italian gesture.

'Oh, Andriena Sagati! I do indeed remember her. The most beautiful, the most mournful – and yet, the most humorous of ladies . . . I do indeed remember her.'

'I am glad to hear it. I am Andriena's daughter.'

He observed her more closely, taking off his glasses, then assuming them again. 'Yes, the nose, the shape of face, the brown eyes . . . And you are well developed, as was she . . .' He removed his spectacles once more, the better to shade his eyes with his hand. 'Fancy! It's strange! How old are you, Maria?'

She told him she would be forty on her next birthday.

'So you were just a child when your mother and I . . .'

'How do you mean, *just* a child? Does a child have no significance?'

'You were not yet grown-up.'

'Quite so. I was a vulnerable child. Extremely vulnerable.'

'Andriena was often away from home. I was working on a dig quite near Naples . . . Yes, I remember that time well.'

'You two were lovers, weren't you?'

He hesitated. 'It is such a long time past. One does forget.'

'But you *were* lovers, weren't you?'

'Come, now! I greatly admired your mother.'

'You were lovers, were you not?'

'Yes, Maria, we were. I am proud to admit it. You see a miserable old man now, but those were the happiest years of my life.'

'But not of mine, Professor.' Maria drew herself up, looking stern. The colour rose in her cheeks. 'While my mother was away on business — *monkey business*, as she used to phrase it — she used to leave me with an older man and woman who lived nearby.' She fell silent, then added, 'Meanwhile, you were both enjoying yourselves, you and my mother.'

126

'It was so romantic,' he said.

Maria stood up. When she spoke, it was in her usual controlled way. 'I will not take up more of your time. I was interested simply to see you, to take a look at you.' She picked up her striped parcel. 'This is not for you, Professor, but for my lover. Farewell!'

Valentine rose to his feet with difficulty. 'Why this attitude, young woman? I thought we could have a nice chat, a conversation about old times.'

'Not in a million years!' She walked out of the door and slammed it behind her.

He stood in the middle of his room. He shook his head. There was no understanding people. Certainly there was no understanding women. He sat himself down at his computer. After a while, he began to peck at the keys: 'The desire to be loved is another source of misery.'

Sharon was reluctantly putting aside her latest paperback and getting up from the sofa, smoothing down her dark satin dress. 'Must we hold the committee meeting here? Why not in Henry's house?'

'Because this is what we arranged,' Stephen said. 'Please don't be difficult, Sharon. They won't be a nuisance. I'm sure you will like them.'

'I want to go back.' She spoke in a low voice, looking down.

He glared at her, without comprehension, and asked her what she was talking about now.

'Don't be so unkind to me, Stephen. Why are you always so unkind? You used to be nice to me. Isn't life bad enough? I just feel I want to go back. I'm sick of this place. I have no life.'

'Where would you go back to? Cheapside? Switzerland?

Upper Silesia, or wherever it was? Or do you mean back to the Middle Ages?'

She lit a cigarette with trembling hands. 'That's the trouble. I don't know. The salmon, born in freshwater rivers, suddenly gets the call to swim into the Atlantic.'

'Sorry, Sharon, no natural history. People will be here at any minute.'

'It gets the call to swim into the Atlantic. But there is a time when another call comes to swim back, up waterfalls and all kinds of hazards, back to the headwaters where it was born. It's inexplicable in a way, isn't it?'

'Well, we're not salmon, that's certain. Sharon, I know there's a sense in which our lives are incomprehensible, but you're making them impossible.' Moved by sudden sympathy, he crossed the few feet of carpet dividing them and took her into his arms. 'Back to a concentration camp, is that it?'

'Oh, maybe, I don't know! Please never leave me, dear Steve! I do know I'm awful.'

'I won't leave you,' he said, with infinite pain.

The doorbell rang.

The committee was gathering. Sharon had asked Andrea to come and help look after the guests. Sharon wore a grand black dress and overplayed the role of hostess. Stephen looked glum. He settled Henry Wiverspoon by the fireplace with a glass of whisky. Andrea handed round canapés.

Jeremy Sumption arrived, looking somewhat ill at ease; but Stephen had liked him even more since Jeremy had hit Greyling for a racist remark. He poured Jeremy a Beck's. Rodney Williams arrived, still with baby powder on his trousers. Penelope came in, was calm and polite to all, and talked for a while to Sharon, her chin held high. Sharon enthused about a watercolour she had

128

bought from Penelope's lodger. 'It's a view of the church. Not too accurate but cheerful.'

Ah, then Bettina can afford to pay her rent! thought Penelope. She avoided Stephen's eye, knowing he was anxious to receive some sign of approval from her.

Sam Aziz arrived, bustling as usual, abuzz with enthusiasm and curious to see the interior of the Manor. He went over and made a point of shaking Henry's hand. Everyone wanted to hear the latest news of his son. 'I was this afternoon at the John Radcliffe Hospital,' Sam told them. 'Sammy is definitely getting better. Definitely. He is on pain-killers, but tomorrow he must have another operation on his leg. He does not look forward to such a thing, of course, but he is cheerful and he thanks all the people in the village who so kindly chipped in to buy him a new mountain bike. When I described it to him, Sammy said that it was decidedly better than his old bike.'

Everyone was cheered at the news and Stephen pressed a glass of white wine on him. He insisted on a toast. Lifting his glass, Sam said, 'Happiness to our beloved village!'

They were all embarrassed in an English way, and drank, mumbling, 'Our beloved village.'

The Reverend Robin Jolliffe was the last to arrive. He accompanied Miss Hetty Zhou. Hetty entered like a vision, very aware of her youth and her foreignness, very poised. She was cool and elegant, and the Vicar introduced everyone in the room in turn. Hetty was dressed in a grey suit, beautifully cut. She wore grey high-heeled shoes. Her hair was curled. Her makeup was perfect. She was a source of amazement to the men; it was as if some rare and beautiful migrant bird had settled in their midst.

'*Cloisonné!*' exclaimed Henry, struggling to get to his feet to clutch her hand.

129

'I am sorry. I am not familiar with that word.'

'Oh, cloisonné . . . It is a perfect enamel ornament, which is what you are, Miss Zhou.'

'Thank you, sir, but you will find I am something more than an ornament, believe me.'

'Quite, quite,' said Henry, aware that his compliment had not worked out as he had hoped. He wiped his lips on a handkerchief and sank back into his chair.

Stephen announced that they would retire to the adjoining room and sit round the table. The room commanded a view of the garden and the swimming-pool, over which the swallows were still sweeping.

'What a lovely pool!' exclaimed Hetty. 'That's rare in England, isn't it?'

'It's lined with Portuguese tiles,' said Stephen, moving to her side.

'May I swim in it at some time?'

'I'd be delighted. You can swim naked, if you like, as we often do.'

'I certainly would not think of doing so.'

They seated themselves at the table, with Stephen at one end and the Vicar at the other. Sharon entered the room, glass in hand, then tiptoed away to Andrea to order coffee for everyone.

'You are all welcome here,' said Stephen, opening proceedings. 'Particularly you, Miss Hetty Zhou, as a new resident in the village. I am hoping that you will all serve on my committee to celebrate the stability and continuance of our local church through the last one and a half millennia. First of all, and most importantly, we must ask our Vicar if he will consent to our holding the proposed celebration. We would like, sir, to hear what you think about the matter.'

Perhaps for dramatic effect, Robin let silence ensue

130

before he spoke. 'You will possibly remember that when Jesus was tempted by the Devil on the mountain, he said, "Get thee behind me, Satan." I feel that you are offering me similar temptation. But I am not the man our Saviour was. I shall give in to temptation. And I thank you for your kindness, one and all.'

He held up a hand, as his audience murmured in approval. 'There is a condition, though. I want it to be clear — to be recorded — that this planned celebration was not of my instigation. I could not afford to think of such an event. The celebration — or perhaps I might say 'commemoration' — is for St Clement's Church itself, and for all those holy men who have served in it, often in desperate times, more desperate than now, and for all the countless people, rich or poor, who have worshipped beneath its roof.'

Sam Aziz started to clap. The others followed his example.

Stephen was beaming. 'We shall be honoured by your blessing, Vicar. However, there is one thing I must point out to you from the very outset. This committee, which will run the organization and the celebrations, is composed entirely of Jews, atheists, a Hindu and a Chinese lady. We couldn't get anyone else to stand. Do you have any objection to such a pack of unbelievers?'

A slight smile gathered over the Vicar's rubicund face. 'I did say that these were desperate times.'

'Thank you, sir. We take that as an acceptance of our failings.'

'I shall convert you all to Christianity before we are finished. You have already started on the road by this Christian act.'

As they were all chuckling, Sam Aziz said, 'By the way, I hate to mention it, everybody, but I am converted to

Christianity, although I am so busy I never enter the church. For which I apologize.'

Hetty Zhou also spoke up: 'Mr Chairman, I am indeed Chinese, as you say, and proud of it, but I come from Hong Kong, which was a British colony until five years ago. Consequently, I am Roman Catholic. And not only that, I am a capitalist.'

'Welcome to the fold,' said Robin, eyeing her benevolently.

'I intend to be an active member, Vicar, which is why you find me here,' she replied.

'We are delighted to have you,' said Jeremy, who had managed to sit next to her. Murmurs of agreement sounded round the table.

Rodney Williams spoke: 'If I might just say, Vicar, Judy and I never come to church but we do intend to get the baby baptised, so that's why I'm on the committee – to support our church. If I can help in a legal capacity, I shall be only too delighted.'

'I, too, am happy to be one of the company, Vicar,' Penelope said. 'I am not a believer, as you know. I also have had little to do with anyone in the village because of my commitments elsewhere. I just want to say that I hope to make up for my separateness and look forward to working here with everyone. May I also say that I admire you personally?'

The Vicar nodded and blinked.

'Thank you, Penny,' said Stephen. 'I would agree that to some extent we all have a separateness, as you put it, which we might care to shed . . .' He smiled at her, but she did not meet his eye. 'Now, let us get down to business. First of all, we should attempt to determine how much money we will have to raise for the celebration.'

Henry raised a hand. 'May I enquire if we are sure that

132

St Clement's is as old as we assume it is? Are there records? Is the date on this stone 503? I went to have a look but couldn't make it out. Vicar?'

Robin stared hard at the table. Below the table, he crossed his fingers. 'All written records were destroyed at the time of the Black Death. And, yes, the date has been officially read as 503.'

'It's such a long time ago,' said Sam. 'A few years here or there hardly matter, do they?'

Henry said nothing. Stephen returned to the question of how much money would be required.

'First of all,' said Robin, from his end of the table, 'I suggest that you should decide how you will commemorate the event. I have to bring to your attention the sad plight of our bells. One is cracked and all of them need rehanging. The tower itself is unsafe. Possibly a flying buttress might make it more secure and would not look unsightly. I must admit, I have always liked flying buttresses, and would not be averse to seeing one adorning St Clement's.'

'Where do you get flying buttresses?' asked Jeremy, mystified. 'Excuse me asking – I was born in a backstreet.'

'We could try B&Q for a start. And we do really need a church room for meetings and Sunday schools. It is not right that we should have to use the school, as we have been doing.'

Rodney cleared his throat. 'I have an alternative suggestion. Clearly, a considerable sum of money would have to be raised if we were to finance all these alterations to the church. I would have thought that the money would be morally better spent on the poor of the parish. Better housing, improved educational facilities – that sort of thing.'

Silence fell.

It was Jeremy Sumption who broke it. 'I grew up in a lousy district of London. It's given me a bit of an attitude. Otherwise, no harm done. Sorry, Mr Williams, but whenever some big project is proposed which is either going to change the world or raise people's morale a bit, there's always some miserable geezer who gets up and says, "Let's spend it on the poor!" I've heard that when Christopher Columbus was planning to set sail, someone suggested the money should go to building a hospital for the destitute instead. Where would America be now if they'd done that?'

'Yes, but—' said Rodney.

Jeremy overrode him. 'Then when the USA was about to start up the Apollo programme to land a man on the moon, oh, no, someone gets up and says, "Let's spend the dough on the poor!" Always in the name of morality! Frankly, I've nothing against the poor, except that they're an undeserving lot of losers, but this concept, "The Poor", it's like a sponge that could mop up money for ever. Look at Africa! No, my friends, let's be sensible. Let's go for this flying-buttress stuff.'

'Well, I don't think that's any way to talk,' said Rodney, looking upset. 'There is morality in everything.'

'Even without Jeremy's rather specious argument,' said Henry, 'I would certainly prefer to opt for what he terms "the flying-buttress stuff".'

'I'm afraid I'm on the side of the buttresses too,' said Stephen. 'What do you say, Penny?'

'We are celebrating the endurance of the church, are we not? We should ensure its continued endurance. Sorry, Rodney, I'm also for the buttresses.'

'And me,' said Sam. He thumped the table for emphasis. 'We shall be glad to see this splendid thing every time we pass the church. It will cheer the mind.'

'I hope you won't *pass* it every time, Sam,' said the Vicar, drily.

If Stephen was at all taken aback by the possible expense of the Vicar's proposals, he did not show it. He understood there would be other unforeseen difficulties ahead. But none so difficult as dealing with Sharon.

When the committee meeting was over, and very little decided, Stephen Boxbaum showed his guests to the door. He seized the chance briefly to press Penelope's hand. His pressure was not reciprocated. 'I'm cross with you,' the hand said.

Jeremy stayed close to Hetty Zhou, asking if he might see her home.

'I shall not get lost,' she said.

'But monstrous things haunt the streets of Hampden at night.'

'You must show me.' She spoke lightly but formally.

They disappeared together into the night. Stephen returned to the sitting room. Sharon was standing by the fireplace, lighting a cigarette. She had a gin and tonic close by.

'B&Q! The Vicar's a card, and no mistake.'

The remark was lost on Sharon.

'So, now you are a well-integrated Yiddisher member of Hampden society,' she said.

'I have been for a long time. I would advise you to follow suit, Sharon.' He lit a cigarette and helped himself to a drink. 'It may make you happier.'

After a pause, she asked him why he had invited that old fool Henry Wiverspoon on to the committee.

'He's a useful man. He needs a boost after the accident. He has connections. His brother, Andrew, was lord lieutenant of the county at one time. And he has money,

135

which we are certainly going to need. He was telling me something of his earlier days, when he ran a chain of hotels in South America. Quite an adventurous life.'

'He was never in South America.'

Her flat denial startled him. She rarely surprised him, and he had come to believe that all her surprises were somehow unpleasant. He asked her what she meant.

'I mean what I say.'

'Don't be annoying, dear. Explain.'

'Andrea used to work for Henry. He told her he had spent his days in North America. He started a bottled-water company in Ottawa, which made his fortune. So he said. The man's a liar.'

Stephen thought about it. 'Don't be so ready to be unkind about Henry. He's a nice man but he's getting on a bit. Sometimes, the old like to embroider their past – perhaps because they feel they missed something when they were young, and now regret it.'

'But you don't have to lie.' She turned to stare at her husband as she flung out this remark, which seemed designed to make him uneasy – to make me feel I'm living a lie, he thought.

He watched her drink her gin and tonic. 'I can never please you, Sharon,' he said heavily.

'That's an eternal truth, if ever there was one.'

Silence fell between them, watertight and shatter-proof. She propped herself against the mantelpiece, staring bleakly at the wall. Her pose recalled to Stephen the canvas *Ennui*, by Walter Sickert: the woman with her back turned, the man at the table, leaning back in his chair, with a glass on the table, half full, half empty. It was boredom that had made them grow slowly apart. Could it have been boredom that drove him to Penelope?

136

He sighed. 'Well, Sharon, I'm off to bed.'

She spoke without turning her head: 'Go and sleep in one of the spare rooms. I don't want you any more. You don't care about me, except for sex. So that's going to stop.'

'I'd say it had already ground to a halt.' He crossed the expanse of carpet and headed for the staircase.

Sharon continued to smoke, staring at the wall.

On leaving the Manor, Penelope Hopkins lingered in the shadows at the entrance to the close, so as not to catch up with Hetty Zhou and Jeremy Sumption.

She felt the deviousness of her delay. Quite why she did it she could not say, but she was as yet unprepared to be on terms of close friendship with them. She felt nervous beside Hetty's coolly commanding personality, suspecting that she had earlier been guilty of patronising both her and Judy.

She waited only a minute or two before she continued her walk home, heading eastward, then taking the turning down Clement's Lane, where street-lights were few and far between.

A slight breeze had risen. The trees on the south side of the road, heavy and bushy, weighted down with ivy, leaned over the pavement with a restless motion. Penelope had always admired them. At present, in her depressed mood, she perceived them as threatening. She hurried on, once looking back nervously.

For some reason, Bettina Squire's obsession with the city of the dead came to her mind. She wondered, as she moved from shadow to shadow, what she would do if she were confronted by her dead husband, Greg, emerging from it. The notion pursued her, although in the rational side of her mind she regarded Bettina's idea of the city of the dead below as impossible as the City of God above, of which the Vicar had spoken.

The front door of her own little house opened directly on to the pavement. She slipped into the shelter of the porch, whose trellised sides were covered with honeysuckle, already coming into bud. The security light flicked on. Why did she feel so wretched? Nothing bad had happened. She unlocked the door, pushed it open, went in, closed and locked it. Turning, she almost stepped on a blue and pink plastic lorry parked by the mat.

Penelope's was a small late-Victorian house. A stained-glass panel was set into the panel of the front door depicting an eagle with a man standing behind it, posing – unsuccessfully, Penelope always thought – as Robin Hood. The flooring that led from hall to rear rooms was tiled red and black, in an ecclesiastical pattern. A narrow staircase led to the first floor, from which came the sound of voices and stifled laughter.

Penelope sniffed the air. The smells of pot and coffee greeted her nose. All the upper rooms, bar the boxroom, were let to Bettina Squire. Penelope took two, three steps up the stairs to listen. Bettina was talking. A man's voice said something in return. Their tones were lazy and contented.

It came forcefully to Penelope that she was surrounded by couples, private in the night, together, wanting or getting something from each other. She was alone, and had been so for many years – ever since Greg had died.

Back to her came the grieving face of Greg's mother, saying to her, 'The loss of my son will inevitably fill the remainder of my life but you are young, Penelope, and you can have another life.' Had she had another life? Certainly she had been well occupied: but that was not quite the same thing.

And she had used her involvement with work not to maintain contact with Margery Culverson, Greg's mother, a woman of whom she had been fond. Margery was probably dead by now. Standing there on the stairs, in almost total darkness, she felt the solitude of her life like a tight cold girdle.

Had she been hoping for a chat with Bettina, or had she been intending to avoid one?

She backed quietly downstairs and went softly into her living room–kitchen, switched on a light and the radio, then poured herself a glass of Chardonnay.

Since that unexpected oasis in the desert, when they had kissed, a week had passed in which she and Stephen had barely seen each other. There had been a second meeting in the Café Regale, which she had spoilt, as she realised later, by insisting that he leave either his wife or her. 'Make up your mind,' she had said.

The truth had dawned on her belatedly that she had been foolish to press him so hard. Did he not understand that in that kiss she had given him her heart? A tear of self-pity stood in one eye.

That evening she had phoned him to apologise; Sharon had answered and Penelope had rung off. The next morning, Stephen had phoned her just before she left for work, asking her not to ring him at the Manor again. He must think I'm a horrible creature . . .

She snapped off the radio, thinking she had heard laughter. She went to the door and listened. All was darkness and silence upstairs. No cry from the child. She was sure that he, whoever he was, was staying the night, sleeping with Bettina in her bed. Both of them naked . . .

She poured the Chardonnay remaining in her glass down the sink, made herself a cup of tea and retired to her bed. She wore a pair of bright green silk pyjamas with silver lapels. Just in case, she told herself.

The north-facing room in the upper floor of Penelope's house was full of dying flowers in jam-jars and water-colours of flowers alive and dying. Most of the paintings were executed on A3 cartridge paper. Stacks of them were lodged on a long shelf; others were enclosed within a portfolio that had once belonged to Bettina Squire's mother. A faded photograph of this lady, smiling bemus-edly into the camera, hung framed on the wall near the door.

A chair and desk occupied much of the room, which otherwise held only a small electric fire with a trailing cable. It was a cheerful, untidy room, dedicated to painting, as many Windsor & Newton brushes, tubes and tubs of colour testified.

Bettina worked here whenever she found time. She had followed her mother's example: what was good enough for her was good enough for Bettina. She visu-alised her mother in a room identical to hers, just a few feet underground, in the city of the dead, moving in her earth-choked space. She regarded her paintings as an attempt to capture life on the wing, as it flew by. She occasionally exhibited them, mainly sketches of vegeta-bles, at the vegetable stall she manned with Dave Cotes on the Cotes Road. Sometimes passing customers professed themselves delighted with a study of lettuce or apples and would buy her modest pictures. Having heard of the possibility of a celebration of the antiquity of the local church, Bettina was determined to hold a proper exhibition and was preparing to approach the committee about it. That would be fame! Her mama would be so pleased!

140

Bettina was a small, dark, nervous woman in her early thirties, one of a large family of which she was the youngest. She regretted that all the other members of the family were living elsewhere, in particular her brother Mark, of whom she was extremely fond: he was in the Cook Islands, where he had a boatyard and a black mistress.

Bettina was the mistress – she preferred that term to any other – of Dave Cotes of Cotes Farm. He came and slept with her occasionally, planting his broad, strong body against her slender one. They tried always to make love quietly because not only was there an envious landlady downstairs but, perforce, in the same room slept young Ishtar, Bettina's one-year-old daughter.

Ishtar had been unwell, but Bettina's Auntie Ann, Nurse Longbridge, had recommended some antibiotics and the little girl had recovered her health. The sale of a sketch of the church to Mrs Boxbaum had been a windfall. It paid the antibiotics bill, for which Bettina had paid privately.

Since the vegetable stall was manned only at weekends, and not all the year round, Bettina worked also in the local hairdresser's. She had a mop of curly black hair, which the owner of the shop, Mrs Aylet, regarded as a good advert.

Bettina, Doreen Aylet and the other assistant, Kyle Bayfield, got on well together. Doreen was the motherly type, a large expansive woman with a ready smile. She had a three-year-old daughter, Cherie. Her sister looked after Cherie and Ishtar in the back parlour while Doreen ran her hairdressing business. Occasionally childish giggles filtered into the salon.

In an idle moment, of which there were plenty in Salon Française – as Doreen had christened her shop – they were discussing their recent customers.

'That Italian lady,' said Bettina, 'she was so sweet. Well dressed. Wouldn't you like to be like her? Spoke English as good as you or me. I wondered if she was at all artistic.'

'How do you mean, autistic?'

'I said artistic. Fond of art.'

'A bit overdressed, if you ask me,' Doreen replied. 'But yes, I agree, very nice. She has to be – she's on Italian TV, so she was saying. She spoke at one of the colleges the other night, I'm not sure what about. What she's doing in Hampden Ferrers, God only knows!'

They laughed, and Kyle suggested, 'The usual.'

'She gave a lecture at Wolfson College,' said Bettina. 'Mrs Boxbaum was telling me. And I heard they all went mad afterwards. Wasn't there something about it in the *Despatch*?'

'If so, we must have it somewhere. Never read it myself.'

They fished among the piles of *Hello!* and *OK*, provided for customers, and finally retrieved the local paper. On the front page, sharing space with the story of a local man of eighty who had cycled up Kilimanjaro with his pet dog in his bike basket, was an article headed 'HALLU-CINATORY HAPPINESS IN WILD WOLFSON.' The report told of a gigantic statue of the college founder and past president, Sir Arthur Berling, being thrown into the lake while an Italian opera singer sang an aria from an Italian opera. The report was accompanied by a photograph of the Countess of Madera.

'That's her!' said Doreen. 'And to think she was in here and we never knew she was a countess! We might have been a bit more polite if we'd known!'

'You can't believe everything you read in the paper.'

'But fancy! She was in here, in my salon, and I did her hair!'

'What sort of tip did she leave?'

142

'I'm not telling you.' They both laughed.

Kyle was looking out of the wide plate-glass window. 'I don't go for royalty. Do you think she'd be related to the Queen? I mean, Prince Philip, he's Italian, isn't he?'

'No, he's Greek,' corrected Bettina.

'Watch out!,' called Kyle from her vantage-point. 'Here comes that miserable old bitch Marion Barnes, dragging her poor dog along! You can do her rotten hair, Bettina. Catch me doing it!'

'Don't worry,' said Doreen, undisturbed. 'She wouldn't come in here to save her life. She knows me and Bettina are unmarried mothers.'

Sure enough, as Doreen Aylet had predicted, Marion Barnes passed by the Salon Française, dragging Laurel along on a lead, heading for Hill's Stores, with never a glance towards the nest of unmarried mothers.

'Oh, well, let's have a fag,' said Doreen, but at that moment the door was pushed open by a small Chinese lady, who looked about her hesitantly.

'I'll do it,' said Doreen, from the corner of her mouth. 'They have lovely hair.'

As she went forward, Bettina said, 'Goodness, more foreigners!'

Kyle was up on village gossip. 'This one's going out with that Rupert Boxbaum, the songwriter, so-called.'

VI

The Piranesi Period

Kyle Bayfield was awake. She was lying against the sleeping Duane in his narrow bed, in his narrow house. Duane slept heavily, his mouth open.

Dim morning light was filtering into the room. Kyle was staring at the chair by the bedside and, beyond it, at a small piece of furniture on spindly legs. She had worked out that perhaps it had been designed to hold a chamber pot; now the end of a bicycle pump protruded from the half-open drawer. Above it hung a framed photograph. As far as Kyle could make out in the gloom, it depicted a woman in a long coat standing in the middle distance. A large bush occupied the foreground, with trees in the background. The woman stood alone, not looking towards the camera. Kyle wondered about her. She thought it funny to be alone like that. It was not the way people were generally photographed.

She slid quietly out of bed and peered out of the window. The time by her watch was five seventeen. The garden was depicted in tones of grey: the blossom on the apple trees was grey. A mist hung over the distant fence, rendering anything beyond invisible. It was rather

144

like looking at eternity. How much of the day was spent just looking?

There was no point in looking at eternity for long. She spoke to Duane: 'Sweetie, is it okay if I go down and make myself a cup of tea? Do you want one?'

He propped himself up on one elbow and asked drowsily what the time was. She told him.

'Shit! I said I'd be at Aziz's place at half past. I'm doing the newspaper round for him while his kid's up the hospital.'

'Lucky I woke you, then.'

'You could have given me a call sooner.'

'I'll go and make us some tea.'

Kyle made her way quietly down the winding staircase, past Andrea's room. Poor old Andrea, she thought. It was the day of Arthur's funeral.

The *Daily Telegraph* fell though Jeremy Sumption's front door at eight ten. He was up, looking out of the back door and eating an apple. He had a problem. The central character in the novel he was writing was getting ready to assassinate President George W. Bush. For this act, he was to be paid a considerable sum of money, given a false identity, and installed on a small private island in the Caribbean. The character suspected the murder was financed by a Middle East government. What Jeremy had to decide was whether the Muslims or a sinister secret US organisation was behind the plot. He considered the pros and cons as he bit into the apple.

A knock came at the front door, sharp and peremptory.

Jeremy felt immediate guilt. Was it the Muslims or a sinister left-wing organisation coming to get him?

When he opened the door, he discovered two

important-looking men standing there. One was young and tall with a long neck and prominent Adam's apple; he resembled an ostrich – a recently defeathered and polished one. The other was middle-aged and portly with blue-black jowls. Both wore suits, the young man a shiny blue one with three pens clipped into the breast pocket, the other a hairy brown suit, which made him look somewhat like a teddy bear of exceptionally poor antecedents.

A fat man with a florid complexion stood behind them. His arms were folded across his chest. He went under the assumed name of Langdon, and had talked with John Greyling in the Bear on the previous evening. He stood back and watched events, evidently with some satisfaction.

The older of the two men immediately put a heavy boot into the hall so that the door could not be shut. 'Morning, sir, my name is Detective Inspector Paul Lorryload, and this is Sergeant Ivan Arsich of the Scottish Division of Thames Police. I myself am in charge of Street Crime, Pavement Crime and, in some cases, House Crime, and we wish to ask you a few questions, if we might come in, sir, thank you.'

Lorryload was a ferocious-looking man, prominent teeth lending weight to his air of threat. By the conclusion of his weighty pronouncement, he had already entered Jeremy's house and was looking about him with sharp thrusts of his neck, like a bird about to peck.

Sergeant Arsich fixed Jeremy with a cold stare he seemed unable to deflect. He spoke in a thin voice, evidently feeling he had not been sufficiently well introduced. 'Sorry to call so early, sir. That's the way we catch 'em. Off guard. You seem somewhat surprised to see me. Due to my alien appearance, my colleagues on the force call me "Mr Other". It's a friendly joke. All good friends down the station. But to you I am *Sergeant*, okay?'

'I see,' said Jeremy thoughtfully. 'So you are actually Ivan "Other" Arsich . . .'

'Perfeckly correct, sir. But to you I am Sergeant, okay? Just to keep everythink polite and formal.'

The fat man had also entered the house, to stand with his back to the door, his arms still folded. He had not been introduced.

'What do you want?' Jeremy asked, looking from one to the other of the two police officers.

'It's not a question of what we *want*, sir,' said Arsich, laboriously. 'To be specific, we don't *want* nothing, not Detective Lorryload nor myself either, nor our comrade here. It's not our business to *want* nothing in the circumstances, however suspicious those circumstances may be. Say rather it is a case of what we are going to *give*. Which, in this case, is a few questions, a spot of the old interogation, like.'

Jeremy was still clutching his half-eaten apple. Annoyed by Arsich's pompous manner, he said, 'I haven't finished my bloody breakfast yet, *Sergeant*,' and flourished the apple.

Genially, or at least with mock-geniality, Detective Lorryload warned him, 'If I was you, sonny, I'd put that there apple down in case it gets construed as a dangerous weapon, leading to your prompt arrest and subsequent questioning down the station.'

Now really annoyed, Jeremy asked, 'Look, what the fuck do you two sods want?'

'We should enjoy the speaking of proper English for a start, sir,' said Arsich, the Adam's apple bobbing above the blue suit. 'Without all the blasphemous surplus wordage added, so to speak, like. Now, sir, where were you on the night of the crime?'

'Crime? What crime? I've committed no crime!'

147

Arsich and Lorryload exchanged understanding glances. 'They generally start by denying everythink.' They gave a dungeon-stained chuckle.

Lorryload came very close to Jeremy. 'I expect you have heard of buggery, sir? Begging your pardon, I mean to say bigamy. Would you say you have ever heard of bigamy?'

'I've heard of it, Of course I've heard of bigamy. So what?'

Arsich had moved away and was studying a printout by Jeremy's computer. 'Are you denying you're a crime reporter, sir?'

'Yes, I do deny it. I'm a thriller writer. That's a bit different, if you don't mind.'

'I do mind, sir. I see it says here, printed like, "Police were baffled."' He waved a sheet from Jeremy's novel.

'Oh, Christ, you're loonies.' Jeremy threw himself into a hardbacked chair, fumbled for a packet of Benson & Hedges and lit one of their soothing cigarettes.

'I'll make a note of that remark,' said Lorryload. He produced an electronic notebook and wrote, pronouncing the words as he did so, 'Smoking on the premises.' He then drew up a second chair and sat down, facing Jeremy.

He glanced over his shoulder at the man standing by the door, as if seeking affirmation. On receiving a nod from this dignitary, he directed all his attention at Jeremy. To do this, he frowned intently, resting his upper teeth over his lower lip in the attitude of a man about to bite open a can of pilchards.

'Now, sir, we had better get at the truth for a change, forgetting all deception. If you can be frank with me, we will get this painful process over all the quicker.'

Jeremy blew smoke over Lorryload. 'What the hell are you talking about?'

148

'We are led to believe, sir, as you were married to *two wives*. Could you tell Sergeant Other Arsich and I if that, in fact, is the case.'

Jeremy blew out more smoke and coughed a little. 'Yes, I had two wives. Not at the same time, of course. Consecutively, if you understand the word. Nothing illegal in that, is there?'

'On the face of it, no, sir.'

'He could be lying,' said Arsich, from the background, again fixing Jeremy with his icy stare.

'Are you prepared to divulge the names of these so-called *wives* of yours, sir?' asked Lorryload.

'Divulge? What do you mean, "divulge"? There's no secret about their names.'

'I would advise you not to get sarcastic with me, sir. I irritate easy.' Indeed, the hairs of his brown suit seemed to stand irately on end. His teeth came into display again.

'Yes, he irritates easy,' confirmed Arsich, not shifting his stare.

'Oh, fuck! All right, their unmarried names were Joy Langdon and Polly Armitage. Polly was from Northampton.'

Lorryload wrote the names painstakingly in his electronic notebook. 'Would you be good enough to spell Northampton, sir?'

Jeremy did so.

'Now, sir, I gather you are acquainted with a gentleman calling himself John Greyling.'

'Well, yes. Sort of.'

'You are acquainted, sir, or aren't you? One or other or neether. This is not a court of law.'

'I am.'

'Thank you, sir.' Another note was made. A look of extreme cunning made its laborious way over the

149

inspector's blue-black jowls. 'Similar to you, sir, this gentleman calling himself Greyling, though we have reason to believe his real name is Feather, also had two wives. One is called – let's see now – Paulina Pardal, a foreign name, sir, and the other is called, yes, she is also called Joy Langdon, same as you said. Now, sir, would you reckon these two Joy Langdons were different persons or one and the same person?'

'I married Joy after her divorce from Greyling.'

So pleased was Lorryload by this response that he glanced over his shoulder to make a meaningful face at the man beside the door, who responded with a brief nod of approbation.

Lorryload leaned so far forward that his stomach rested on his knees. Then he launched his triumphal question at Jeremy: 'So that was your motive why you attacked this gentleman called Greyling on the street on yesterday's date. A matrimonial disputation.'

'No, it wasn't that at all.' Jeremy was vexed to find that his hand was shaking. He drew deeply on the cigarette. 'I hit Greyling because he made an uncalled-for racist remark.'

'I see, sir.' He wrote down 'racist remark', held the notebook away from him to survey it better and murmured, 'Racist remark,' to himself for his own satisfaction. 'And does that explain why, as of this morning, Greyling has turned into a donkey?'

Jeremy frowned, unsure whether he had heard right. 'A donkey, you said?'

'Yes, sir, donkey, *equus asinus*, to employ the Greek term. You sound surprised.'

'Certainly I am a bit. Are you surprised I'm surprised? Where did you find this donkey?'

'In Greyling's house, sir. We proceeded there to arrest

150

him on a charge of buggery – pardon, bigamy. The beast or mammal was seated on the sofa, still wearing Greyling's jacket and attempting to digest a copy of the *Oxford Despatch*.'

The sergeant interrupted: 'We also noted the animal concerned had made a mess on the sofa from its rear end.'

Lorryload briefly showed his teeth to indicate that he resented the interruption, and said forcefully to Jeremy, 'Naturally you fall under the suspicion of being implicated in the crime of bigamy. Which is why we are calling round here at the present time, because of the connection of identical matrimonial females.'

Jeremy felt himself at a loss. 'But how did – how could Greyling turn into a donkey?'

'That's not for us to say, sir.' Lorryload inclined his head gravely, in the manner of one who reluctantly shakes an earwig from his right ear. 'Neither the how of it nor the why of it. Science holds many mysteries, withheld from we lesser mortals.'

Speaking from the background, Arsich said, 'Besides, Pinocchio turned into a donkey. It's not all that unusual.'

'It bloody well is in Hampden Ferrers!' said Jeremy, and burst into wild laughter.

'You may find it amusing, sir,' said Lorryload, severely, 'but we have to take these matters seriously. If you wouldn't mind coming down to the station with us, sir, to answer a few questions?'

'What? You're arresting me because a man I hardly know has turned into a donkey overnight?'

'We don't know as it was overnight, sir. It could have been as late as seven this morning. We just want you to help us with our enquiries, as the expression goes.' And the detective inspector winked at the sergeant of the Scottish Division.

151

Jeremy stubbed out his cigarette. 'What a precious insight into police methods!' he exclaimed, as he rose.

Marion had a little wind-up clock in a tortoiseshell case on her bedside table. It told her it was ten minutes past nine, and high time she got up. She tottered about the room, barefoot on the floorboards, looking for her spectacles. Laurel sat up on the bed, scratching herself in a reflective manner.

Marion found the spectacles on her dressing-table. She rested for a moment with her hand on the window-sill, then went to the bed, reached down and brought out her chamber-pot to empty.

A knock came at her door. The dog growled, low in its throat, as if asking itself who it might be at that hour.

'Now who might that be at this early hour?' Marion asked herself.

She returned to the window, opened it and called, 'Who are you? What do you want?'

In a couple of bounds, Laurel was at the window, paws on sill, wondering who it was and what it wanted.

A young man in a suit backed away from the front door, looking up at the window, waving. 'Oh, hello, ma'am! We're collecting for Help the Aged, ma'am,' he called. 'All contributions gratefully received.'

'What do you mean, you stupid fellow? I *am* the Aged. Can't you see that? You got me out of bed!'

'Sorry 'bout that, ma'am! But perhaps there are some worse off than you.' He smiled up at her, a wide, false smile.

'No one's worse off than me!' Marion shrieked.

She lifted her chamber-pot and tipped its contents over the young man's head. He ran off, screaming and shouting abuse, down the street.

Marion cackled to herself. 'I'll give 'em Help the Aged . . .' She favoured Laurel with a confidential nod. 'Won't I just?'

In the BBC television studio on the third floor, Maria Caperalli, Contessa di Medina Mirtelli, had been speaking about Otzi and the examination of the mummified Neolithic body. She was being questioned by Ernie Crickson, a well-known interviewer of easy manner and ready wit.

'Is there a special attraction in looking back down the deep well of the past?' He asked her.

She replied that there was. 'But it lies within a category of what the Englishman de Quincey described as "insufferable splendours", of those grand and terrible things that possess us at times, visions we cannot reach in ordinary lifetimes, that threaten us and yet we seem to need. In a way, I find the Neolithic terrifyingly beautiful.'

'You speak of de Quincey, author of course of *Confessions of an English Opium-Eater*. But I believe that you, Contessa, have had personal experience of opium. Is that so?'

Maria had agreed to speak about this subject before-hand.

'De Quincey calls his early experiences "an abyss of enjoyment". For me it was the same. There was certainly enjoyment, and also the abyss. Frequently, accompanied by grand music, I found myself having to wander through bejewelled underground cities, the very grandeur of which was oppressive. Perhaps you recall the underground city of Eblis in Beckford's novel, *Vathek*. And there's Milton's magnificent City of Hell. Oh, yes, I have studied the drug literature. As you say, I had a personal interest.

'In some of those infernal underground places I was the Queen of Sheba. Flaming torches lit my way. The stones beneath my feet were of gold, the vaulted roof overhead of the finest ivory. Yet always there was fear – a sense of repressed evil.'

'It was opium itself you took, I understand?'

'Easy to get hold of in Rome of that day, then as now.'

'What prompted you to take it?'

Maria gestured with one hand. 'It was a bad time of my life. I was only in my teens. Difficulties beset me. I was in real distress. I had tried to drown myself. At first opium was a refuge. But I was never addicted, not properly addicted. And then my father got me expert psycho-analytic assistance, and I came out of it.'

'I understand you sought this assistance in England?'

'Yes, I stayed with my aunt in Kensington. She was married to an Englishman. She knew a good analyst. It was then that I picked up my English – and my love of this country.'

Crickson nodded. 'Have you tried drugs again since those distressing times?'

Maria gave one of her most dazzling smiles. 'No. I have had problems enough. Those narrow buried chambers through which I had wandered, bemused, became too dreadful. I am now in control of my life, or so I believe. I stick to wine.'

'To close, what would you say to Britain's youngsters who are tempted to try hard drugs?'

She hesitated only for a moment. The question had not come up in the preliminary discussions. 'Perhaps you expect me to say, "Stay off them." Of course, addiction is a terrible curse, as we all understand. But there are romantic or rebellious spirits who have to visit those infernal regions. To them, I would say, "Go there! It may

154

enrich your spirit." The infernal, after all, has meaning for us. Just make sure you get out again.'

'Contessa di Medina Mirtelli, thank you for talking to us.'

Afterwards, the producer told Maria reassuringly that the interview would go out on *The World Tonight*, 'on BBC2, *after the nine o'clock watershed*'.

Everything was designed for the practical in Brookes University. Penelope Hopkins's office was a small glass cubicle furnished with the regulation desk, computer, filing cabinet and coffee machine. It looked out on to the wall of a neighbouring building. Between the two buildings, a strip of wasteland gave succour to a horse-chestnut striving in a dispirited way to look into the windows of the first floor.

Penelope was engaged in her usual work of filling in forms. The government had devised a new questionnaire for educational establishments employing more than sixteen persons of either sex. She was punching in a response to question 25A on her screen: 'State whether Caucasian, Irish, Slav, Asian, Polynesian or American (N or S)', when Leonora King-Jones poked her head round the door. 'Still ferreting away, darling?' she asked, expecting no answer. She sidled her way in to perch an elegant buttock on the side of Penelope's desk. Leonora was given to tight grey suits in office hours. She was admirably slim, wore red lipstick and silver earrings of a minimalist kind.

'How's the Reading Club going?' Penelope asked, referring to Leonora's latest project.

'Oh, please, darling, *Book Club*, if you don't mind. You mustn't suggest to the students they are going to have to *read*, not initially. Of course it will be confined to paper-backs. Can't afford hardcovers, not at Brookes. The usual

mixture of Fay Weldon, Jane Austen and William Boyd
. . . Oh, and opening next week with Jean Auel!'

Penelope smiled. 'And what masterpiece did Jean Auel
write, whoever she was?'

Leonora tapped a pen on the Formica desk top for
emphasis.

'You mean you've never heard of Jean Auel? She writes
Stone Age fiction – sort of science fiction in reverse. *Clan
of the Cave Bear*, would you believe? Four books in the
series so far, and they have sold – oh, don't ask, over
thirty million copies worldwide. Funny how easily one
says "worldwide" these days. Anyhow, that's the book
we're going to kick off with. It's no good anyone
complaining they don't like it – you just have to say,
"Well, it sold thirty million worldwide."'

'Is it any good?'

'You can't ask that question. It's like asking, Is rock 'n'
roll any good. It must be *important*: it brings in loads of
money.'

She eased all of her bottom on to the desk. 'Sometimes
I despair of our culture, except it is sort of exciting to
see it all going down the tubes. I mean, that's capitalism,
isn't it? Everything gets measured by what it grosses.'

Penelope replied, half teasing – she had heard her friend
on this subject before, 'Capitalism certainly encourages
greed, and greed does nothing to encourage happiness.'

'Full marks! The mad quest for happiness leads to
misery . . . Serves us right. Speaking of which, how's the
love-life?' She leaned over and made a pretence of staring
hypnotically into Penelope's eyes.

'Well,' Penelope started to say, 'it happens that I have
met a man—'

'Don't tell me!' shrieked Leonora. 'I know! He's lovely
but utterly inappropriate. He's either married or gay or

a hunchback! I ran into a gorgeous guy on Saturday at a party. It's true we were drunk, but I ended up in his bed. Directly I was there, I regretted it. Pissed though I was, I thought the pillows were smelly, you know? So was he. I went right off him. But once you've gone that far, it seems kind of wimpish to start getting coy. So—'

'You're lucky to have got that far,' said Penelope. 'It's more than I have.'

However, there had been a time in her early adolescence when she had almost gone that far, long before she met Greg. She had had a crush on Adam, a curly-haired youth who sang her some of the songs from *My Fair Lady* in an alluring Scots accent. He had been too timid to carry the affair through. Adam had grown up to be an academic and something eminent on the board of some society or other, Penelope had forgotten what. He was now the portly Dr Adam Hamilton-Douglas, unbearably learned and a boring fellow.

Penelope had withstood the boredom and she and Dr Hamilton-Douglas met for lunch about once a year. He always paid the bill. Grant him that. She was glad of the acquaintance now, and as soon as Leonora had left her office she dialled his number on her mobile.

He answered at once and announced that he was busy thinking. They exchanged pleasantries, during which Hamilton-Douglas announced that he was thinking of getting married. He had told her this during their previous meeting.

'Adam, I have a friend whom I think may be in some kind of psychological trouble. I want your advice. She appears to think that there is a city of the dead underneath our village, almost identical in structure but, of course, full of earth. The dead live there. I find it very creepy and—'

'Hang on, which village is this?'

'Ferrers. Hampden Ferrers.'

'Oh, where you live? You still live there? I suppose it's cheaper than Oxford. A very leafy village, eh? Full of trees. Lot of hornbeams along the upper road, yes?'

'Isn't it psychologically weird of her to—'

'Oh, the Melanesians have similiar beliefs. Probably to do with trees, *au fond*. It's all a matter of perception. Their underworld is a sad and dreary place. The dead pursue their old activities as best they can. Their characters remain always the same. It's no wonder they keep trying—'

'Adam, we're talking Oxfordshire, not Melanesia, and what I want to know—'

'But, you see, dear,' came Hamilton-Douglas's droning voice in Penelope's ear, 'this whole notion of cities in the air or cities underground is pretty universal. As I say, it's all a matter of perception. We cannot stand too much reality or, for that matter—'

'So my friend's just—'

'Sorry to interrupt, but you must listen to what I am saying. In the Bronze Age, the peoples of the Aegean area constructed corridor tombs with vast corbelled vaults and multi-chambered graves. Much like a small city. Mankind has always tended to explain the phenomena of nature – in which, of course, I include life and death – theologically, not least—'

'But that's the Bronze Age, Adam,' she said patiently. 'I mean to say, nowadays—'

Hamilton-Douglas's laugh boomed in her ear. It was the laugh, among other things, that had put her off him. 'You imagine the Bronze Age is long ago? Believe me, in geological terms it is just yesterday. In fact, for you folks stuck in leafy Hampden Ferrers, I'd say the Bronze Age was still in progress!'

★ ★ ★

The plot of ground behind St Clement's was cold at this time of day. It lay in the shadow of the church – which however, had been warm for the service. Some of the congregation present for Arthur Ridley's funeral were wearing no coats; the days when everyone had had one were long gone. As they filed out to the freshly dug grave, they felt the chill in the air.

Rog and Dave Cotes were the gravediggers, standing respectfully by with their spades. Other members of the Cotes clan represented there were Yvonne, wearing a thin grey raincoat, and Jean Parrinder, Rog's friend, standing by Joe Cotes, who was leaning on a stick. Joe was attending, despite his lameness, because funerals gave him a melancholy pleasure.

The Reverend Robin Jolliffe spoke by the open grave, prayer book in hand. 'My dear friends, it is natural that we should feel sadness when one of us passes over from this present world, this world ruled by Sin and Time, yet we know as Christians that we should also rejoice to think that he or she has made the passage into a better world, the world of God, that infinite hereafter, compared with which this world of ours is just a moment. Arthur Ridley endured his share of sorrow and hardship. He served his country in the British army when a youth—'

'He was in the Ox and Bucks Light Infantry, Father,' interposed Andrea Ridley, who stood dry-eyed by the coffin.

'Yes, thank you, Andrea, so he was indeed. He served in the Ox and Bucks—'

'Aye, but that were after the war were over,' said Joe Cotes. 'Arty were younger 'n me. I were in the Ox and Bucks in the war. Where do you think I got my gammy leg from?'

Father Robin nodded. 'Quite right, Joe. Thank you.'

'That were at Anzio beachhead, and I bet none of you ever seen anythink like it for carnage.'

'Yes, I'm sure, Joe.'

'What's more,' Joe Cotes continued, carried away by reminiscence, possibly because the grave with its tumbled piles of earth reminded him of the trenches in the First World War, 'my grandfather were killed by a German shell at Passchendaele when my dad were only a year old. 'S terrible to think of them times!'

'Indeed, very terrible,' agreed Robin. 'We all have to make our way through a world of trouble. So let us stand in *silence* for a moment, and think not of ourselves but of him who has left us. Arthur's was a modest role in life. He served for many years as a porter at Oriel College—'

'Excuse me, Vicar,' interposed Henry Wiverspoon. He had arrived in coat and scarf, and stood with a stick. 'Arthur served as a porter at University College. I was up at Univ, which is why I am here attending this service, in his memory. I remember Arthur well, and I have to admit he was somewhat of a heavy drinker in his day.'

'Thank you, Henry,' said the Vicar. 'We are here today, on this calm English morning, to remember not Arthur's faults but his many virtues, a loving husband to Andrea and a loving father to Dotty—'

'Step-father to Dotty,' corrected Dotty, piping up. She had been allowed the morning off from Debenham's to attend the funeral.

'I'm sorry, yes, Dotty, of course, a loving step-father to Dotty and to, er – to Duane. We must all speak up for ourselves in this world, but Arthur Ridley was a quiet man and a modest one. We value his modesty as a virtue,

160

and we respect his passing. He died as he had lived, without fuss or protest.

"'Man born of woman hath but little time to live. He cometh up and is cut down like a flower.'"

Arthur Ridley's coffin was lowered into the open grave by the two gravediggers. Andrea and Dotty threw little bouquets of choisya on the box as it descended into the hole.

As the soil was shovelled in, Father Robin intoned, "'Forasmuch as it hath pleased the Almighty to take unto Himself the body of Arthur Ridley here departed, we commit his remains to the ground. Ashes to ashes, dust to dust, in certain hope of the Resurrection, and of eternal life: through our Lord Jesus Christ. Amen.'"

Andrea and Dotty clung to each other. Both shed a few tears, horrified by the finality of the earth hitting the box with a dull and dreadful thud; whether they cried for Arthur or for themselves was hard to determine – perhaps for all mortals. Father Robin went to them and offered some gentle words of comfort.

As the few mourners made their way through the churchyard to the street, Joe Cotes, limping, said to the Vicar, 'It gets to you, certainly. You're right what you say about us coming down and being cut up like a flower. It'll be my turn next, you bet. I need a drink after all that, Robin.'

'How do you think I feel?' Robin asked, with a mischievous gleam in his eye. 'Never did a parson meet with a more obstreperous lot of parishioners . . .'

Joe shook his head. 'I'm sorry about all the interruptions. Have a pint on me, Vicar. You're a good man.'

The specialist in the white overall, Bertram Vissick by name, was growing bald; his high forehead had receded

161

even further until it had reached the crown of his head unimpeded. His wife, Brenda Vissick, was a celebrated pastrycook who had appeared more than once on television. They lived in a detached mock-Tudor-fronted house in Blenheim Drive, North Oxford, with two bay trees in tubs beside the front door. In the hall stood a rocking-horse Brenda had first ridden as a child. Both Brenda and Bertram were kind to their wire-haired terrier, Bloggs; they had no children of their own.

Nothing of this was in Bertram's mind as he stood by Detective Inspector Lorryload, contemplating the donkey strapped to a bench in the laboratory.

Bertram tapped the beast's muzzle with a spatula to see how it would respond. It reacted as might have been anticipated, by struggling to get free.

'Genetically, it seems to be a perfectly normal donkey, Inspector. Tell me again what leads you to suspect it was once a man.'

Detective Inspector Lorryload inspected his electronic notebook before he spoke.

'The former man, going under the name or sobriquet of Greyling, was suspected of bigamy committed while resident in Argentina and the British Isles respectively. Also, financial matters requiring investigation. Together with my associates, we went to place him under arrest at a house known as the Pink House in Hampden Ferrers, near Oxford, the site of some funny goings-on recently, whereas upon entering we found that Mr Greyling had transformed himself into the ass you see before you in an attempt to evade arrest. The giveaway was that the animal was still wearing Mr Greyling's jacket, containing a pen, some dirty photographs and an opened packet of chewing gum, together with a bag of a spicy foodstuff commonly known as Bombay Mix. We found no trace

162

of drugs. Nevertheless we formed the decision to take the animal into custody.'

Bertram Vissick nodded seriously. 'A strange case, Detective Inspector. I had to deal with something similar in the Boars Hill area, back in 1981. There the victim was a retired head of college. Apparently he had spent much of his headship in a – well, in a more or less donkey format.

'Our best plan will be to leave the donkey here in its present position with the television cameras trained on it, and see if it shows any inclination to change back into a man.' He attempted a joke: 'It's what I call a sort of *Jekyll and Herd* case.'

Lorryload put his head steeply to one side, showing his prominent teeth in the manner of one about to make a profound suggestion. 'Might it be possible to communicate with the animal, sir? For instance, since the only noise it can make appears to be the traditional "hee-haw" of its species, it might become feasible with skill and patience to train the beast to signify "yes" with a "hee" and "no" with a "haw" – or vice versa, of course. We could thus interrogate him and discover what he's up to.'

'A clever suggestion. But perhaps it is best to leave him under observation for an hour or two.'

This decision by the veterinary surgeon was adhered to. Lorryload uttered a few terminal remarks and quit the building.

Bertram Vissick phoned Brenda Vissick.

'So, is the Inspector still hanging about?' Brenda asked.

'He left. He said he was on another job. I suspect he was going to have a drink. Probably two or three.'

'This story of a man transformed into a donkey – it's all poppycock, isn't it?'

'It could be, dear. It's what I call a *Jekyll and Herd* case.'

163

'Turn the poor animal out into a field. If you arrest a donkey, it will be the law that looks like an ass.'

'Okay. I'll do as you suggest. What's for supper, dear?'

The honeysuckle in Penelope's porch was coming into full flower. She paused before entering the house, inhaling its fragrance.

Inside, the smell of cigarette smoke lingered, filtering down from Bettina's room. The door was a little stiff. Hearing it closed forcefully, Bettina stuck her head over the banisters. 'A letter came for you, Penny. I've put it on your table.'

'Thanks,' said Penelope, annoyed. It was no business of her lodger to pick up her letters, or to put them in her kitchen. She counted this as interference.

She had had a busy day at Brookes, conducting three interviews with overseas students, two of whom she considered quite unsuitable. Perhaps she had been less patient with them than she should have been.

On an impulse, she crossed to the small front room, rather dark at this time of day, went to her hi-fi and slotted in a CD of one of her favourite pieces, Shostakovich's Sonata for Viola and Piano. She knew something of the composer's difficulties under the tyrannical Stalin. She also recalled, with both irony and hope, that a critic had said of Shostakovich that his new work would 'make the world a better place'.

The dialogue between the two instruments began, essentially music for lonely people. She let it play while she went into the kitchen.

As she began to pour herself a glass of white wine, she noticed the letter lying on the table. Her name, 'Penelope', was inscribed on the envelope in elaborate lettering, which she recognised. It had been delivered by hand. She put down the bottle and pounced on it. In it was a single-folded sheet of A4, on which Stephen had written in holograph,

My dearest Penny,
   I am sorry I have not been in touch. It is not that I have forgotten you or your sweetness, how could I?, but I have some difficulties. Thank you for your note although – I hate having to say it – it is wiser not to write. May I come and see you this evening at somewhere between eight and nine? My pretext is that we need to discuss various committee matters. (I saw the Vicar just now, looking distraught – which gives colour to my alibi!)
   You are so precious to me. I so desire to see you and hold you. It will not be long now.
   Your loving Steve.

While recognising what she thought of as miracles of cowardice in the note, Penelope was pleased nevertheless by the promise of his arrival. After she had filled her glass, she looked about her to see how tidy the place was.

   Another letter lay on the draining-board. This was open and, in her own handwriting, addressed to Zadanka, the cleaner. Penelope always tried to write Zadanka a note, with her week's pay, to make up for the fact that she almost never saw the girl.

   She realised she had left the note but not the money. She uttered a gasp of exasperation. She had had no change that morning before she left home, had intended to get some, then immediately – burdened with thoughts of Stephen – had forgotten the matter.

   Zadanka had left no note of protest. Zadanka never left notes.

Penelope took the wine over to the sofa, where she put her feet up, eased off her calf-length boots and tried to think things over. The Shostakovich still played. The piano was leading the argument.

The sofa was shabby. The framed picture on the wall, a reproduction of a rather dim Puvis de Chavannes, was hanging askew; in it, two thin men were trying to get into or out of a small boat. The carpet needed vacuuming. The busy lizzie needed watering. The truth was that Penelope had become uninterested in her surroundings.

The time was only a few minutes past seven. She could take Zadanka her money immediately: and be back well in time for Steve. Maybe even vacuum the carpet.

Leaving most of the wine, she looked in her handbag. Thanks to a visit she had paid to the Brookes staff canteen for a snatched lunch, she now had the necessary change.

She went into the street, dragging the door shut behind her.

Zadanka lived at 49A. Penelope was vague about where that might be. She knew it was somewhere near Hill's Stores. When she reached the shop, Sam was closing, pulling down a metal shutter over the window. She asked after Sammy Junior and was told he was cheerful. He informed her that 49A was 'round the back'.

The yard behind the shop was piled with rubbish, discarded crates, boxes, a bonfire in one corner not entirely extinct, rotting vegetables, and junk of all sorts. A cat scrambled for safety when Penelope appeared. A small section of the yard had been walled off to form a strip of garden: Sam Aziz's runner beans were growing in a raised bed.

A fire escape, which at one time had been painted a Ben Shahn red, stood against the rear of the building.

166

Rather doubtfully, Penelope began to climb it. She ascended towards a half-open door, close to which was a window with a broken pane patched by a square of cardboard.

As her head rose to level with the bottom of the door, the door was pushed wide open and a young woman asked, 'What you are want?'

Penelope climbed one more step and stopped. She recognised Zadanka: not the neat person she knew, but a woman with straggling hair, barefoot, clad in some sort of gown with a violent pattern of fruit. 'Oh, Zadanka, hello! It's me, Penelope. Shall I come up?'

This information in no way softened Zadanka's challenging attitude. 'What you are want?' she asked again.

A voice from the room behind her called to ask who it was.

Zadanka replied swiftly in a foreign tongue, and was instructed to bring the person in.

She beckoned Penelope with a nod. 'Come on.'

Penelope entered a room that demonstrably served the function of a whole house. A hard-backed chair and a small table were jammed under the window. In one corner there was a small fitted cupboard and a washbasin, in another an iron bed, on which a black man sprawled. He was wearing a faded striped shirt and an equally faded pair of jeans. His feet were bare. She saw how tenderly pink were the soles of his feet.

She felt vaguely alarmed, out of her depth.

Various oddments of plates and clothes lay about the place. A saucepan steamed on a small stove, from which came an encouraging aroma of curry.

The black man sat up and eyed Penelope with a frown. 'What can we do for you?' he asked. 'I've not seen you before.'

'Nor I you,' said Penny, and looked at Zadanka.

Zadanka said, sullenly, 'You come to give the sack to me?'

'No, certainly not, Zadanka. I'm quite happy with what you do for me. I have come to pay you. I forgot to leave your money on the draining-board this morning – as I'm sure you realise.'

The man now sat on the side of the bed, scratching the back of his neck. 'That makes a change, to have someone want to pay money. It's a hard world, that's for sure. Can we offer you a drink, lady?'

Before Penelope could answer, Zadanka said, 'I have not come your house this morning.'

'Oh, why not, Zadanka? I'm sure I underpay you. Is that it?'

Mutely, Zadanka shook her head. The violent fruit on her dress shivered. 'My poor mother is died in Pribram.' As she spoke the words, Zadanka burst into tears, hiding her face in her hands, rocking back and forth. The man hurried over to her and cradled her in his arms, uttering soothing sounds.

'Oh, WW, whatever I can do?', she asked between sobs.

The man addressed as WW explained to Penelope over Zadanka's shoulder that Zadanka's mother had been ill for some while. Then the old lady had caught pneumonia, but Zadanka could not afford to return to the Czech Republic to be with her mother. Last evening, a sister had phoned to say she had died.

While Penelope tried to express her regret, Zadanka howled with a noise reminiscent of wolves in an Arctic night. A banging on the ceiling of the room below followed swiftly.

'Is there anything I can do?'

168

'No, dear, thanks.' WW gave her a wide smile. 'It's okay. Zadanka will calm down in a while. Leave her to me. I am cooking her food to eat. You'd better go.'

'Well, I'll just leave the money, if you don't mind.' She put it on the table.

'Hush, hush, my baby. All of the world's mothers got to die some day. It's a rule fixed by God. Else the world would fill up with old mothers, and that would never do. Hush, now!' Zadanka howled the more, as if even WW's comfort brought fresh wounds.

He turned back to Penelope, with another reassuring smile. 'Sorry for all this. Your mum dying is a serious matter for all of us. She will be okay pretty soon. She needs to have a cry.'

Almost in a whisper, Penelope asked if Zadanka wanted to go back to the Czech Republic. WW gave a confused answer, saying she and her mother had fled there but were originally from Montenegro, although their origins were somewhere else in the Balkans. He confessed he did not know that part of the world. Why should he? Penelope thought. 'She has quite a lot to be sad about,' he said, with a solemn look at Penelope, as if testing to see whether the truth of the remark penetrated.

She felt deeply ashamed. Tears came to her eyes.

'I'm so sorry. I shouldn't have intruded.' She held out her hand. The man took it. His clasp was warm and gentle. When his smile ceased, he looked extremely sorrowful.

Back in her house, Penelope listened in the hall. Silence upstairs. Perhaps Bettina was painting in her little room, with Ishtar asleep beside her. The heels of her boots clicked on the tiled floor, and she kicked a toy out of the way before she entered the kitchen to pour herself

169

a vodka. She switched on the radio. Someone was talking about youth and Israel. She switched it off again. She walked about the confined space. She opened the back door and stood in the small garden, glancing about her absently. The smell of cats came to her nostrils, vying with a lingering scent of philadelphus.

The bell rang. She went and opened the front door. Stephen stood there. He came in and they clasped each other briefly, without kissing.

'Would you like a vodka?'

'Have you got a beer?'

'Sorry.'

'A vodka would be fine.'

'Come into the front room. I'm afraid it's in a bit of a mess.'

'You look a little gloomy.' He spoke tenderly.

'I am gloomy,' she said.

He removed two days' newspapers and sat on the sofa under the window, where Penelope brought him the vodka. She said she needed a cigarette. Stephen provided one – not her favourite brand – and took one himself. After their cigarettes were lit, he said, 'Frank Martinson is throwing a party this evening – you know; the historian who lives at West End.'

'I know him by sight, yes. Nice man. He sometimes gives lectures at Brookes. He's an expert on Stanley Baldwin.'

'Indeed? Penny, I feel very bad about neglecting you. Come with me to Frank's party. We can turn up at nine. It will still be going strong.'

'I haven't got a party dress.'

'It's not that kind of a party. We can go as we are.'

'I could wear my blue-and-white stripe.'

He smiled. 'So you'll come, then?'

170

Penelope sucked on her cigarette. 'What about Sharon? What will other people think if they see us together?'

'Come on.' He captured her hand. 'No one will mind. It's the twenty-first century!'

'What? Even in Ferrers?'

He laughed. 'Yes, even in Ferrers the ghastly twentieth century is over. Apparently Frank has acquired a new ladyfriend so she'll be on display. How about it?'

'Mmm, maybe. If I'm not too tight. And too tired. And generally fed up with life. I just feel I've been a bitch without realising it.' She told him of her visit to Zedanka's flat. 'Zedanka lives so poorly in one room over Aziz's shop, with a strange black man. I've been exploiting her for months.'

'Surely you've given her gainful employment – isn't that the phrase? She was happy enough, wasn't she, before her mother died?'

'She was an exile, Steve. *Is* an exile. That can't be a happy state.'

'Probably she's an illegal immigrant. I don't wish to seem unsympathetic, but it may be she is living better here, certainly more safely, than she did in – wherever she comes from.'

Penelope was silent. At last she muttered, 'Somewhere in the Balkans . . .' She settled herself, nursing her glass, beside him on the sofa, aware that he was regarding her enquiringly. Finally, she asked, 'Were you born here? In England, I mean.'

'Yes. Also my brother – just. My mother was pregnant when she and my father landed, in a small boat mooring at London docks.'

'This was from Germany, yes?'

'Sure.' It seemed he was going to say no more. He busied himself stubbing out his cigarette, and then, 'My

171

mother was quite ill. She gave birth to Herby in a small hotel in – Cheapside, I believe it was. We were lucky. Many of our relations, including my mother's sister, did not get away from the Nazis in time. I was born ten years after my brother, by which time we were slightly more prosperous.'

She put an arm round his shoulders.

He said, 'I grew up determined to be English. My mistake was to marry another Jew.' He sipped his vodka.

They sat in companionable silence, regarding each other. 'My brother Tom died in a car crash at the age of eighteen. Did I tell you? No, of course I didn't! You realise, Steve, we have hardly spoken to each other . . .'

'It's been my fault.' They went on to talk about fragments of their lives. Things almost forgotten, some amusing, some less so, came floating to the surface.

Penelope got them more vodka, and stood the bottle nearby, on the window-sill, next to her busy lizzie. They scarcely took their eyes from each other's gaze; she felt the dazzle of his.

Stephen began telling her something of Sharon's history. It seemed he fell into the theme almost inadvertently. His eyes were elsewhere as he spoke, conjuring up an immense snowbound landscape, so unlike the dear, dowdy little room with a fly buzzing drowsily in which presently they lingered.

As far as the human eye could see, the flat landscape of the Vistula estuarine land was covered with a shelf of ice, Stephen said, traversing his hand before him, palm downwards. It might have served as a representation of eternity. The drab whiteness was scarred by black craters, caused by exploding bombs and mortar shells. It was the winter of 1944. Nothing lived, except a cluster of four figures making slow progress westwards.

172

The figures were ill-clad against the extreme cold. They had sacks or blankets wrapped about their bodies and over their heads. Such boots or shoes as they wore were bound to their feet with strips of cloth. They moved slowly and automatically. Two of the group were aged men in their late sixties, bearded, one was a gangling adolescent, one was a woman in her late teens. They bore no kinship to each other. What they had in common was their flight from the city of Elbing two days previously, when a Soviet tank battalion was already entering its eastern gates.

They were heading for the doubtful shelter of the city of Berlin, many miles away. Behind them, growing ever closer, came Stalin's invasion force, terrible in its strength and indiscipline, the almost legendary terror from the East. Fear kept them on the move. All four were close to starvation.

The dull dead light of day was fading, the temperature dropping. The little group came on the ruin of a cottage, destroyed by shell-fire but nevertheless offering at least partial shelter from the strengthening gusts of wind. No other feature could be seen. With looks and grunts, they decided and forced their way in over a fallen roof beam.

A corpse lay in one corner of a room. Its head was buried under fallen debris. The cold had prevented much decomposition. The man wore a Soviet-style tunic, although whether he had been Russian or Prussian was open to doubt: the men snatched what clothes they could, and this might have been a dead man in another dead man's suit. One of the old men searched the corpse's uniform and found, in its pack, a chunk of iron-hard bread and a sliver of salami.

As far as their frozen hands were able, they divided the morsels into four and ate as they crouched. They fell

173

asleep huddled together to conserve body warmth. The woman's name was Martha Beierstein; she was Sharon Boxbaum's grandmother-to-be.

At some time during the night, a blinding light was shone into the ruin and a man shouted at them to get up. Martha Beierstein and the youth helped each other to their feet. The man, evidently a soldier, held a light machine-gun. In fear, they raised their hands into the air. The night was pitch black, without a star, and the wind whistled in the broken roof.

The two older men were slower to rouse. So numb were they that they had trouble struggling to their feet. They had been lying across the corpse.

It seemed as if the Soviet officer – as they assumed him to be – was maddened by the sight of the corpse. Possibly he assumed the men had murdered the dead soldier. Or else it was late, he had gone without sleep, he was drunk, he was gun-happy, all of those. He opened fire. The two men uttered no sound as they fell dead, sprawling in the trampled snow.

Martha went into hysterics. The officer, stepping forward, grasped her arm and dragged her out of the ruined cottage. The youth followed, arms still above his head. He was shaking with fear. The officer turned, saw he was being followed, and hit the youth a blow in the stomach with the butt of his gun. He fell to his knees, gasping, in the snow.

There, in the purgatorial dark, could be glimpsed Soviet T-34 tanks, various vehicles, and Cossacks on horseback, swathed in rugs or shawls, silent, immobile. A miscellaneous soldiery could be glimpsed, several clinging together in a temperature far below zero. This was the army, all conquering, that had swept across Poland and was due to cross the Oder to enter Berlin, answering

174

Nazi violence with their own terrible brand of vengeance.

Martha Beierstein, who had dyed her hair blond, had become the mistress of a German *Feldwebel*, and so far escaped the fate of many Jews. She was three months pregnant. The Soviet officer dragged her into a Lend-Lease Studebaker. Before the door had slammed shut and he had given the signal to advance, two fiends in the rear of the vehicle had seized her and were tearing off her shreds of clothes, to rape her back and front. To stifle her cries, they stuffed a filthy rag into her mouth. She lost consciousness.

When she roused, dawn was filtering through cloud. Another ghastly day was advancing, resembling an old whitewashed wall. The vehicle had stopped. It was empty, one door swinging open. She lay battered and damaged, half on the rear seat, half on the floor. Ruins were all about the Studebaker, ghostly in snow and frost.

'Oh, why am I telling you this?' Stephen wondered.

'Because it haunts you? Go on. I assume Sharon's grandmother did not die?' Penelope took a sip from her glass, avoiding his gaze.

He regarded her closely, as if her reassurances had failed to reassure him.

'What happened was that Martha escaped from the vehicle while the soldiers – the rapists – were having something to eat, or being briefed. Who knows? She crawled into the shelter of a church. She was sure she was dying. However, she was fortunate to fall into the hands of a German pastor who gave her sanctuary. He and his wife looked after her. He was preparing to get away to Switzerland. He had always been anti-Nazi, and saw that the end of the Third Reich was coming.

'This man, essentially kind though he was, was a rabid

175

anti-Semite. He blamed all that had happened on an international Jewish conspiracy. He never asked Martha if she was Jewish. He and his wife kept a vehicle, which had not been confiscated by the Wehrmacht. They had hidden it. In it, they drove to Switzerland. Switzerland was a more or less neutral country, although decidedly pro-Hitler. Martha was extremely ill but did not lose her baby.

'She became very withdrawn. For two years she worked as a servant for the pastor in his modest new home. She and her child lived in an outhouse. I believe it had been a cowshed. The pastor had connections among the clergy, and life was not too bad for him and his wife, unlike the millions of other people who continued to suffer long after the war was over. In the way that some of us still suffer. Including my poor wife, Sharon.

'Sharon's mother was brought up in Switzerland, in a village near Zurich, by Martha, this deeply traumatized woman. She had a fear of all Germans. Eventually, when she was just a teenager, she made her way across Europe and crossed the Channel to England.

'To cut a long story short, she took a job in a shop and eventually rose to be under-manager. This was in Harrow, I think. There she married Sharon's father, but the marriage was not a success. However, it was from that marriage that Sharon was born. Her parents separated when she was five. A distant relation brought her up.

'When Sharon and I were married, we seemed happy at first, but gradually I have witnessed her falling into a psychosis, the roots of which I am sure lie in the past.'

'Do you blame yourself in any way?'

'I do. I feel I've failed her. But history is a heavy burden,

176

after all. Sharon goes to psychoanalysts, but seems to get no better.'

Penelope found herself increasingly unsympathetic to all this. She did not understand why he should waste their precious time together telling her of the past, which did not even involve his own past. Increasingly, as his narrative unfolded, she recalled a novel of Stefan Zweig's, *Beware of Pity*. Beware of pity indeed! She wondered if anyone read Stefan Zweig's novels nowadays, and thought probably not.

She believed she had seen somewhere that Zweig had committed suicide, in Brazil or South America at least. It might be interesting to discover more about him.

And now Stephen, not Stefan, was speaking of his own problems.

'It is as if some terrible thing hovered over me – as if there were kilometres of black ocean above me. I seem frequently to be paralysed by it.'

'A fear of death?', she asked, randomly.

'Worse than that, because it has no name. Death at least has a name. We understand death. It lies in wait, not entirely unwelcome. Maybe it is something horrible that happened once and I have – I've just edited it out. I'm sorry.'

Penelope jumped up, reached for a packet of Marlboro, shook out a cigarette and lit it. She blew smoke from her mouth.

Her foot tapped impatiently on the floor as she spoke. 'If we dwell on such morbid things, we'll never get anywhere. Although I am not averse to such sorrow – indeed, I hear sad stories from my young students all the while – I believed, I *hoped*, that you were coming here perhaps to utter words of love. Obviously, I was presumptuous.'

177

'No. No, it's not like that! I only wanted you to know—'

'Forget it!' She spat the words at him. 'I didn't want to know! What I wanted to know was if you bloody well loved me, and it's clear you don't. You're too wrapped up in yourself.' She turned her back on him.

'Penny, please—'

'Oh, shut up! Why does it always have to be the past? The sodding past.' She was annoyed to feel the sudden exhilarating burst of anger leave her.

Stephen stood, holding out his hands. But she had folded her arms across her chest, either protectively or confrontationally.

'Penny, dearest Penny, I did not mean to offend. Indeed, I did come here to speak of love. I'm sorry if my explanations ran away with me.'

She was not going to let him get away with it so easily. Puffing at her cigarette, she said, 'Oh, stick to your boring explanations if you wish. They're nothing to me.'

'That may be the case. They were intended to show you – maybe to warn you about – the sort of man I am.'

'Huh, well . . .' she breathed. 'Have another drink.'

She turned away again but, as she did, he took hold of her, putting his arms about her waist, kissing her hair from behind, her ear, her cheek. 'I don't want a drink, Penny, I want you. You're such a brilliant, beautiful woman. I'm sorry about all that past history. It was a mistake. I know how you feel—'

She turned within his embrace, to say, half laughing, half sneering, 'Don't you think it absurd the way we pretend we know how someone else feels? What an arrogant assumption to make – especially when one hardly knows what one feels oneself.'

'It's more of a hope than a claim.' He would not let

her go, and now he kissed her lips – at which she did not protest.

She put her arms about his neck and kissed him in return, because she, too, had her needs. 'All right, let's go to this sodding party and be cheerful. You'd better leave now. I'll do myself up and you can collect me at nine.'

'Great!' He kissed her again.

'Pick me up in your car.'

When he had gone, closing the difficult door behind him, Penelope paced about the room, digesting the meaning of his lengthy account of Sharon's mother's survival. It was clear to her now: Stephen was a victim of pity, as in Zweig's novel. He had been saying that he could not leave his wife. Yet.

Jeremy Sumption was in Hetty and Judy's house, perching on one of the chairs he had lent them until theirs arrived. He and the girls were drinking tea.

Judy looked at her watch. 'Now, then, where is that blinking furniture van? Half an hour late!'

He yelled, 'Oh *blinking*! I love it! That's what I call swearing!'

She had been into Oxford in the morning and ordered some furniture from Court's megastore in the Botley Road.

'Don't worry,' said Hetty. 'Perhaps there's a traffic jam.'

'In Kowloon they would lose their jobs.'

Their scheme had been to buy a dining-room suite and a sofa to furnish the downstairs of their new house for the time being while they looked around for antiques.

Jeremy's fascination with these two self-assured Chinese ladies knew no bounds. He set down his cup and saucer and said, firmly, 'Whether your furniture arrives or not, we are going to the party at Frank Martinson's place. There's a really successful writer for you!'

179

'It's a nice house, is it?' Judy asked.

'Brilliant, so I'm told, and elegant grounds. Lots of booze.'

Judy clapped her hands. 'We must go in fancy dress, is it?'

'Of course.' He liked teasing Judy, the more excitable of the two. 'You can go as the Queen of Sheba.'

'Where exactly is Sheba?' Hetty enquired.

Jeremy had recalled an old joke, and did not respond. 'Did you hear about the married couple who were going to a fancy-dress ball? They didn't know what to go as. Then the wife comes downstairs absolutely naked, except she's covered in garden cloches – you know, those glass things. The husband's a bit taken aback and asks what she's supposed to be.

'"I'm going as the Crystal Palace," she says. He rushes into the garage and come back naked except his old man is stuck in a mouse trap.'

Jeremy looked at them to make sure they were following so far, and suddenly realised that the punch line was going to be difficult to put over.

'So the wife says, "My God, what's that all about?" and he says, "If you can go as the Crystal Palace, then I'm going as Hampton Court"!'

He roared with laughter. The ladies looked blank.

'Hampton caught. Get it? His hampton was caught in the mouse trap.'

'Is it this Hampden you mean? We're strangers here, you know. I'm sure it is a very funny joke, Jeremy dear,' said Hetty, 'but as a suggestion regarding how we go to Frank's party, it is not useful at all.'

He grabbed her and kissed her. 'I love you, Hetty. You are utterly marvellous! And it's not fancy dress this evening. You and Judy go as your own sweet selves.'

180

'Of course you are mad, Jeremy!' She kissed him in return, with equal fervour.

An hour later, the furniture van arrived.

West End was all lights. The garden glowed with a chain of lamps, knee-high beside every path. Chinese lanterns shone like domestic moons in cherry trees. Musicians played at one end of the long terrace.

Extensive preparations came smoothly into play. The caterers had arrived, clad in evening dress and white tie. A cleaning company, Chores of Oxford, had whisked through the entire building, making everything extra clean and wholesome. Wheelbarrow Bingham had been given a Cotes lad to help manicure the flower-beds. Nurse Ann had been hired to look after Fred, just in case the incursion of so many people alarmed him.

The evening was warm enough for the guests to wander in or out of doors, seeking old friends and new, holding brief conversations, laughing, posturing, being something more than their usual undramatic selves.

Frank was dressed informally in a deep blue sports shirt and white slacks. Maria was also informal, in a floral chiffon blouse and flared white cotton trousers, which laid emphasis on her neat little bottom. Together, they wandered among the guests, where locals mixed with academics and their partners. A trio played light music, currently offering selections from Offenbach's *Orpheus in the Underworld*.

Maria was talking to a group of admiring men, mainly from Wolfson, including the poet John Westall, and Sydney Barraclough, as well as Rodney Williams, the only man without a drink, enabling him to stand with his hands behind his back.

John was declaring his love for Italy, and asking eagerly where he should take his wife for a holiday.

181

Maria said, 'I have a friend who is manager of a hotel south of Naples, on the coast. Hotel Castellabate. I know the owner quite well. His name is Vincenzo Mandolfi. It's a sweet old-fashioned hotel. I sometimes visit there when I wish to get away. My mother used to stay there with a lover of hers, but I don't let that put me off . . .'

The men laughed.

She permitted them the benison of her smile. 'Castellabate is just so beautiful – beautifully situated, with steep cliffs all about and a nice deep sea to swim in. I went there to rest once when I was recovering from my breast cancer.'

The men showed interest, but Maria did not confide further.

Stephen and Penelope entered and were shown to where oysters, canapés and other delights were on offer. A waiter poured champagne for them. Jeremy and Rupert were there with the two Chinese ladies, Hetty and Judy, dancing decorously in the Blue Room. Other guests were still arrivng, mainly people from nearby houses on the Cotes Road.

Henry arrived late, accompanying Valentine Leppard, who was ensconced in an electric wheelchair. Frank came forward to greet his distinguished guest. 'I'm sorry to see you in a wheelchair, Professor.'

'Don't worry. Don't fuss. It's comfortable. Also, fewer people will talk to me while I'm in it. People hate bending down to talk. As I can see you do.'

'No, no.' Frank smiling. 'Not at all.'

'Well, we won't argue. I came only to set eyes on your Kiftsgate, which I understand is just coming into bloom.'

'Yes, I'll show you.'

'Just don't introduce me to people. I loathe and detest

small talk. I like to think of England as a quiet place. Whenever you see news reports on the television, or hear reports on the wireless, from places like Bangladesh, the entire population seems to be shouting. We don't want to behave like that, do we?'

'Of course not. Perhaps you and Henry would care for a glass of wine?'

Valentine ignored the offer, and said, as he chugged along, 'By the way, Francis, this new Italian lady of yours is an insolent little body, isn't she?'

At this juncture the insolent little body was talking to Hetty Zhou in the Blue Room.

'I have been made very welcome in Hampden Ferrers,' said Hetty. 'It's extremely kind, thank you.'

'Oh, I'm only a visitor myself. But, yes, almost everyone is very pleasant.'

Hetty smiled disarmingly. 'I have been told you are in love with the historian, Francis Martinson. Is it true or just a rumour?'

Maria was slightly taken aback by this frankness, and said only that she happened to be staying with him for a few days.

'Perhaps my question was too direct. I apologise. You see, I believe I have unwisely fallen in love with this terrible man Jeremy here.' She squeezed Jeremy's arm.

'Careful,' Jeremy said. 'Remember I've been in the cop shop all day. I did shower afterwards, though.'

Hetty kissed his cheek, then turned back to Maria, asking her if she had not fallen in love.

'Miss Zhou, I tell you this in the confidence that must exist between women. Jeremy, you can turn away. Yes, I am in love with Frank. I have been for many years. But unfortunately I have a husband.'

Hetty almost shrugged. With a bright smile she said,

'But if the husband is in Italy, there is no obstacle, is there?'

Maria could not help laughing. A gaunt figure stalked into the room. It was Sharon Boxbaum. She looked about her angrily, and declined a proffered glass of champagne.

'*Mamma mia*!' exclaimed Maria. 'Jeremy, please rush into the garden and warn Stephen Boxbaum his wife has arrived. I will hold her in a conversation. Rupert, do help me detain your mother.'

She and Rupert crossed the floor. 'Oh, Mother, could you let me have a Marlboro? I desperately need a puff.'

Sharon eyed her son. 'Where's your father?'

'Not a clue. Is he here?' Rupert strove to look brainless.

She did not answer. She opened her handbag and produced her cigarettes. She offered them to Rupert, then pointed the packet at Maria. 'Do you smoke?'

'Thank you. I would love one. Very kind. I cannot give up the habit.' Maria gave little gestures to indicate helplessness. 'It's disgusting, I recognise.'

They all three lit up. Over her burning tip, Sharon shot Maria a look of hatred. 'Not as disgusting as the drugs you used to take. I just saw you on TV, admitting freely – boasting! – that you took heroin.'

'No, Mrs Boxbaum, I was on opium.'

Sharon shook her head, as if to free it from the images that had been conjured up. 'I shall go and find my husband. Excuse me. Goodnight.'

'Excuse *me*, Mrs Boxbaum, I understand you have a rather stunning swimming-pool at your property. Do you think I might come to see it?'

'Some other time!' With that, Sharon was off, into the garden.

★　★　★

184

Valentine, meanwhile, had manoeuvred himself in his chair more deeply into the house and had entered Frank's book room. Henry followed rather aimlessly, clutching his glass.

The study shelves were lined with history books; many ancient and many more modern authors were represented. There was also, he noted with approval a philosophy section. And some fiction, much of it of an earlier date. As he was poking about on the shelves of forgotten authors, Eric Linklater, R.C. Hutchinson and others, Valentine gave a cry. 'Goodness me, look at this, Henry! Rosamund Lehmann!'

Valentine extracted the Lehmann novels from the shelves to inspect them and found they were all first editions, still clad in their dust-jackets. *Weather in the Streets* was dedicated to Frank's mother, Lavinia Martinson, and signed by the author.

'Poor fellow! Frank a sentimentalist! Who'd have thought it?' Valentine shook his head gloomily. There was no trusting anyone these days.

'He has never been a particularly serious historian in my view,' Henry said. 'Too often on television. An inclination towards personal grandeur – always a sign of iniquity. I observe he has now taken up with an Italian contessa.'

'Quite so. Would you believe it? The rude little creature came to visit me. I used to know her mother quite well, long, long ago. Very nice woman. Daughter's a different kettle of fish. We were just starting to have a really pleasant chat when she ups and is away in a most impolite manner.'

Henry smiled over the top of *Dusty Answer*. 'I expect you offended her, Val.'

'Not at all. I was courtesy itself. She might have been

185

expecting her period, of course. When you're as ancient as I, you tend to forget women have these upsets.'

Stephen Boxbaum and Penelope Hopkins were dancing close together on the terrace, with other couples, while the trio played dreamy waltz tunes. They had struck up with an old favourite, 'Destiny', when Stephen, over Penelope's shoulder, saw his wife approaching.

'Quick, Penny, there'll be a row! You'd better beat a retreat.'

She turned and saw Sharon, puffing angrily on her cigarette. 'I shall stay with you.'

Sharon had become angular with anger, all elbows and fists as she confronted Stephen. 'This is what you get up to, is it? You rat, you wretch, you faithless sneak!'

Stephen put on his spectacles to regard her more formally. 'Please, let's not have a scene here, dear. Oh, this is Mrs Hopkins, by the way. We've just met. I don't think you two know each other?'

'You lying schmuck! I know you've been carrying on for years.' Sharon launched into a furious delineation of his character. The other dancers stopped, either to listen or to flee. The music ceased. Penelope stood and let the invective wash over her.

'When you have finished, Sharon, I will take you home.'

'You'll do no such thing! You'll not touch me. I never want you in the house again.'

Penelope said calmly, 'You are interrupting the dancing, Mrs Boxbaum. Why should your husband and I not dance together at a party?'

'Oh, I know you! Dance at a party, prostitute yourself at some sordid hotel! This dirty little affair has been going on for years. You are just a cheap little flirt! Gutter behaviour! That's you, that's him, gutter behaviour!'

186

'You lying minx!' Penelope exclaimed. 'You totally misrepresent everything!' Even as she spoke, she felt it was a feeble protest.

'Keep out of this, Penny,' Stephen advised. 'You are innocent. I will deal with Sharon.'

'Oh, no, you won't!' cried Sharon. 'I've finished with being dealt with! I've had enough of your dealings altogether!'

Rupert had come up, with Judy tripping behind him. He looked desperate, that she looked excited. He took his mother's arm. 'Mother, darling, please, this is someone's party. Don't make a scene!'

'Let me alone! I will make a scene. Anyway it's not of my making. I'm guilty of nothing. Your father is the adulterer. Typical of you to take his part!'

'Mother! I must—'

'Son, stay out of this, please!' said Stephen, protectively.

'Adulterer!' shrieked Sharon, hot tears of fury bursting from her eyes. Having found the word, she was not going to let it escape.

Stephen took a step forward, perhaps hoping to protect his son. Immediately Sharon flung herself at him with such force that he took two steps back. His heel went over the edge of the terrace. Next moment, husband and wife were sprawling full length in the grass. Fortunately, the drop was only a shallow one. Stephen's glasses went flying into a lavender bush.

Sharon crawled away, sobbing. Her dress was torn. She got to her feet and ran limping from the scene. By this time Frank had come up, attracted by the shouting. He motioned to the trio to start playing again. The strains of the 'Destiny' waltz honeyed the air once more. Penelope, Frank and Rupert helped Stephen to his feet. He had hurt his back and was clearly shaken.

'I must go home and soothe her.'

'I'm so sorry, Steve. Are you all right?'

'She's been drinking. She'll be okay. She's been drinking. I'll see to her. She's often like this. Where are my glasses?'

'And how about us?' Penelope enquired, in a low voice. 'Do you give a thought for how I feel?' She was trembling.

'Penny, dear, my wife is a sick woman. Please understand.'

Rupert saw the expression on Penelope's face. He kissed her cheek. 'Don't worry, Penny. Sorry for what's happened. It'll be okay. Dad's not himself.'

'Oh? Who is he, then, I'd like to know?'

Her question remained unanswered. Judy had retrieved Stephen's spectacles and he was limping away, uttering excuses. Rupert hovered uncertainly.

Frank, Judy, Maria and others gathered round Penelope. She was crying openly. 'It's so horrible. So unkind. I feel so ashamed.'

When Rupert put an arm round her, she sobbed, 'This awful situation – this awful—' but could say no more.

The little group made their way slowly towards the house. The strains of 'Destiny' were left behind.

Watching this scene from his bedroom window was Fred Martinson. He told his nurse that people were fighting. He was scared in case they entered the house and found where he was. And they would be bound to kill his guinea pig.

Nurse Ann put an affectionate arm round him. 'It's all over now. Don't be frightened, Fred.' She spoke softly, smiling into his anxious face. 'No one will harm you. Come and lie on the bed with me. I'll look after you.'

He went with her as meekly as a child. But he was no child.

The party was almost over. Valentine's electric chair was trundling slowly down the drive, with Henry hobbling after it.

Soon the waiters were clearing away the uneaten food and unopened bottles. All the guests had departed. The musical trio drove off in their car. Most of the garden lights were switched off.

A few champagne glasses remained, lying unbroken in the grass.

It was still warm enough to sit out. Frank and Maria were ensconced on a stone bench in a remote corner of the garden, heads close together over glasses of Chardonnay. Moon daisies flowered all about them. 'What a party! What a scene!' they said, almost in delight.

The house, lights still agleam, was moored like a beached ship in the distance. They were alone. Behind them the fence was adorned with a sprawling mass of honeysuckle and jasmine, whose scent reached them like the sound of recent music. Beyond, the fields rose gently, ceasing before a line of trees and then the dark wild bulk of the Molesey hills.

'Well, that was a barney.'

'I don't know whom I feel most sorry for.'

They were calm, without regret, having reached an agreeable plateau. No thought of the morrow, or even of the next hour, reached them. It was as if fate could not harm them. That they had known each other, however briefly, so many years before, was the taproot of their love.

'Your letters when you wrote and confessed you had been on opium were miraculous. I feared for you in retrospect, but I admired what you had said – what you had experienced.'

'Mmm, it's okay to talk about those times now. But we must enjoy sanity more than insanity. Insanity is the more confining prison of the two. If there's a choice to be made.'

A lantern burned just behind them, a false moon wrapped in folded paper. A bird was singing to it, long after its bedtime.

He asked her now about the cancer. It had dominated her life for a long while. 'I feared to die so young,' she said. She clutched his hand. She wore expensive rings and bracelets, he was pleased to notice. 'I longed to fulfil the potential I felt within me. My husband became tired of my illness dragging on. Poor Alfredo! I did not want my child near me. It was awful. *I* was awful. That was when I needed the spiritual assistance your letters gave me.'

She ran a hand through her blond hair. The bracelets on her wrist jingled. 'But let's not talk about it now. It is true that I am haunted by the fear of death, but the bad days are over, at least for a little while. And for now I am safe in your house.'

She smiled at him and giggled. 'Alfredo and I are now on better terms. Although we have few interests in common, I recognize what a kind person he is, and how popular with other people.'

He did not wish to hear that.

She shivered, and he was all concern, saying it was too cold for her to be sitting outdoors. She protested that she enjoyed the fresh air.

'It must be almost midnight.'

'Don't look at your watch, darling. Maybe time has stopped.'

190

'Yes, probably it has. Just in this garden.'

'So I shall never see Roma again.'

She produced some bright coins from her purse, laying them on the table in front of them. 'They're euros – no use in England,' she said, half laughing. 'But if time has stopped, it doesn't matter.'

She turned some of the coins over and indicated that, while most were from Italy, one was from Germany, another from Belgium. 'So we see how far these coins have travelled . . . How nice when I can find an English one in my purse . . .'

He was thinking how perfect she was. When had a woman charmed him as much? They would go to bed soon; there was idle pleasure in the anticipation of her warmth, her perfumes, her embraces.

She asked about his childhood. Frank said it had been privileged. His parents had been wealthy and lived in a large, rambling house in Hampshire. His father, rather a distant figure, had been managing director of a major biscuit and confectionary company: 'the Martinson', on which their fortune was founded, was a recipe of his great-grandmother, who had, no doubt, got it from her grandmother. Frank's mother, Lavinia, was kind and tolerant but somewhat remote, in the manner, he seemed to think, of mothers at that time. Frank had attended Oriel College at the University of Oxford, reading PPE, and had graduated with honours.

'But you see, Maria, my parents were into commerce. They were ruled by money. Yet in the wider family, we had always had artists, even a poet. They cared not a hoot about money. I always respected that. My great-uncle, Troy Martinson, made a small name as a painter in the early years of last century. He could not bear England, with its Philistinism, and went to live in Montmartre in

Paris. Was a bit of a Casanova. Then there was Hugo Martinson in the nineteenth century – a poet, not very readable now. In his time, a friend of Byron and Tom Moore, author of *Lalla Rookh*. A bit of an Orientalist, when the Orient began in Belgrade. Those were the men I admired. Free spirits. As you are, my beautiful Maria! And a woman too, a sister of my maternal grandmother, Amy Phipps. A nice painter of wildlife in Scotland. I'll show you some of her Highland cattle in the morning . . . *The Smell of Highland Cattle in the Morning* . . . But despite these illustrious creative examplars, you see in me a terrible propensity for making money out of the *biscuits of history* . . .'

She snuggled against him. 'You make too much fun of yourself. It's the English vice.'

'I thought that was something else.'

In the long vac, when Frank was an adolescent, the Martinson family had always gone to Italy, to spend some weeks climbing mountains and the rest of the time lazing by the Adriatic. That was where Frank had learned to speak Italian.

They held hands and smiled at each other.

'I wonder what you were like as a little girl.'

'My earliest memory is of sitting on my father's knee while he sang to me.'

'Sit on my knee, Maria. I promise not to sing.'

When she had made herself comfortable, and put an arm about his neck, Maria explained that her family had come down in the world. She spoke in her usual rather detached way. Her paternal grandfather had been a diplomat under Mussolini. She made a face as she pronounced the dictator's name. Her parents lived in a small, ornate house near the harbour. The family had had another home in Tuscany. Her mother had loved her and

192

made much of her, always kissing and playing with her, but she had to be away on business a great deal, as she pretended. She entrusted her precious Maria to the care of an elderly couple who lived nearby.

Maria paused, sipping her wine, wondering whether to tell Frank of her visit to Professor Leppard, but what purpose would it serve?

She continued with her story. The couple who looked after her had no children of their own and treated Maria as if she were their daughter; Maria regarded them almost as grandparents.

She took out her cigarettes and began to smoke one. Frank empathetically did the same.

But when Maria was growing up, the man began to molest her sexually. For some years she told no one. She was miserable and degraded, and dreaded her compulsory stays with the couple when her mother was away. She became anorexic, and was suicidal. All this she related, with seeming calm, while puffing on the cigarette.

She eventually told Andreina, her mother, what was happening, one evening after she had tried to drown herself in the harbour. Her parents were distraught.

'Mother was furious! So, so angry I was terrified. Angry beyond reason. I even wished I had said nothing. This was when I started to take refuge in drugs. I call it my Piranesi Period.' She gave a chuckle. 'Though I believe Piranesi took opium only as a cure for malaria. That was the way it used to be. Italy's history is as much influenced by malaria as by drugs . . . Now I see that time differently. At least I believed when all this confusion was going on that Andreina was on my side. I can now perceive that she felt much guilt at having left me to the monster while she enjoyed herself elsewhere . . . She brought a lawsuit against the elderly reprobate who had sullied me. I begged her with tears not to do so. He fought the case. He was quite a respected member of the community, the old bastard. It was awful. I was adolescent by then. I had to tell all things in the court. Everything, what he did . . . I was interrogated, can you imagine? The whole matter became public.'

She laughed unhappily, and clutched Frank's hand. Her bracelets rattled.

When the elderly man was finally convicted of the abuse, he committed suicide. She had felt guilty about that.

She took a gulp of the Chardonnay and coughed.

'Then I was despatched to my aunt in Kensington. A haven of calm! The psychoanalysis also helped, but it was the calm . . . So healing . . .'

Frank squeezed her waist. 'Kensington has changed since then.'

'It's so quiet here. It's as if everyone in Hampden Ferrers was dead. Were dead.'

'It's gone midnight, after all. Do you want to go in?'

'That would break the spell . . .'

'I can see how terrible for you all this must have been, Maria.'

'Oh, all that stuff. And the pain then of discovering that my mama had never been faithful to my poor father.'

'Have you ever traced her lover?'

She was discreet, and wished to change the subject. There seemed no good reason to mention Professor Leppard. 'Well, it's over now, like the cancer. And I enjoy a little fame. How I love your college of Wolfson! Don't you think that fame and popularity are a defence against oblivion? Do you live longer if you are famous, I hope?'

Frank laughed. 'Success certainly helps.'

'Yes, even a little success.'

They sat together, holding hands. The coins glittered on the table before them. Eventually, by mutual assent, they moved to go inside to bed.

No sooner were they indoors than rain began to fall. It came softly at first, from the hill, as if tiptoeing up to the house, then more heavily. Then it was a downpour, sousing everything.

Penelope got herself back to her little house. In the dark, she almost fell over a toy in the hall. She made herself a mug of tea before crawling into bed.

A dream came to her as she slept. Greg was alive again. They were living in a bungalow by a great river. Sun shone into the rooms. She could discern that he was unwell. They seemed to be happy, but there was a large fly in the room, a fly like a black beetle, which greatly bothered them, buzzing about their heads so that they were unable to talk.

The fly settled on a table edge close to Penelope. She slammed her hand down on it. The fly felt hard and brittle, with a soft interior, like a kind of chocolate. She could feel it in her dream. The body fell to the floor. She and Greg were close again, as once they had been, many years past. In the dream world they were young. She wore a green dress.

The fly was not dead, only injured. It began to climb rapidly up Penelope's naked leg.

Deepest, bluest night up on the Molesey Hills. Clouds, no sign of moon or stars. Grass wet from the recent downpour. Worn paths, thickets of bramble, tall grasses still dripping, studded with nettles and daisies. Things moving. Hedgehogs, bats, frogs, birds, rats, a feral cat, a fox.

195

A line of ancient oaks, heavy, sullen, sempiternal. One had been struck by a bolt of lightning when George IV was on the throne of England. A branch and a major part of the bole had peeled away and back like a banana skin. It still lived, spreading its dull leaves above the ground – and providing an ideal bed or couch for lovers.

The nurse, Ann Longbridge, was Bettina Squire's aunt. She was the reason why Bettina had come to Hampden Ferrers. Ann was well into her fifties, and a portly figure. Her hair, normally controlled under a bandana, was long and dyed jet black.

She lay now, all but naked, her legs spread, back arched against the woody gizzard of the oak, sighing wordless words of encouragement to the young man mounting her. The ancient branch creaked to his pleasure.

Ann had initiated many young Ferrers men into the delights of *al fresco* sex: the Cotes boys, Rupert, Duane, many others, owed what prowess they had in lovemaking to Nurse Ann at the oak. Even Jeremy Sumption, even the owner of the Bear, all had come to this unruly abandonment. This was the way she liked it, with midnight and the secretive trees all about, a place in which an ambience of the primeval still lingered. If it rained, so much the better, the randier, the closer the grind got to the mannerless matings of nature. It was the antidote to civilisation, practised long before the days of King George.

She reached her orgasms readily. She hugged the man close, this anonymous man. They had no remembered names, only movement. Only the vital thing within her, driving home.

By day, you would not know her for the same woman. No one knew her. Nor would she acknowledge her men by any special sign.

Across the ancient hill came movement. A river had

196

severed it long ago from the White Horse Hills to the south, with their prehistoric Ridgeway. The river that had roared its way through the chalk during the decline of the Ice Age had become the tame Hampden Brook, babbling its way southwards to join the unimportant river Ock.

Night seemed to reunite the high ground. Heading south-west, like phantoms came the wild dogs, running, running, mouths open, tongues lolling, sharp teeth shining, dogs and bitches, running in a pack.

They ran close by the line of oaks. They paid no attention to Nurse Ann and her lover, nor she to them. She never saw them.

None of the young men who enjoyed this pagan rite on the Molesey Hills ever spoke of it to others. Nor did they mention the wild dogs.

Morning brought different activities. Humans, cars and buses were about. The noises of human occupation filled the village air.

The bus from Marcham was dawdling along on its way to Oxford. Green fields lay all around; trees were dressed in their lightest foliage, as yet innocent of high summer; cow parsley cast its sporadic snow along all the ditches. The night's downpour had slaked the county's thirst. Sitting together, Judy Chung and Hetty Zhou were saying how wonderfully unlike Hong Kong it all was.

'A field of cows! Look!'

'Yes. They are in black and white. Where has the colour gone?'

'What are those other things? Oh, yes, sheep. Real sheep!'

'Hey, what's *that* animal?'

They had not seen a donkey before. Certainly they

had not seen a donkey such as this one, which was falling about on its back in the damp field, kicking up its hind legs – hind legs that sprouted human feet and toes instead of hoofs. Everything changed as they watched. Human arms were sprouting from the shaggy body. The long head was altering shape. The strange mixture of animal and human resembled something in a Francis Bacon canvas. It was possible only to watch with fascination spiced by terror, as if a ghastly myth were being enacted.

'Should we stop the bus? Such things cannot be happening!'

The youth in the seat ahead had a shaven skull. He turned to address the ladies. 'It's amazing,' he said, 'but we're just getting to a stop. Then we can have a better look.'

Judy was frightened. 'Do such things happen often in Oxfordshire? I thought it was a nice county.'

'No. There was Apuleius's Golden Ass, but that happened quite a way from here. Aliens change shape all the time.'

Sure enough, the bus was slowing. The youth got up and went to speak to the driver. He beckoned to the two Chinese women.

'The driver has seen what's happening. He's a bit aghast. His name's Harry. We'll wait a moment and see if we can help.'

'Oh, he's awfully handsome,' Judy whispered to Hetty. 'This boy, I mean, not that awful ass . . .'

The bus stopped abruptly. Harry got out of his seat to announce what he called a bit of an emergency. 'Nobody panic.' Nobody did panic. The passengers were silenced by the struggle taking place in the field nearby.

They stood staring over the hedge to where the trans-formation was taking place, where the grotesque figure

198

was fighting with itself. No metamorphosis is without pain: its open mouth, wide in agony, showed a graveyard of big yellow teeth. Passengers crowded to the windows, trying to open them so that they could lean out.

'Them windows do not open, thanks,' the driver announced. 'It's against bus-company rules.' He was a good family man, pushing forty-six, who had given up smoking a year ago, supported Swindon City, read the *Mirror* every day and believed every word of it.

The tubby donkey body was stretching, writhing into a thinner shape. Hide faded, whitish-brown skin appeared in patches, together with much else. Some women on the bus were tittering at what was being revealed. Now the creature was standing — tottering about on its two hind legs, falling to its knees, staggering up again. It held its long head, appearing to wrench at it with two malformed hands.

It gave a final hee-haw, then shouted for help in a choking voice.

'Over here!' the driver shouted, waving from the step of the bus. 'We're friends! Can you make it?'

A woman passenger called shrilly: 'Don't let that monster on this bus!'

'We're friends!' It's just like *Star Trek*!' exclaimed the shaven-headed youth, in sudden delight.

Hetty Zhou remembered her camera; she had planned to use it later, when they went to car showrooms in search of a new car. She got a shot of the naked man – almost all man now, though still with distorted cranium, long ears and furry tail – as he attempted to climb a five-barred gate out of the field. Twice he fell back, to lie uttering hollow groans amid a clump of nettles, only to rise again and attack the gate anew. His limbs lacked co-ordination, but at last he was over the barrier, falling to his knees in the grass. As he staggered towards the bus, he was seen to grow a goatee beard.

He fell exhausted at the step of the bus, a trail of saliva issuing from his jaws. The driver climbed down to help him. 'That was a bit of donkey-work, mate,' he said, offering the man his arm. 'You'll be okay. Don't worry, it could happen to anyone.'

So the poor forked creature stumbled aboard the bus, guided to the nearest seat. The driver gave him a copy of the *Mirror* to cover his most vulnerable parts. 'Shame!' exclaimed one of the female passengers, and several women laughed.

'What's your name?' asked the driver. 'Where do you live, apart from the field?'

'Heeee . . . sorry! I'm Greyling, John Greyling. Ooooorrrr . . . Or I think I am. Get me to a hospital.'

'Hospital's off my route, mate. Sit tight and you'll be okay.'

Greyling was panting heavily. He still sported two ass's ears, although his skull was now becoming more human, less animal, in shape.

The bus started on its way once more. Everyone was talking, generally in incredulous tones. The majority opinion was that it was *drugs*. Again Judy asked the youth in front of her if such things happened frequently in Oxfordshire.

'It must be a trick of some sort. This bloke could be a professional magician, like.' Such was his guess.

'Why was he rehearsing in the field?' asked Hetty Zhou.

'Dunno. Perhaps he owns it.'

Hearing this remark, a man in a seat on the other side of the aisle said, 'No, he doesn't. That field is Oxford Preservation Trust property. This is a political matter. I shall phone my MP when I get to the office.'

'You do that, mate!' The youth turned to face the ladies over the top of his seat. 'My name is Barrie. I'm a professional movie actor. They call me Starman. I know you, like, just moved to Ferrers. How are you?' He smiled pleasantly.

Judy was first to clasp his hand. She clutched it as she introduced herself and asked where he lived.

He told her.

'But that's very near our new house.'

They got into conversation. But all the while Barrie's eyes were on Hetty.

VII

El Kakkabuk Appears

Since it was a Saturday, Sonia, the Vicar's wife, was at home. She was in the kitchen, singing to herself as she prepared elderflower cordial. She was squeezing lemon juice into the bowl when Father Robin came in. He put an arm round his wife's shoulders. 'Would you mind coming with me into the vestry, love?'

'What a proposition! How could I resist?'

He explained what he had been doing when the angel in the dirty T-shirt had advised him to do: vandalising Church property and knocking a hole in the back of the ancient cupboard in which hymn books were kept. And he had seen something. He needed her as support and witness.

She turned and looked at him over her spectacles. Sonia was the sort of woman who blossomed when helping people: as plants flourish with a helping of compost round the roots, so Sonia increased in stature whenever anyone imposed on her. On this occasion, however, her stature remained stationary. She peered into her husband's eyes as if in the hope of discovering lunacy.

'Robin, pet, you don't think you set too much store by this so-called apparition of an angel? You say it was wearing a dirty T-shirt? That's not the customary dress of your usual angel, is it? Correct me if I'm wrong.'

'Of course you're not wrong, love! When were you ever wrong? But you suspect I was seeing things, don't you? Too much red wine? You think religion has gone to my head, along with the *vino*. Accompany me to the cupboard and see for yourself. My firm belief is that there is something rather unpleasantly unecclesiastical lurking behind one of the panels.'

'Do you see what is lurking in this bowl? Do you or do you not want some elderflower cordial this winter, dearest?'

'In this case, I want to have my cake and drink it.'

They were both laughing as Sonia, wiping her hands on her apron, went with him to the church.

The silent, twilit atmosphere embraced them. Their footsteps sounded on the stone flooring. The faint aroma in the air was of candles, incense and antiquity. This was where Robin Jolliffe was at home. He and Sonia had come, nine years earlier, from a poor London parish, where the church had been larger and more showy; but it was in St Clement's that the Vicar had created a special mingling of the reverent with the welcoming – mainly by improving the lighting, creating pools of light and dark, and by installing effective central heating. It was a church one was pleased to enter, a refuge.

The doors of the ancient cupboard stood open. The Vicar's mallet and chisel lay on a shelf within it. A small hole, the size of a prayer book, had already been made in one of the rear panels. Peering into the cavity newly revealed, Sonia saw a corner of something leaden in appearance. She recoiled from it. 'Pet, do you think you should go any further? Why not nail a bit of boarding over the hole and forget all about it?'

'Did you feel something evil is lurking in there? I did. But what could be evil that has rested so long in the House of God? The angel told me to look, so look I must, love. But I certainly want you standing beside me.'

Sonia shivered and said no more.

Robin glanced at his watch. 'Three o'clock, near enough.'

He got to work on the panel, banging away. Echoes of the mallet strokes rang through the church. He stopped once to listen. The noises went on.

With renewed vigour, he attacked the wood. Woodworm had weakened it. All of a sudden, a section crumbled away like old cake, revealing a shallow alcove. In the alcove stood a stone tablet, almost as large as a sheet of A3 paper. Robin and Sonia peered at it, unwilling to touch.

Eventually, Robin reached in and withdrew it. 'It's quite a weight.'

It was as if, to an external viewer, the structure of the church elongated upwards at great speed, while the two human figures shrank. As the globe on which they lived spun round on its course in space, they were no more than fleas in the fur of a fleeing cat, unaware of the complexity, the immensity, of the expanding galaxy of which they formed an insignificant and imprisoned part. The holy man was himself unaware of how small and anthropomorphic was the god he worshipped in terms of the scale of a universe itself, but one bubble of a multiple vastness of universes.

The tablet was hot to the touch, and seemed to adhere to Father Robin's hand. He was mildly scared. His wife, equally scared, reached into the recess and withdrew from it an item previously concealed behind the tablet, a parchment folded and sealed into the shape of an envelope.

'What on earth have we got here? Let's take it outside for a better look,' he muttered.

They went out to stand by the church porch, where the edge of the grass was ablaze with clumps of bright poppy-like eschscholzia. The sun shone also on Robin and Sonia and on the stone they held, which glowed in return. They heard the rumble of thunder overhead.

Robin blew dust off the stone, the better to study the curious inscription cut into its surface. 'It's a sort of cuneiform, love,' he said, 'only the letters seem not to hold still . . .'

Sonia was breaking the seal on the envelope and opening up the stiff parchment. 'Goodness gracious me,' she exclaimed, running her eye quickly over it. 'This is a letter written by the Reverend Tarquin Ferrers. He signs it at the bottom and dates it May, in the year of Our Lord 1814.'

'Yes, but what does he say, love?' asked Robin, with a hint of impatience.

'It's funny handwriting, pet. He says, "I wish to warn the inquisitive not to touch this tablet, and in particular not to carry it forth into the sunlight." Well it's a bit late for that.

'He goes on, "This is a tablet of the Early Ethiopian Church which, to my everlasting regret, I stole from a church in Aksum. It contains the magical writing of a mystic by name El Kakkabuk. In my African travels I sat at the feet of the aforesaid Kakkabuk who saw far beyond the environs of our Christian Lord God. By means of flight and meditation, aided and abetted by occult sciences, he claimed to have caught a glimpse of the Great Originator of our universe, known by the name (I translate) of OPCEAN, a name formed from the title, Original Pantocrat Creation of Eternal Antiquity and Nemesis.

205

'"This monstrous being exists as 'strings among the stars', according to the word of El Kakkabuk, strings that tie the universe together. Unfortunately, Opcean indulges a malignity towards all sentient life, which it regards as rivalling its rule in some way."'

'Where is the human soul in all this?' cried Robin.

'It doesn't seem to mention the human soul, pet.' Sonia went on reading from the letter: '"The very knowledge of Opcean's existence causes doom. The mystic El Kakkabuk himself was found hanging from the branch of a deodar shortly after he had inscribed this tablet.

'"In my folly, I have brought the tablet to my native land and shall immediately hide it away in the church of which I am minister. Holy surroundings may quell its power. Already I feel myself accursed by this Pantocrat Creation."'

Robin had become increasingly nervous.

'Oh dear dear, and this same Reverend Tarquin was the very chap who was devoured by a pack of wild dogs,' said Robin. He glanced involuntarily at his wristwatch. 'And that was in 1814.'

'Lucky there are no wild dogs nowadays, dearest.'

'Wild parishioners, though . . . What are we going to do with this confounded tablet? Put it back where it was? Move the family rapidly to Paraguay or Uruguay?' He was looking about anxiously, as if hoping to see the countries he had mentioned.

'Don't make jokes about it, pet. This is serious. You notice it is called a "creation", not a creator. Doesn't that suggest it is a mindless force, with nothing remotely human about it? Anti-soul. Hadn't you better ring the Bishop of Oxford?'

He stared into the distance, too burdened to answer her question.

206

'It's a hoax, isn't it? All of it. We know what a blighter this Tarquin Ferrers was. Opcean? What is it? Eternal Antiquity and Nemesis? We mustn't allow ourselves to take this seriously. It deeply undermines our faith.'

Marion Barnes happened to be passing, her dog on a lead as usual, on the other side of the low church wall. Robin forced a smile, waved, and called, 'How's Laurel today?'

A wind was getting up, a sudden, furious gale. Tarquin's warning letter, was snatched by the wind from Sonia's hand. She made a grab for it but it was gone, whirling into the distance. The gale pulled at Robin's surplice, as if to strip him of it. Rain and hail came pelting down. Tucking the tablet under his arm, he ran for the shelter of the church, Sonia following close behind.

Once he was inside the building, the Vicar placed the tablet on a pew and mopped his face with a handkerchief. Husband and wife stared at each other.

'We'd better not tell anyone about this,' she said.

'Don't you see? I cannot continue as a priest of the Church of England if any item of this monstrous statement is true. I have always thought – I've voiced my doubts to you, love – that the scientific perception of the universe dwarfs the idea of our God, sitting above us to guide and judge us. Is He busy doing this on a million other planets? There is no trace of such a concept in any of the scriptures. Not that *I* have come across.

'As you say, we mustn't tell anyone else about this find . . . That this universe-creation – you might say it's a sort of vast machine – is a neuter thing, I mean, does it not preclude any idea of God or a soul?' He gazed appealingly at Sonia's troubled face. 'If it's true, that is. Tarquin thought it was true.'

Sonia, face pallid in the decent gloom of the apse, said, 'Opcean's malignity—'

'Don't mention it by name in case that summons it!'

'Sorry, pet, you're right. This *thing's* malignancy is what scares me. Why are humans constantly having to battle against bacteria and viruses, most of which threaten our very existence? It could be they are this thing's agents, dark and blind . . .'

He put a hand on his wife's arm, to find that she was shivering. 'We must not allow ourselves to start believing any part of this anti-religious hoax. Let's defeat it – let's turn it to good. I have an idea. We'll put this ghastly object up for auction at Sotheby's. It might fetch enough money for us to repair the church tower.'

Sonia buried her face on Robin's chest. 'I'm frightened, Robin, pet. And we must retrieve that letter, or no one will believe it's genuine.'

'They'll believe it's genuine if I get eaten by a pack of wild dogs.'

Outside, the sudden storm was already dying. With a final sigh, the air became still. Perfectly, sullenly still. As if waiting.

'Typical English weather,' said Sonia, trying to make the best of things.

Jeremy Sumption had spruced himself up in order to call on the ladies newly resident at number twenty-two. He had brushed not only his hair but his old green corduroy jacket, and had sprayed himself here and there with Inca – 'Inca for stinkers,' he said – underarm deodorant.

Hetty Zhou opened the door, smiling sweetly. He thought how wonderfully neat she looked. She was wearing jeans and a light fluffy sweater, with pink sandals on her feet. Her high cheekbones and the epicanthic folds around her dark eyes merely added to her attractions. Jeremy almost licked his lips.

He could not help wondering what she would think if she knew of his meetings up on the Molesey Hills, under the oaks.

'Hello, Hetty. We have a committee meeting tomorrow evening at six.'

'I had not forgotten,' she said. 'But thank you for reminding me, Jeremy.'

'I *had* almost forgotten. I was wondering if you would care to dine with me this evening.'

'How kind of you. I am very busy now, settling in, as you may imagine, but will you come in?'

He entered, passing close by her and inhaling her scent. It was dark in the hall until Hetty opened the door into the front room. The front room was bare, except for a bucket of water, a scrubbing brush and bottle of Dettol standing in the middle of a wet patch of the floorboards. 'I don't know why, but at three this afternoon,' she said, 'I suddenly had a sort of vision that the world was full of filth.'

He looked puzzled. 'How odd! It was about three when I suddenly thought something amazingly evil was going to happen. But happily I met you instead – which is amazingly pleasant.'

Hetty threw him a teasing smile and explained that the floor was disgustingly filthy: she had decided on the spot to scrub it before laying a carpet. She had bought a new pail from Mr Aziz. Jeremy looked at her in fresh amazement. 'You were down on those gorgeous knees scrubbing the floor?'

'We have no maid as yet, and Judy has gone off with Rupert Boxbaum.' She giggled. 'You see how we foreign ladies are integrating with the local population.'

'Well, Hetty, I was hoping we might integrate this evening.'

She regarded him rather slyly, still smiling. 'How far do you think this integration might lead?'

Feeling uneasy, he explained that a Swedish publisher was going to give him dinner in Oxford, and had invited him to bring along a ladyfriend for company, since his wife would be with him. Then maybe, afterwards, Hetty would like to come back to Jeremy's place for coffee.

Hetty let a moment's silence elapse. Looking at him through her almond eyes, with what he construed as a benevolent gaze, she said, 'I am delighted to be asked. It is most flattering and kind of you, when you must have many English girlfriends. May I say to you that I will be glad to accompany you and even to return to your home for coffee afterwards. But it would perhaps save some misunderstandings and disappointments if I tell you now that if you are thinking of seducing me, well, I am not averse to being seduced. It has happened before, naturally. But before I become complaisant, the suitor must turn an invisible key to the lock – to my lock. I cannot say exactly what that key is, but I assure you that I will know and you will know if you happen to turn it.'

It would be true to say that Jeremy was agog at this frankness. That this delicate female person, standing before him in fluffy sweater and pink sandals, could speak so legalistically was cause for astonishment. He thanked her for the warning, stuttering a bit.

At seven o'clock he called for Hetty in his old red Toyota. He was wearing the clothes he had had on earlier. Hetty had changed, and was arrayed in a shimmering satin trouser suit, with matching blue high-heeled shoes. She wore a pearl necklace at her throat and pearl earrings.

210

He watched, almost faint with lust, as her tidy bottom came down to rest in his car seat.

'God, you're gorgeous, Hetty. If I can find that key to your lock, I will. I sure will.'

They parked in Oriel Square and walked to the nearby restaurant, Ma Belle. Hettie took his arm. Warm sunlight slanted down on the street.

The Swedish publisher, Goran Holmberg, was a man in his sixties, silver of hair, thick of stature, with a rather severe appearance. His wife, Ingrid, was considerably younger, a smartly dressed woman who laughed easily. The four of them sat at a downstairs table, ordered drinks and talked.

Goran Holmberg explained that he had enjoyed Jeremy's thriller *Piggy Bank*. One scene had been set in Stockholm. This had given him the idea that Jeremy should come to Stockholm as his guest, staying for perhaps a year and writing two thrillers set there. There was the distinct possibility of a film to be made, maybe two. 'Europe must be made more aware of our magnificent city – even of its dark side.' Goran went into detail, all the while squinting at Jeremy to see how his proposal was being received. A considerable sum of money was guaranteed.

'It sounds very exciting,' said Jeremy. 'Would I be staying in a hotel? A four-star hotel?'

'Mr Holmberg, you would probably wish to control the Swedish rights for the books,' Hetty said. 'Mr Sumption would have complete control of all other language rights, I gather, including English?'

'We – um, we could negotiate, of course.'

'I don't think such rights are negotiable, are they, Jeremy?'

'Well, no. I'd have to ask my agent.'

The discussion was interrupted by a study of the menu.

211

The food was ordered, and a good Australian Shiraz that Goran was keen to try. By the time the first dishes were served, Jeremy had agreed to go to Stockholm and write at least one book for him.

'I was an architect before I became a publisher,' said the Swede. 'I have a nice little house where you can stay. You will not be interfered with.'

'That's nice to know,' said Jeremy. He did not look at Hetty as he spoke.

Goran tucked into the food and wine with enthusiasm. As he was finishing his duckling, he ordered a second bottle of the Shiraz. 'I frequently visit your country, you know,' he said. 'I like it quite a lot. Ingrid and I stay often at the old-fashioned Brown's Hotel in Mayfair. Do you also stay there? No? Well, never mind. Unhappily, our role was not too friendly to Britain in the Second War of the World. It's different now.'

'We don't need to talk regarding that period, dear,' said Ingrid, warningly. 'It's a long time ago.'

'But I can tell you a curious story regarding that time, in which my wife's family was involved.'

'Please, Goran, not that awful tale again.'

He gave her a wolfish grin. 'Because it is awful, we like to hear it. You see,' he turned to Jeremy and Hetty, giving them both a swift glance, 'my wife was a part of the celebrated Foch family before her unfortunate first marriage. The story does her no discredit.

'You will remember that Hermann Göring was the air marshal of the Nazi Luftwaffe. But long before that he was an air ace in the First World War, and a daredevil pilot between the wars. It was then he met a charming Swedish lady, by name Karin Fochsdotter. Although we may say Hermann later went to the bad, I believe he always retained his love for Karin.'

212

Goran went on to say that this marriage perhaps accounted for a certain lack of hostility between Sweden and Nazi Germany. Ingrid lit a cigarette with a bored air.

'Put that thing out,' Goran said. 'It shortens your life.'

Karin, Goran told them, died of a mysterious illness and was buried with some ceremony within the extensive grounds of Hermann's hunting estate, north of Berlin. A mausoleum was created for her. When the war was over, and good old Hermann was dead, the estate came within the Soviet zone, with all the terror that that implied. It happened that Ingrid's grandfather was newly appointed Swedish ambassador to Western Germany. He had visited Hermann's grand mansion in earlier days.

One day in the cold January of 1946, a poorly dressed woman came, said Goran, to the Swedish Embassy. After waiting many hours to see Ambassador Sven-Henri in person, she spoke to him privately, telling him that the estate was becoming overrun by Soviet troops. She feared that they would establish a headquarters there. She was a faithful old retainer who remembered Sven-Henn's visit to Karinhall before the war. Karinhall was now a ruin, blown up by Hermann's own hand, and she feared that the brutes of Soviets, as she termed them, would desecrate Karin's mausoleum. So she had taken Karin's corpse and, with the aid of her aged husband, had buried it in the woods.

Still she was afraid. Afraid that the Soviets would happen accidentally on the body, afraid that she would die – she had tuberculosis – and that the body would be lost for ever.

'As if it mattered by this time,' said Ingrid, still smoking.

'It mattered to the previous generations of your family, my dear,' said Goran. He gestured, with a knowing look.

213

'All over Europe at that time there were thousands and hundreds of thousands of lost people, dispossessed of everything, and all sorts and kinds of lost properties. Not to mention the bereaved seeking the graves of loved ones.

'I would say that this was the most dreadful time Europe has ever known, including the time of the Black Death. Only because of the terrible lessons learned was it possible later to aspire to the united European Community.'

'I am afraid that my husband is obsessed with the end of the Second World War,' Ingrid said apologetically to Hetty.

'In the East it was just as bad – a massive upheaval,' Hetty said. 'My great-grandparents had been very wealthy, living in Nanking. When the Japanese armies came, they lost everything and became fugitives.'

'So that's how your family finished up living in Hong Kong, is it?' Jeremy asked.

Hetty nodded. 'Eventually. But please continue with your story, Mr Holmberg. I find it very interesting.'

Goran inclined his head and gave her a smile.

He went on. Sven-Henri was touched by the little woman's faithfulness to her late mistress, Karin. He sent her to a hospital in the American sector for tuberculosis treatment, and arranged to collect the corpse of his fellow-countrywoman from the grounds of Karinhall. It was not easy.

'This was now the Soviet Zone, remember,' said Goran, frowning as he regarded Hetty and Jeremy.

Sven-Henri obtained both a lorry and East German credentials and went himself with the lorry driver to Hermann's old estate. The pretext was that he was going to repair something or other. He then searched in the woods, according to a map the old retainer had drawn. All this had to be done at dead of night, of course: the

214

fact that it was several degrees below zero meant that the Soviets were indoors, keeping warm.

He found the body by a frozen watercourse. It did not stink too much because of the frost. It was slipped carefully into a body-bag.

He and the driver slid Karin's body into a specially prepared locker under the driver's seat. They then drove back to the western zone. They were searched at the frontier post, but only in a cursory manner.

Sven-Henri had Karin's corpse cremated in the embassy grounds, a messy night-time cremation, with the smoke blowing over the barbed-wire-crowned wall into the chill German night. The ashes were put into an urn and sealed. In the same week, he drove in his Jaguar car, with the urn beside him, via Hamburg to a little village just on the Swedish coast facing across the water to Denmark. An ancient relation of his lived there, maybe a second cousin. She was superstitious and did not wish to keep the urn, but Sven-Henri left it with her, hidden among the coats in a little cupboard, and returned to Berlin where his presence was required at a meeting.

'So we come to the end of the whole business, to my wife's obvious relief,' said Goran, shooting a foxy look at Ingrid. Frowning, she raised her wineglass to him and drank.

'Either that week or the next, he drove in the Jaguar again, collected the urn and took it to be presented to the Foch family in their grand mansion just south of Stockholm. Of course he had phoned ahead to say he was coming. The whole family turned out, all dressed in black, including a teenage girl, also called Karin, who was to become the mother of my dear Ingrid here. There was great formality and ceremony. All went into the house, where every blind was drawn down, and prayers were said. It was virtually another funeral.

215

'And that's the end of the story,' said Goran. 'Let's have some more of this excellent wine.'

'What happened to the old woman with tuberculosis?' Hetty asked. 'Did she recover at all?'

'History does not relate,' said Goran, dismissively. Turning to address Jeremy, he said, 'I thought maybe, Jeremy, you might turn this tale into a good thriller, with both Nazis and Soviets as baddies.'

'It sounds promising,' said Jeremy. 'Is it true or did you make it up?'

'Oh, there are many similar tales from that period. You can take your pick when you reside in Stockholm.'

When Jeremy and Hetty were driving back to Hampden Ferrers, they discussed Goran's offer. Jeremy pointed out that he had not said whether his Karin story was true or invented. When she asked why he should have made it up, he had no answer. 'He didn't strike me as particularly straightforward.'

'No. Nor me. But you are a thriller writer, bound to sniff out villains.'

'I think it was just the apprehension of evil I had this afternoon, lingering on. Gone now . . .'

The village was silent. He stopped the Toyota at his door.

He turned to Hetty and asked if the invisible key had turned in her lock.

'There was a moment,' she said, 'when *he* said that you would not be interfered with, and you said, "That's nice," without smiling at all. At that point, I felt my lock give a little.' She gave him a demure look.

He clutched her hand. 'It happens I have a key we might just slip into that lock.'

They hurried into the house, arms round each other.

★ ★ ★

Duane Ridley took Kyle to the Bear for a drink. He was used to standing at the bar, but he meekly took two lagers over to the table where she had seated herself, and sat down beside her.

At the next table sat Zadanka and the black man with whom she lived. Zadanka was looking more cheerful than previously as she sipped a glass of white wine. The man she called WW had a Guinness before him. He produced a packet of cigarettes. He and Zadanka lit up from his lighter, breathing out smoke with evident relish. Duane remarked to Kyle, 'It's hell trying to give up. I could do with a fag meself.'

Hearing the remark, the black man turned and proffered his packet. 'Have one of mine, mate.'

Duane looked at him doubtfully, at Kyle, then back at him. 'Great! I could just go one, ta.'

As he took a cigarette from the packet, the man leaned forward with his lighter ready and said, 'My name is Wally White. A bit unfortunate on both counts, like. Call me WW. Everyone does.'

'We're pleased to meet you,' said Kyle politely. To Zadanka, she said, 'I've seen you on the bus, I think. Do you live here?'

'I want to go Prague. I want WW come with me.'

'We'll find the bread, old girl, don' worry,' said WW, comfortingly.

Two men barged into the public bar and went straight to the gaming machine, arguing loudly about the World Cup, the first games of which were just about to commence.

'England haven't got a fucking chance, not a fucking chance,' the fair-haired one was saying.

His pal, a fat little muscular man, had a different opinion: 'We just gotta beat fucking Argentina and we're away.'

217

'Nyah, Argentina will fucking eat us, like what they done last time. You'll see!'

Keeping his voice low, so as not to be included in this belligerent conversation, WW said to Duane, 'We got a good chance, don't you reckon, if Beckham's foot heals?'

Duane said, 'That goalie, Dave Seaman, is bloody brilliant, I reckon. There's never been anyone like him.'

The two men started talking football. Kyle and Zadanka sat silent, exchanging occasional glances of boredom. Kyle did not care for the look of Zadanka. She herself had had a free hair-do that afternoon, in the Salon Française, and was elaborately coiffured. Since she was being taken out, she had been careful to put on shiny plastic trousers and a provocatively cut satin blouse that revealed the cleft between her generous breasts. Zadanka had lank hair and wore an old nondescript dress; her breasts were not greatly in evidence. There was, thought Kyle, summing her up, nothing provocative about her.

'What do you do for a living?' Kyle asked, rather contemptuously.

'I clean.' The reply and its flat delivery did not encourage further discourse. But at length Zadanka spoke again, directing her voice confidentially towards the other young woman so that the men's conversation was not interrupted. 'My mother used to fear that our family was – what is it in English? – oh, like *common*. We were poor but we read literature. Now I am sat here in this public house. I don't know you. I think you maybe don't like me. These males we are with – have they ever read Dostoevsky's novels? My poor mother would hate to see me. I live in one room. I am become *common*.'

'Don't see what you're on about,' said Kyle. 'You live as you can, don't you?'

'It's about that I complain.'

218

The exchange languished.

An hour later, the four left the pub together. Dusk was gathering. The philadelphus outside was casting its innocent perfume on the air.

WW said to Duane, 'Wasn't you the bloke as duffed up them two queers outside the Carpenter's?'

Duane was instantly alert for trouble. 'What's that to you?'

With a wide grin, WW said, 'I just wanted to say good on you. Why do you think I give you that ciggie?'

The sun, fitful during the day, blazed out after eight that evening, sending long shadows of trees across the greens of Knoleberry Park. Frank and Maria were walking, arms linked behind each other's back, across the park. In the distance, the tower of St Clement's Church could be seen, bright in the sunlight.

They had dined early in Wolfson and were taking a stroll before retiring to West End for the night. They were talking of marriage. Maria was saying that she was troubled because she was now enjoying a better relationship with her husband than she had done for years. She recognised his kindness and forbearance; even though they had little in common, she had been contemplating settling down with him into a comfortable middle age, until meeting Frank again had reawoken her feelings for him.

Then breaking off this debate, she turned to kiss his lips and say, 'Where would we live if we were married?'

Frank pulled her against the trunk of a horse-chestnut and kissed her in return. 'Oh, you're so desirable! We don't have to marry. We can live here and there – anywhere!'

'I am devoted to Rome, now I have this job of teaching adults English and English literature, as well as the science

219

and TV-personality stuff. I like it all. It has made me a more balanced person. I am able to give people something.'

Frank laughed. 'You certainly give me something.'

'Yes, I can feel it.'

'Let's go back to my place.'

As they hurried back to West End, Maria exclaimed on the strange things that happened in England, such as the report she had heard that a donkey had changed into a man. She asked Frank if such things happened all the time.

'Every year the *Fortean Times* reports on similar oddities. Science can't account for them. I understand that this donkey had been a man originally. He was living in Ferrers. I heard that he was bigamously married to the writer Jeremy Sumption's first wife. The police arrested him.'

'For turning into a donkey?'

'As yet there's no law against that. For being bigamously married and apparently for drug-smuggling.'

Back at West End, they rushed to the bedroom and tore off their clothes. He submerged himself in her supple, subtle body. For her part, she experienced him as a breakwater against which the seas of her existence surged. In that intensely personal embrace, they went as one beyond the personal into the oceanic world of the purely physical.

Lying there afterwards in each other's arms, Maria said vaguely, 'I often used to imagine I did not exist. It was not only because of the sexual abuse I suffered but because my grandfather almost died before my father was born.'

She told Frank a story about her grandfather, Ernesto Baldini, of the distinguished Baldini family, who had become an admirer of Mussolini and was promoted to high diplomatic rank by the Duce. In the Second World War, Ernesto had headed a top-flight Italian delegation to Japan, an ally of Hitler's Germany and, consequently, of fascist Italy. The war was going badly for Italy; support from Japan would be welcome.

Fortune was against them. Hardly had the opening speeches of the conference in Tokyo concluded than a report came through that Italy had changed sides and from now on would fight with the Allies against the Axis powers, officially as co-belligerents.

Here, Maria burst into laughter. 'Oh, it's so funny! Can you imagine? What a fix for my grandfather and his delegation! Of course, the conference immediately collapsed. The atmosphere turned to ice. The poor Italians retreated to their hotel. When they tried to order a meal, the hotel would not serve them. They were now the enemy. Italians without food and drink! Awful!'

Frank, too, was convulsed with laughter. 'What happened to them?'

'Eventually, at midnight, a party of Japanese officers in uniform, very formal, arrived and were received into my grandfather's suite. There they ceremoniously presented my grandfather with a large *samurai* sword. Of course, the expectation was that he would commit hara-kiri with it, according to Japanese traditions of honour. Our delegation entirely misunderstood the intention. They knew nothing of the bizarre tradition of self-disembowelling. They thought the Japanese were attempting to make friends and show sympathy. So they presented the Japanese in return with a small Italian-made dagger . . .'

Maria and Frank collapsed with laughter. The bed shook with their mirth.

Finally, Frank managed to ask what had happened in the end.

'Oh, the Japanese retreated in bafflement. Next day, our delegation was escorted under armed guard to a ship that sailed them back to Italy. The Japanese behaved perfectly honourably. Fortunately my grandfather behaved dishonourably and did not cut open his stomach, as you are supposed to do with *samurai* swords – and, in the following years, his wife gave birth to my papa!'

'Excellent story! I shall now kiss you all over as a reward.'

Maria feigned horror. 'How disgusting!'

'I hope so.'

A slender moon rose over Molesey Hills to render the intertwined bodies in silver. From the viewpoint of the moon, such details, unimportant in themselves, were part of a whole landscape of struggle for admiration, companionship, power and success: a struggle that would never end while human beings found it necessary to fight for position in the stressful societies they had created.

For Marion Barnes, there was little social standing to be had. She sat alone in her dark little parlour, on an old dark chair, with Laurel lying beside her, giving herself the odd scratch.

'Stop it, Laurel, dear!' Marion would order at intervals. 'She's got fleas,' she told herself. She was drinking from a dark brown bottle containing the cheapest brandy Sam Aziz could sell, by name Beauregard. This was her Saturday-evening treat. It accounted for the redness of her withered cheeks.

The television set cast its flickering light about the room. Marion was watching *Relations You Hate*, a merry programme of humiliation of the unfortunate, conducted by a slightly well-known comic personality called Pete

222

'Con' Crete. It was Marion's favourite show. Cackling with laughter, she almost choked on her Beauregard.

The commercial break came up. It was then that she fancied she heard a footstep in her back yard. She rose unsteadily to her feet. 'You stay where you are, Laurel.' The dog took not a blind bit of notice and followed Marion to the back door.

She unbolted it, top and bottom, and peered out into the gathering dusk. No one was there. 'Hello! Who is it?' No one answered. 'Clear off, you blighter, whoever you are!'

Seizing her chance, Laurel leaped out of the door, rushed down the yard and jumped the low fence at the bottom. She headed instinctively for the hills.

'Laurel, Laurel, bad dog! Come back! Laurel!'

The Labrador said furiously to herself, 'What does she mean, "Laurel"? Doesn't the old hag know my name is Grozzkel shnarr Snammawar of the Snamms?' She ran along the footpath past the allotments, splashed through a small stream, tributary of the Isis, and began the long winding ascent to Molesey Hills. 'Free at last!'

By the times Grozzkel reached the great green shoulder, she was out of breath. 'That's what comes of living off Pal,' she told herself. She rested in a patch of long grass, watching darkness descend and the moon rise in its cunning fashion over the world.

Grozzkel sat up on her haunches and began to howl. She knew exactly the note that set on edge the teeth of her fleas. No longer were they needed as a hobby. They could not bear that particular discord and left their old home in droves, to try to make a living off the vegetation or a passing hedgehog. Many would die of starvation – the eternal fate of immigrants everywhere.

Once she was free of her passengers, Grozzkel shnarr

Snammawar of the Snamms changed her tune. Her full-throated cry echoed repeatedly over the hillside.

Very soon, she could hear an answering sound, like a growing wind. It grew louder, nearer, more savage. Sedges bowed before it.

She rushed forward to meet it.

Out of the murk it came, a colour, a phenomenon, a legend, a pack of wild dogs, the phantom hunt. The dogs surrounded the newcomer, snapping and snarling at her. She snapped back, making the leader of the pack yip with pain.

She pissed on the ground. They sniffed and accepted her.

Then they were off again, eternally in pursuit, eternally after victims. Once, many generations back, they had tasted human flesh. They sought it again – though not exclusively. A fox in their path was torn to pieces and devoured as they ran, ran, ran, eyes aglow, teeth agleam. And Grozzkel shnarr Snammawar of the Snamms was of their number.

Distantly to Marion Barnes as she stood in her yard came the sagacious bay of hounds. The cry died away, like a sigh made in sleep . . .

Shedding acid tears of grief and fury, Marion went in, slamming her back door, remembering to bolt it top and bottom.

She returned to *Relations You Hate*, and the consolations of her Beauregard bottle.

The Committee for the Celebration of St Clement's was assembling at the Manor. The time was a few minutes after six o'clock.

Stephen Boxbaum greeted the members with the rather haughty friendliness customary to him. He was wearing a brown suit with a white shirt and a gaudy tie picturing children's books of yesteryear, as if to state that he understood fun when he saw it and was certainly not against it in small doses. He had persuaded Sharon to stay and greet people as they entered the rather grand old panelled room that overlooked the garden, where a Rambling Rector was in the display, rambling across a timber gazebo.

Hetty Zhou and Jeremy Sumption arrived together and settled in two chairs near the head of the table. Jeremy sought to hold Hetty's hand secretly, but she whispered that she did not wish him to show off his conquest.

Henry Wiverspoon came in, walking with a stick, closely followed by Rodney Williams, the solicitor, entering with his customary stalk, hands clasped behind back. Sharon was rather afraid of Henry's sharp tongue, and thought he was on her husband's side. She lavished attention on Rodney, therefore, enquiring solicitously after his newborn son's health and weight.

'Yes, yes, thank you, Sharon, he's fine.'

'And Judith?'

'Yes, thanks, she's fine too.'

'No signs of post-natal depression?'

'Not as yet, thank heavens.'

'I'm glad to hear it.'

Then Sharon realised she was being impolite to Henry by ignoring him. Fearing Stephen's wrath, she scuttled after the old man, who was making slow progress to the rear room.

'Henry, excuse me. I was being neglectful. You're looking well.'

He stared at her over the snowy hedge of his moustache. 'You surprise me, Sharon. I would be more surprised if I believed you. How many years is it since I last, as you amusingly put it, looked well?'

'How are you getting on with your book? *City Entirely Collapsed*, isn't it? Nearly finished now, is it?'

'An inspired if inaccurate guess. I see you have not been reading your Seneca lately. I have chosen a less exciting title than the one you mention, *City Utterly Fallen.*'

'Of course, yes. I was almost right. A powerful if not entirely cheerful title. I shall remember it in future, though, Henry!' She gave him a broken-hearted smile.

'You will have plenty of time before, if ever, it is published.' He took her arm, but she pulled away. 'I am an unfortunate who observes the writing methods of Flaubert. I write, shall we say, a paragraph in the morning and delete it in the evening.'

Yvonne Cotes, newly enlisted member of the committee, arrived and said hello solemnly to the other members. She sat at the table and industriously polished her glasses. Sam Aziz entered briskly, rubbing his hands and nodding cheerfully to people; he refused Sharon's offer of a drink. One wall of the room was lined with mahogany bookcases, inhabited by ancient books, many of them in sets, bound in calf. Sam regarded them with curiosity.

Last of all came Penelope Hopkins, catching Sharon having a quick smoke and a glass of something in the anteroom off the hall. Passing into the committee room, she suppressed a desire for a cigarette and had a special smile for Hetty Zhou. It was warmly returned.

Stephen Boxbaum settled himself at the head of the table. 'Good evening, everyone. Thanks for coming so promptly. We have quite a lot to discuss, so perhaps we had better begin. The Vicar phoned to say he might be late. So, Penny, as our new secretary, perhaps you would kindly read the minutes of our last meeting.'

226

Penelope read out from her printed notes that a firm of ecclesiastical contractors in Oxford, Benskin and Dzokwa, had presented their estimate for making certain alterations and renovations to St Clement's Church, including reparations to the tower, at a cost of not less than £183,585, to include a flying buttress.

She handed round photocopies of the Benskin estimate.

A new commemorative stained-glass window had been commissioned from a Mrs Maureen O'Rourke, a well-known local artist. The total cost of the window, including installation, would be in the range of £259 to £300. This window would quite possibly carry VAT at 17.5 per cent.

Photocopies of the O'Rourke estimate also circulated.

Sam asked why there was no VAT on the work Benskin were proposing to do.

'Because it's a church. Churches are immune from Value Added Tax. A stained-glass window is a different case – a luxury.'

The question of a brass commemorative plaque was also under consideration. They were talking to memorial masons in Horspath, Banbury and Abingdon. The committee would have to decide whether the inscription was to be in copperplate or roman.

'That's a tricky one!' exclaimed Jeremy.

The matter of where the considerable sums required for these works would come from had yet to be resolved. Mr Rodney Williams had suggested a raffle.

At this point, Hetty spoke up: 'Excuse me, Madam Secretary, if you please. As a new resident in this village, I hope I do not speak out of turn. Mr Chairman, the question of these finances has already been resolved, I am happy to say.' She gazed round the table, making sure she had their attention. 'I have spoken on the cellphone to my father in Hong Kong. He has readily agreed to foot the bill – you say that phrase still? – and will forward a percentage of the total sum required to my bank over this weekend. The rest to follow as needed.'

In the stunned silence that followed Hetty's announcement, Jeremy was heard to squeak, not entirely admiringly, 'This is naked capitalism!'

Hetty added, 'Father sends good wishes for our enterprise, and hopes to visit Hampden Ferrers to attend the final ceremony.'

'How amazingly kind,' said Stephen, amid exclamations of wonder all round, while the company clapped – except Henry, who spoke up now.

'Miss Zhou, this is extremely generous of both you and your father. I include you because, no doubt, you found it expedient to put some daughterly pressure on your pater. I do not wish to appear ungrateful if I voice what will no doubt be a minority opinion when I say that in my judgement the improvements to our local church should be paid for by local people and not by an unknown magnate in Hong Kong. A matter of principle is involved.'

'Quite so,' agreed Rodney. 'A matter of principle.'

The phrase brought to Stephen's mind his visit to the church of Sveti Pantelimon in Macedonia the previous year when he had been prevented from putting money into a collecting box for repairs to the old building. A man had told him that local people alone, of the Orthodox faith, should contribute to the fund. Only now did he understand the reservation.

It was a matter of pride, of principle.

He brushed aside the betraying thought.

He was stern. 'Penny, please note Henry's reservations,

228

and Rodney's, in the minutes. Does anyone else agree with Henry's rather surprising viewpoint?'

Silence, and a certain avoidance of eye-contact. Henry sat motionless.

'Yours is a solitary voice, Henry, I'm afraid, apart from an echo from Rodney. Miss Zhou and her father lift a considerable burden from our minds. We are more than grateful for this splendid intervention, and I would like to suggest immediately that a brass commemorative tablet be struck recording Mr Zhou's name, his generous contribution to the church and its upkeep in this next anniversary year. I'm sure we are all — except for Henry, that is — delighted by this connection with Hong Kong, which is now, after all, a territory of China itself. I consider this to be globalisation in its best sense.'

'Still, Mr Chairman, please, I trust this will not put any of us off making our own humble contributions.' This from Sam. 'I mean to say, if it is only presenting some nice new hassocks.'

Even as he was speaking, Father Robin Jolliffe entered, almost at a run. His grizzled locks were flying wild. He stood at one end of the table, and began to talk without apology. 'Gentlemen, ladies, there is a good reason why we cannot possibly celebrate the continued existence of our beloved church. Perhaps it would be better if the church were burnt down.'

Roars of surprise and dismay from all present. Henry Wiverspoon was heard to bless his cotton socks. The Vicar continued to talk over the hubbub: 'I cannot explain, simply cannot explain. This afternoon, Sonia and I — we broke into an old cupboard in the chancel and discovered a tablet, a long-hidden tablet. I don't know whether this makes sense to you. This tablet — it's ancient, centuries old, and it contains . . . I hardly dare mention what it contains.'

Sharon had followed Robin into the room. She urged him to sit down. He rejected the proffered chair. She rushed out, to return with a glass of water. He waved it away.

'There is a thing, an entity, a vast, all-encompassing entity that rules all.' He spread his arms wide by way of illustration. 'The tablet was stolen from the Early Ethiopian Church. It mentions – I mean to say, it is written, carved, by an ancient mystic called Habbakuk. No, no, Kakkabuk, I meant to say. El Kakkabuk.

'Stolen by the Reverend Tarquin Ferrers, early in the nineteenth century – Tarquin's name is still reviled in the parish. He was minister of our church for some years. You remember the legend which has it that he was devoured by wild dogs up on the hill?'

'What about this tablet, Father?' Penelope asked. 'What does it say?'

'It tells us . . . it tells us that the entire universe was created by an entity. I daren't pronounce its name—'

'You're safe in here, Father,' said Stephen drily, somewhat amused by the Vicar's flustered state.

'No, I'm not safe here. Or anywhere. Nor are you. Any of you.' As if somewhat reassured by his own statement, Robin took the glass Sonia was still holding. He drank from it, after which he appeared calmer, and spoke more normally. 'This entity is non-living. It is a sort of process, a cancer on a tremendous scale.' He paused, as if awed by the vision his own metaphor had created. 'Perhaps it will eventually become the universe. It manifests itself in strings of stars. It is vast. It owns everything down to the minutest particle. It has created the universe. It *is* the universe, in fact. I suppose through the Big Bang, or something similar – opening like a cancer cell in the human body. And it is malign, an enemy of intelligent

230

beings, such as humans. It therefore conjures up all that is bad and destructive within us.'

He wiped his face with a handkerchief, looking distraught. 'I can hardly . . . well . . .' His voice faded away.

Rodney was frowning with concentration. He said, almost to himself, 'So we're talking the Devil here, aren't we?'

'But you mustn't think of it in any anthropomorphic way. It's just a – well, it's a *process*. Like cancer.'

Peering through her thick lenses, Yvonne asked, 'Vicar, where does God come into all this morbid cosmology?'

'We regard, *we must regard*, Our Lord as intelligent. Intelligent and benevolent. This entity – I suppose I should say this process – holding sway, presiding over, the entire universe since the beginning of time, is an enemy of Our Lord. So if – I say if – *if* we regard Our Lord as prevailing only over this planet Earth, and perhaps over the other planets of the solar system, but probably not over planets of distant stars . . .' His voice died away. 'Sorry, I'm feeling faint.' He sank down on a spare chair under the window. 'It makes the Lord God so . . . so insignificant . . .' Sharon patted his shoulder.

'I rang the Bishop of Oxford about it,' he said.

All the committee began to talk at once.

Henry rose rather shakily to his feet. 'My dear Vicar, you must be imagining things. Or, if you aren't, then Tarquin Ferrers, who inscribed this tablet, was imagining things. Or, if not he, then this Kakkabuk was imagining things. Who is this chap, El Kakkabuk, anyway? I've never heard his name before. Can't we check up on him?' He glanced round at the ranks of solemn books on the shelves behind the chair where he had been seated.

Robin's head had sunk between his hands, and his reply was scarcely audible. 'The tablet is in some unintelligible

231

script. The accompanying letter from Tarquin Ferrers provides a translation, and he says that the mystic hanged himself after carving the tablet.'

'So where is this letter from Ferrers? Can we see it?'

'Yes, can we see it before you burn the church down?' asked Jeremy, smirking. 'Don't believe a word of this,' he advised Hetty in a whisper.

'We've lost the letter,' Robin confessed. 'It blew away.'

'Blew away?' echoed Stephen in disbelief.

'What will happen now?' asked Sam Aziz. 'Why you don't just throw away the tablet?'

'It's not as simple as that, Sam. According to Tarquin, you need only learn about this entity to find yourself doomed. I suppose that our sudden knowledge of its existence acts as a signal. At first, I thought to keep it to myself. I thought it was Tarquin's anti-religious hoax. But how can you suppress something so terrible? I had to come and tell you. I can't let the celebration continue under false pretences.'

Yvonne spoke up in her tremulous voice: 'Vicar, why don't you see this as an anti-religious hoax? How is it that this mystical Kakkabuk chap is the only person to discover this crazy truth about our universe?'

Stephen answered her: 'Let's suppose for a moment this revelation is true. It may have been discovered any number of times. But if all who discover it die shortly thereafter, then the secret remains secret.'

'So you believe all this, Steve?' Jeremy asked. 'Can we possibly believe it? It's exciting, of course, but isn't it all a bit of a fib?'

Stephen's response was cool. 'I don't know. But look at it this way. It makes about as much logical sense to me as any other religious theory. Hebrew. Christian. Hindu. Muslim. There are any number of crackpot faiths,

232

all endeavouring to explain why we exist here on Earth. This one sounds to me more likely, more all-embracing, than the others. Wouldn't you say this entity or process, or whatever it is, is made for the twenty-first century?'

'Steve, I'm unused to considering higher theological matters. As far as I'm concerned, the world goes on in its usual way. This tablet thing belongs to some ancient century.'

'It was biding its time.' Stephen gave a mirthless laugh. 'Unlike you and me, Jeremy, this cancerous entity is time-less. One can afford to wait, if waiting means absolutely nothing.'

'So you don't think I'm mad?' Robin asked, looking from one to another.

'I think you're crackers, to be honest. Sorry, Vicar!' said Jeremy.

'Yes, sir, you may be mad,' said Hetty. 'Or else this El Kakkabuk may have been indulging in a drugged nightmare.'

Stephen shrugged. 'You may have been driven mad, Robin. Religion can do that to one. No disrespect.'

Sharon, standing by the window, exclaimed on her husband's impoliteness to their vicar. He turned on her. 'He's not *my* vicar! Okay, so what possible motive could Tarquin have to perpetrate such a hoax? Hoaxers like to see their hoax work – the carefully balanced bucket of water fall on the victim's head – don't they? They don't lock their joke away for centuries behind a cupboard.'

A silence fell.

Penelope turned to Hetty and asked her what she thought about it all.

Hetty was hesitant. 'I really don't know. We ought to look at the tablet, oughtn't we?

233

'I'm inclined to agree with Stephen that our religious beliefs, or whatever, are crackpot. How can we estimate if this "process" is impossible or not when we really do not understand the function of our universe? We all have electronic things in our houses which work twenty-four hours a day almost for ever. The electric charge of the universe has not been calculated. Could it not power such an entity perpetually? That might really be the entire object of the universe, for all we know . . . Nor do we really understand how our biological systems work, what the role is of bacteria, for example.'

'But you said that Robin was mad.'

'Sorry for that. What I was really thinking was that when faced with such tremendous questions of existence we are all mad, nonrational. Because we are facing the irrational.'

Hetty paused. They were all looking at her. 'Suppose we are inclined to believe what this weird mystic has revealed. Isn't the stumbling block to believe that this process should be − what was the word? − *malign*? Then if it were malign, why did it permit intelligence into its system in the first place?'

'That's a good point,' Jeremy said.

'So, what do you think?' She turned to him.

'Me, I'm just a thriller writer, Hetty.'

'Isn't this thrilling enough for you?'

'I was sort of thinking . . . It all sounds so unscientific. Is it just a religious theory that people held in the old days? Like, I mean, in Ethiopia. But, then, isn't there a scientific theory, the string theory − or is it superstring theory? − about how all elementary particles were somehow linked when the universe began? In which case − well, that might have been the birth of this malign process. That's all I know. Not much, I admit.'

Hetty nodded and flashed Jeremy a supportive smile. 'Okay, so malign in the sense that you, Vicar,' with a nod to reassure Robin, 'phrased so well: malign in the way that a cancer is malign, malign without intention, but simply destroying life.'

'That's good,' Robin confessed. 'You put it well, Miss Zhou: "Malign without intention but simply destroying life."'

'I don't see why we should give this ancient writing credence,' said Rodney. 'One of Miss Zhou's earlier remarks made sense to me – that this was simply a drug-induced nightmare, experienced by some highly suspect mystic. They're two a penny out there still, aren't they?'

'Not really,' said Hetty. 'They've all moved here.'

While this exchange was continuing, Henry Wiverspoon had risen from his chair. Leaning against the bookcase for support, he was consulting one of its ancient volumes. He blew the dust from the top of it. Holding the volume open, he addressed Sharon. 'Dear lady, might I have a glass of water for my throat? The volumes are dusty . . . I feel quite inclined to have a coughing fit.'

'Of course, Henry. Perhaps you would care for a glass of wine?' She bestowed on them all a nervous smile. 'Perhaps in this moment of grave discussion you would all care for some wine?'

'No, dear, of course not,' said Stephen, looking severe. 'We need clear heads just now. No wine. Get Henry some water, as he requests.'

The poor woman left the room without a word.

Penelope folded her arms and stared hard at the grain of the table.

'Here we are,' said Henry, addressing the committee from the vantage-point of the bookcase. 'I am consulting Volume Two of 'The Encyclopaedia of Ancient Religions and

235

Religious Ceremonies, published by T. Frederick Unwin of Henrietta Street, Covent Garden, in AD 1814. Bless my cotton socks, here is an entry on this very Kakkabuk! Here the name of Kakkabuk is given as "Kakhabuh".' He spelt it out. 'We can safely assume it to be one and the same man.'

Stephen interpolated a remark: '1814 was the year in which the old Manor burnt down – on the site of which this present house stands.'

Henry shot him a look of contempt for the interruption, and began to read from the encyclopaedia in a louder voice than necessary . . .

"'Ahura Kakhabuh was a Zoroastrian, born in the fourth century BC. He forsook his religion in middle age to pursue a mystical investigation into the nature of stars. A mixture of certain herbs and drugs assisted his introspection." How well they wrote in the old days. Don't you like "assisted his introspection"?

"'He wrote a treatise on light, which in his regard was the thought process of an all-encompassing mind, illuminating all things. His controversial teachings on the evil pervading our world, to the contradiction of established savants, forced him to flee his native Persia and seek refuge in the mountainous regions of the Horn of Africa where he founded a short-lived church. His extreme and distasteful doctrines led him eventually to be hanged from a tree by angry disciples of Zoroaster. Kakhabuh's followers in time became Bogumils (*qv*)."'

Nodding towards the Vicar, Henry said, 'And now these extreme and distasteful doctrines have come knocking at your door, Father Robin. A strange turn of events indeed.'

'What is so terrible,' said Robin, 'is that St Clement's should have harboured these beliefs for so long. They have polluted the church.'

'Can't you do an exorcism ceremony?' asked Jeremy, suppressing a grin. Hetty kicked him gently under the table.

Penelope spoke: 'Can scientists explain the nature of light? I couldn't help thinking of a hymn I enjoyed as a girl, which talks about God the Invisible – do you remember? "'Tis only the brightness of light hideth Thee". I was interested in the encyclopaedia's phrase about Kakkabuk regarding light as "the thought processes of an all-encompassing mind". I can't help admiring that idea, particularly as it emerges from four centuries BC.'

'They weren't fools in those days,' replied Henry, tartly. 'That was the Age of Socrates, was it not? Put to death because he introduced strange gods to Athens – though none so strange as the god under our present consideration. Nor were they slaves to global economic machine systems, as we are now.' He looked up as Sharon brought him a glass and a newly opened bottle of Volvic mineral water. 'Thank you, my dear. Kind of you.' He patted her velvet-clad arm. 'You're very sweet.'

'So what are we going to do?' Stephen asked. 'It seems we may have established that this wretched affair is not merely a hoax dreamed up by a bad Reverend Tarquin Ferrers. What do we do now?'

'Go home and have a drink?' Jeremy suggested. Only Hetty and Stephen laughed.

Henry looked at his watch. It was seven forty-two. Addressing Stephen, he said, 'If I might suggest it, Mr Chairman, we need to consult with the most distinguished and learned member of our community, Professor Valentine Leppard. It is not eight o'clock, so he will not yet be in bed. Might we fetch him here, do you think? He is elderly now, but speaks good sense still. We might benefit from his understanding of the message on the

237

tablet and the viability of the cancerous god whose name the Vicar refuses to divulge.'

'I withhold the name only to protect you. Leppard is vehemently anti-Christian,' Robin said. 'He has no business here.'

'I entirely understand your point of view, Father, but your entity, whatever its appellation, is also vehemently anti-Christian – and, indeed, anti everything human. I believe you should not be too offended by Valentine's presence.'

'Yes, I will vouch for him,' said Rodney. 'An acerbic man, but never swears. I acted for him in setting up a contract with a publisher last year.'

'If it requires someone to fetch him in a car, I am happy to go.' This from Penelope, standing up.

So it was arranged.

Despite the warmth of the evening, Valentine Leppard arrived in hat and thick black overcoat. He surrendered the hat to Penelope and Sharon's care in the hall, but refused to divest himself of the coat. The committee stood politely as the old man entered the room. He shook hands with Stephen. A soft-backed chair was provided for him next to Henry. He sank into it, sighed, and looked at the committee through his misty spectacles.

Stephen Boxbaum took it upon himself to address a welcome speech to Valentine Leppard. He explained about the discovery of the ancient tablet, inscribed in cuneiform, with its doleful announcement that the universe had been created by a mindless and cancerous process.

Indeed, he said, it was not entirely clear if the universe were not the process itself.

'Forgive my butting in, Stephen,' Robin interposed. 'I was flustered when I mentioned cuneiform. The lettering on the tablet is not cuneiform. It's possibly written in

Amharic, a tongue classified as belonging to the south-east Semitic sub-family of the Afro-Asiatic group of languages.'

'Thank you, Vicar,' said Stephen, frowning at Jeremy, who was grinning. 'We look forward to seeing this remarkable tablet for ourselves in the near future.'

The committee now sought advice from Professor Leppard as to what credence they should give this inhuman process and what, were credence to be given, they should do about it.

Valentine cocked an eyebrow and regarded Stephen in silence.

Robin spoke again: 'Originally, I had a vision, you see, Professor Leppard. An angel came down and advised me to look into the back of the cupboard where the Kakkabuk tablet was hidden.'

Valentine's eyebrow remained raised as he asked Robin to describe the angel.

'It had wings, of course. Quite large feathery wings. It wore a yellow T-shirt.' He paused abruptly.

'An angel in a T-shirt? Now, that's a novelty! Angels fail to wear T-shirts in the Old Testament. Was there a legend printed on the T-shirt? "Drink More Guinness in Heaven" or whatever?'

'No. Not that. Something else.' Robin was attempting to hide his hostility from this newcomer.

'Do you feel able to tell us what that something was?'

'I would rather keep it to myself.'

'I see.' Valentine appeared to meditate, then said sharply, 'Are you prepared to tell us the name or title of this cancerous entity that claims to prevail over us, or would you rather keep that also to yourself?'

'Professor, it is advisable that I do not speak its name.'

Robin had stood his ground, despite a preference for

shifting sand. But Valentine Leppard's next remark left him unprepared.

'Is the name, by any chance, Opcean? Opcean, an acronym in the English version standing, however foolishly, for Original Pantocrat Creation of Eternal Antiquity and Nemesis?'

Robin placed a hand over his eyes. Overcome by the professor's statement, he asked almost pleadingly how Valentine could possibly have known this name.

Valentine said he would be happy to explain if Robin would tell them all what the message was on the angel's T-shirt.

'Very well. The T-shirt said – I imagine it was a joke of some kind – "King Kong Also Died for Our Sins".'

The tension building in the room was released in a gale of laughter. Jeremy fell about on his chair.

Only Valentine did not laugh. He reached into the recesses of his coat and brought forth a square of parchment, which he unfolded.

He smoothed it on the table before him with his old mottled hands. 'This is the communication from the Reverend Tarquin Ferrers, written in 1814 – incidentally, the year when the Congress of Vienna opened and when the good Pope Pius VII restored the Inquisition.' He had their attention now, and was relishing it.

'You may ask how I came to acquire this vital communication. It was blowing down the street, this historic document, with the other rubbish thrown down by the consumers of junk food who pass by my house. It stuck in my thorn hedge just as I was entering my gate. Needless to say, I took it indoors, read it, and thus made my acquaintance with Opcean. A somewhat disturbing meeting, I must admit.'

'And?' prompted Henry.

240

'So much for the prolegomena,' said Valentine. He folded his hands together and placed them before him on the parchment. Just then the sun came from behind a cloud and shed a late beam, like polished brass, in the room where they were talking. Most of those present took some comfort from it.

'You will recall,' said Valentine, 'if you have any learning at all, that Plato's Symposium or Supper, concludes, after all the discussion of ideas, with Socrates taking a bath and "spending the rest of the day in an ordinary manner". I have always admired that conclusion. However grand and searching the ideas that beset us, nevertheless we can and should spend our days in an ordinary manner.

'Injurious ideas disturb us frequently. It was an archae-ologist by name Gordon Childe, so I believe – I met him once, and took an instant dislike to the man – no, possibly that was someone else. Anyhow, it was Childe who prop-agated a theory that we humans were descended from what he liked to call "killer apes". And, indeed, there was a period last century when it seemed that nations like the Third Reich and the Soviet Union had been taken over by apes of that very ilk.

'Now we entertain the more benevolent belief that we are descended from "hunter-gatherers". "Hunter-gatherers" have a Robin Hood touch: they sound a lot nicer than killer apes. Indeed, despite many horrors insep-arable from what we term public life, we live in an age that does a great deal of gathering – of scientific data and so forth. We have seen most impressive changes affecting our lives in many ways. Nevertheless, men still love women and women men, which is what I intend by the expres-sion, "spending the day in an ordinary manner".

'A conflict of visions continually disturbs us. We see evidence of this in art. We may admire the elegant attire

241

of the élite in the canvases of John Singer Sargent or the distorted forms of the dispossessed in the canvases of Francis Bacon. Or both at once.'

'Val,' said Henry, interrupting, 'we do not at present wish for the history of human evolution, or for a lecture on art, only your thoughts on this cancerous Opcean, if I may venture to pronounce its name without being struck down.'

'Sooner or later, you will be struck down – as we all shall be,' replied the professor, with a show of equability. 'You may then blame it on Opcean or the great god Pan or mighty Baal, as you wish. Nothing will defer your departure . . . We all look forward to the day of our death with varying degrees of fortitude.

'What I am trying to demonstrate is this: that whatever grand theory prevails, we are wise to live an ordinary life, resisting the prevailing idea as staunchly as we can. If you study the history plays of that hasty, shoddy dramatist William Shakespeare, you cannot but be struck by the long-held misapprehension that England owned France. Many gallant men died for that idea – all baloney though it was.'

'However, it has endowed France with many glorious castles,' Stephen interposed.

'Sharon,' said Valentine, interrupting himself, 'you stand uneasily by that window. Do pull up a chair and join us at the table. We are eager to share your opinions. Be at home in your own home.'

She said, 'You are mistaken, Professor, if you have the idea that I regard this as home.'

Nevertheless, she pulled up a chair and at last sat down.

Valentine was shaking his head.

Robin said, 'Excuse me, Professor Leppard, but I cannot wait idly here while you expound – enjoyable though

242

your lectures may be to some of us. Will you or will you not advise the committee on what we are to do about this cancerous thing among us? Hanging over us, perhaps I should say.'

'Oh, but I am advising, Vicar! You and the rest of Hampden Ferrers must go on living your humble, humdrum lives as if nothing has happened, just as you have been doing for three centuries since Tarquin Ferrers wrote what turned out to be his farewell letter.

'You can't do anything about this Opcean. Perhaps Opcean is one more vile idea, like killer apes. You may as well pursue your ordinary days, rich and poor alike, with whatever relish you can muster.'

'You are intolerably condescending to us,' said Hetty Zhou. 'I wish to hear no more of this kind of talk.'

He turned the gleam of his spectacles towards her. 'If you are accusing me of despising the dunce who cuts my hair for being a barber or a plumber for being a plumber, then condescending I am, madam.'

Hetty stood up by her chair. 'It happens that today I engaged a plumber, since I find that my entire house needs new pipes. He asked me for a few minutes alone in which to think. I kept out of the way. He then drew a plan, with a new position for my hot-water tank and a complete radiator circuit for the house, cutting down by about twenty-five per cent on the length of piping required. This man has a wonderful spatial sense that I lack. I admire him and his skills. Please do not insult him.'

'So much for your plumbing, madam. Of great interest to all, I'm sure. Now let us return to a subject of slightly more importance: this creature that rules the universe.'

Hetty was about to leave, but Jeremy caught her arm and, by cajoling, persuaded her to stay.

'First, I must ask you this,' said Valentine, apparently

undisturbed by the hostility he had provoked. 'The proportion of size of a human being to the universe has often been discussed. It seems we stand halfway between a star and an elementary particle. However, it is difficult to judge the extent of the universe. We can measure it in light years, certainly, but I ask you, how big is it really? What in a light year constitutes the actual qualities of time and distance?'

He looked challengingly around the table.

'Let us entertain for a moment a philosophical question, a cosmological question. This is much to the point.

'Let us suppose that what we call the universe is actually an animal's bladder. No, I'm serious. The germs that breed in our mouths may believe they live in a universe as vast as we hold our universe to be. We may all be contained in a pig's bladder.

'You see, we don't have any idea about the answer to such questions. We have no standard for comparison. But, in almost all respects, the answer doesn't matter. Perhaps that is why the question is so rarely asked.

'Now. This uncomfortable thought is directly germane to the question of Opcean. Is it some form of cancer, as implied? Consider our universe to be an animal's bladder, and the animal to be suffering from cancer . . . Can we escape? Might we build a gigantic spaceship of some sort and get out of here?' He gestured dismissively. 'You know the answer as well as I do. We can't do any such thing. We are powerless.

'So we might as well expel from our minds any such questioning, and all get on with our devastatingly ordinary lives. All, that is, except for this eastern lady and her plumber, rejoicing in his ecstatic vision of running copper pipes under the floorboards of a semi-detached.'

'Hang on!' Stephen exclaimed, rising to his feet. 'That's

244

enough of that kind of talk. I'm sorry, Hetty. Professor Leppard's idea of humour is not mine. Let's have a break here. We need to discuss whether we can continue to plan for the church's celebration. We can take a stroll in the garden before dusk falls. And then perhaps,' shooting a look at his wife, 'we might have the glass of wine mentioned earlier.'

Valentine Leppard remained seated at the table. He had thrust his hands into the pockets of his coat. All the others headed for the French windows, except Hetty, who approached the old man. 'You must be very unhappy, sir, to enjoy being unpleasant. Do you regard unpleasantness as a necessary condition of your age?'

He responded quite jovially, if in a frosty manner, 'In my case, it's voluntary.'

'But is it not a means of making yourself unhappy?'

Valentine was seen to shrink back into his overcoat, like a tortoise retreating into its shell.

'I have no one left to care a jot whether I am happy or unhappy. Nor do I care greatly myself.'

She stood looking down at him, swivelling one finger on the surface of the table, as if it were trying to decide for her whether to retreat or talk. It came to a positive decision. 'If I might suggest it, sir, many people care devotedly if happiness anywhere can be increased. Happiness is a form of health. I see unhappiness in this house, between our host and hostess. It is – uncomfortable.'

'What about it? Everyone's unhappy.' But he spoke without his usual conviction.

Hetty shook her head. 'I have a grandfather who lives in Amoy, a port on the Chinese coast. He is approaching ninety and is happy and good.'

Valentine gave a kind of snort. He was gazing ahead,

not looking up at Hetty. 'You're not suggesting I take a trip to Amoy to meet your grandfather?'

'You deliberately misunderstand me. However . . . why not? Fly to Amoy. It would do you an incalculable amount of good to meet my revered grandfather. My point is that he was once a really grumpy man. Nothing pleased him. Many things made him miserable and caused him to complain. He was always a hard man with his workers. He enjoyed a bad reputation. It was said that he liked to see people shrink from him, including members of our family.

'Then one day a young woman came to him. She was married to one of his workers. She told my grandfather that she was sorry he was so unhappy. She kissed him and said something like, "You have a strong will: you can decide to be happy." He took what she said to heart. And so he did become happy. Overnight. Giving up misery, like giving up smoking.'

Valentine turned his withered old face up to her. 'Are you offering to kiss me? I would not object!' He gave a dry laugh.

Hetty also laughed. 'No, that's not at all the deal I have in mind. Your general rudeness is an indication of your misery, not your intelligence, as you may think. My plumber is much more sensible than you because he has contented himself with his station in life, and enjoys his work. You will get a kiss if you say to me, with determination, that you have decided to be happy. You must flick the switch. Then, when I see the magical transformation, I will be glad to kiss you.'

A tear stood in his eye. 'You are playing a cruel game with me, you little minx! Would that it happened more often.'

She shook her head and wagged a finger at him. 'It is

246

not a game. That is just your perception of what I am saying. We understand from science that emotion lies at the basis of all intellectual decisions. I believe that the converse is also true: that intellect can control emotion. The two are closely linked. It is your attitude of mind that makes you unhappy, not the external world.'

He sighed heavily. 'Why do you take the trouble to tell me this? You could be in the garden with younger people.'

She faced him directly. 'I so admire your command of speech and logic, Professor. I liked your cultivation, I liked to hear your arguments. You moved us.'

'I corrupted you by my beauty, eh? Like Phryne before the judges.'

Hetty ignored the allusion. 'But I could see you were such a sad, sad person and I felt – well, I wanted to be near you and possibly to, oh, to wave a magic wand and make you – help you make yourself into a happier person.'

He was silent, digesting what she had said. At the same time, he studied the beauty and calm of her face. 'I was impolite to you. Why should you care?'

'Why should your rudeness hurt me? I am made of steel. Because I care. Because I think relationships are often broken, but can be mended. Quite easily mended. It's a simple trick. Is that not what happened to Scrooge in Charles Dickens's little tale? I rejoice in being able to mend people . . . We all need help so much.'

Valentine found that tears were trickling down his cheeks, choosing the best runnels by which to escape. He pulled out a white lawn handkerchief and mopped his face. 'Listen, Hetty, if I may use your name . . .' He choked back a sob. 'Your concern . . . it's remarkable. Even if it is a trick. It's amazing that you are here in Ferrers. That I am here in this room with you. The two of us.

247

That you are so beautiful and kind . . .' He blew his nose. 'I don't have to become happy. My heart is full of wonder! Is that not the same as happiness?'

'Not quite, but nearly – so you get the kiss anyhow.'

She bent down to kiss his forehead, but he caught hold of her and pulled her closer so that he could kiss her cheek. 'Praise be you didn't bring your plumber along . . .'

They looked at each other, smiling. Val extended a bony hand. She allowed her own slender one to enter into its frail grip.

The Manor garden was full of sweet scents at this hour, poised between day and night. The scabius with its white blossom, a purple ring at the heart of each flower, and the Portuguese laurel, with its spikes of intricate florets like stars, vied with each other to make the evening air delicious. Dusk intensified the sensuousness. The committee wandered aimlessly, for a while not talking. Penelope refrained from lighting a cigarette in order to inhale the atmosphere.

Rodney, hands linked behind his back, set off up the artificial hill in a brisk stalk, as if saying to himself, I'm still a solicitor, whether in a garden or no. Robin, Henry, Yvonne and Sam stood together, enjoying being outside. Sharon had stayed indoors.

Stephen came up behind Penelope and took her arm. He had folded his spectacles and tucked them into his jacket pocket. 'Oh, Penny dearest, you know I am weak and foolish. I am consulting a man I know in London. My divorce will go through and then I hope you will marry me, and live with me, and love me, and no longer be cross with me.'

She wanted to ask him where Sharon would go, but

248

something within her would not let the thought escape into words. Although she imagined that she had realised she did not love him any more, she so rejoiced to have a man courting her that she leaned towards him, saying, 'I know it is difficult for you.'

'And for you, dearest.'

Then, to her embarrassment, she found herself saying that she just wanted to be with him and to live anywhere, it did not matter where. Maybe in Montpellier, which she had visited for a holiday . . . where the weather was good. Not, perhaps, in Ferrers, where too many old memories lingered.

'Oh, I couldn't leave the Manor, dearest. Don't you like it here? I've spent a fortune on getting the place up to scratch. Perhaps we could have a summer cottage somewhere like Montpellier as well . . .'

'You value this place more than me?' How she hated her question and the pain behind the question.

Before it could be answered, Jeremy Sumption was beside them and Stephen's arm was sliding from Penelope's arm, and Jeremy was asking if they really had to put up with Leppard's lecturing when they went back indoors.

Stephen replied that it was easy to see how they had moved into a discussion of the nature of the universe. It was an important and interesting question.

'Okay,' said Jeremy. 'But I'm for taking the old boy's advice, that we just get on with our ordinary lives. You can't really imagine that we're going to kick the bucket just because we've heard the name – well, I mean, the name Opcean? I want to know what we do about the Vicar and whether or not we go on with this celebration.'

'What do you think, Jeremy?'

249

Jeremy gave a short laugh. 'Considering Hetty's pa is going to chip in with — what? About one eighty-five thou, we'd be nuts not to, wouldn't we? When would such a chance turn up again? The National Lottery? Forget it!'

'I'm with you there, but Robin seems to think he's under threat of imminent death.'

'What? From a pack of wild dogs?'

'Perhaps we should ask to see this tablet of his,' Penelope suggested, 'before we make any real decisions.'

'Good idea,' both men said, as one. And they all went back inside.

When the committee had settled back into their places, Valentine Leppard said, 'According to Father Robin, the tablet — which we have yet to examine — refers to the Great Originator of our universe. Supposing the tablet indeed to have been written centuries ago, the concept "universe" would mean something different from what we now understand by the term. For instance, we now know, or think we know, that the universe is almost thirteen billion years old. Such figures would have been even more incomprehensible to El Kakkabuk than they are to us.

'We don't even know what shape the universe is. We may think of it as a balloon ever expanding as mysterious forces blow it up, but there's a perfectly sensible man in London who, if I understand him aright, thinks the universe is flat.

'But we do know the universe exists. In saying that, I am merely conferring intelligibility on our experience of the world through grammar. To talk about "the universe in itself", Kant's good old *Ding an sich*, is nonsense. Why? Because to take away language and grammar leaves nothing, nothing that can be spoken about.'

'Sorry, I don't get this,' said Jeremy. 'Nor do I get any wine, it seems.'

Valentine ignored the interruption. 'I'm not talking idly here, my friends, because this is one of the problems I am wrestling with in the book I am writing, whose title is, as Sharon well remembers, *City Utterly Fallen*.'

'How could I forget it?' Sharon exclaimed.

Valentine smiled across the room at her. 'Oh, remembering is easy. It's forgetting that's the problem.'

He returned to his talk only after he had struggled out of his overcoat, at which task both Hetty and Henry helped.

'That's better. I am trying to be brief, my friends. So I foolishly simplify. Intelligibility is the big problem. Science tries perpetually to make the universe intelligible. Once, theism took on that job, and has been found wanting. Basically, the Vicar's tablet offers a theist approach to solving the problem of the universe and its and our existence.

'But perhaps – just consider this! – the existence of the world, the universe, may be *for ever unintelligible*. If that is the case, then neither science nor any version of theism can compel intelligibility!'

The committee looked at each other uneasily. This was certainly not what they had come together for in the first place.

'Go on,' said Henry. 'What follows?'

'As I have said, the Christian religion, much like other religions, was devised to satisfy our craving for explanations of what we are doing – or supposed to be doing – on Earth. It has made many boss-shots, for which it had been forgiven – for instance, in believing that the Earth was the centre of the universe. But I will resist dwelling on that point.

251

'If we took the God theory on board, we would simply multiply our problems. We would have to ask, "But why God? How God? Where God?" In a way, the Opcean solution is far more ingenious because it seems not to take us outside the bounds of the universe. It is an internal cancer, having no meaning, no intention, no precise location. Certainly no heavenly plan.

'For El Kakkabuk and his followers, his solution must have been immensely satisfying. This druggy mystic discovered a way of feeding the metaphysical hunger that we all feel for a reason behind the existence of the world.

'But his solution will not work. So, he was hanged for preaching this ingenious doctrine. Later, Tarquin Ferrers was devoured by wild dogs. But these are just coincidences, separated by many centuries, dragged in to support the argument. Kakkabuk's guesses have no meaning. They are intelligent enough, but they have no meaning. They cannot have meaning. Why?'

'Blimey, you tell us!' Jeremy exclaimed.

Valentine gave what passed for a smile. 'Because there is no answer to the question of reality. Nothing can adequately describe the workings of the universe or of existence. No formulae, no words, no thought, could reach that far. Or, if there were to be a description, then our brains are not equipped to comprehend it.'

'And where exactly is the human spirit in all this?' Robin asked.

'Where it always was, of course. We aren't going to let a little thing like our position in the universe get us down. We should rejoice or at least be happy that all our world pictures are inadequate, doomed to be inadequate. Our universe is inscrutable. I judge that this tablet and its message are therefore irrelevant.' He made a gesture of dismissal with his right hand, and ceased speaking.

In the silence that followed, Hetty whispered in his ear, 'Congratulations, Val! I heard you say "happy"!'

'I'll say it over and over.'

'All the same, your conclusions are gloomy.'

'Not at all. They're a relief, you splendid lady.'

Stephen Boxbaum rose to his feet. 'Thank you, Professor Leppard, for your analysis of the situation. I, at least, am reassured that you have penetrated to the essence of Kakkabuk's message. That message cannot have the effect on us that it did on the Reverend Tarquin Ferrers. His is just one more guess – a dramatic one – about the nature of the universe. And that nature cannot be encompassed by human thought.

'You, Father Robin,' he turned to the Vicar, 'can also be reassured. Your life is not under threat.'

Robin was hesitant. 'No wild dogs, then?'

'They don't exist. You can frame the tablet as a harmless curio or send it to the British Museum for safekeeping.'

'I vote we keep it for exhibition during our celebrations.' The voice was Rodney's, and for once he carried the committee with him.

Stephen turned to address Valentine again. 'However, Professor, I think your analysis of the situation digs too deep. For most of us, there is no doubt about ordinary reality. Perhaps I should not use that phrase, perhaps "ordinary reality" is an oxymoron.

'Let me tell you that my reality certainly includes Hampden Ferrers itself, and England, Britain. Britain represents stability to me, and the fortitude that stability requires while in the midst of change. In the dark days of Hitler's Germany, when war was declared, Britain stood alone to represent democracy and freedom. Neither the Soviet Union nor the United States of America came to our aid.

253

'That dreadful age is a long time ago now, but many people still carry memories like scars of the days through which their grandfathers and grandmothers lived. We should also carry memories of Britain's courage, when it stood against the insane cruelty of the Third Reich. For me, as a member of a family of persecuted Jews who came here to find shelter and build their lives anew, that courage, that stability, always remains a reality.'

Valentine spread wide his arms and gave a broad smile. 'How can I disagree, my friend? Metaphysics is one thing, patriotism another. Now, who will drive me home to bed?'

Henry looked taken aback. 'Bless my cotton socks, he's actually smiling!'

VIII

Photo Hetty Zhou

The alarm rang. Sam Aziz put out a hand and swatted the bell. He sat up in bed and scratched his temples.

Rima opened a rheumy eye and closed it again.

'Waken yourself, you lazy person!' exclaimed Sam, genially rolling Rima about in the bed. 'Time to rise and shine! I had such a good time last night. My friends on the committee are really intellectual. Often I did not understand what they were saying. Professor Leppard is really brilliant at that.'

'Oh, do leave off, *pyara*!'

'He thinks we all live in a pig's bladder. Didn't I always say so myself?'

'Good, good. Nice for you.' She groaned. She made a faint attempt to get up. Sam had already left the bed.

'This is reality,' he mumbled, as he showered and dressed. 'Bloody reality! The firm of Carr's could make a reality biscuit. "Eat a Reality and Feel More Real." I'm sure it would be a bestseller.' He was a minute or two ahead of his usual timetable. He unbolted the back door and went out into his narrow strip of garden to see how

255

his runner beans were growing. A scraggy cat disappeared over the fence.

The beans looked good. Some were a sprightly four inches high. Sam scattered a few blue slug pellets about the plot and returned contentedly to his shop.

After unlocking the door, he stood on the pavement to gaze up and down the road, awaiting the morning's papers. The street was deserted. He liked this time of day. He kicked an empty beer can into the gutter. As he knew, there was serious trouble all over the world: the continuing economic crisis in Argentina, the difficulties in Iraq, starvation all over Africa, the stand-off between Israel and Palestine, the confrontation between India and Pakistan. Sam reserved his particular contempt for the latter. He was glad he was away from that part of the world, derided its politics, congratulated himself that he was British.

Besides, his son was coming out of hospital today. His legs were intact, thanks to the skill of the surgeon. And the surgeon was an Asian.

Behind him, he heard noises emanating from the kitchen. He detected the sound of slippers on the concrete floor. Rima was up. Probably mixing them both a Cadbury's.

A figure was approaching the shop. Even with the early sun behind him, reducing him to a silhouette, Duane Ridley was easily recognizable by his swaggering walk and his new cockatoo haircut.

'Morning, Sam, how ya doing?'

'Hello, Duane. The papers will be here any minute. Go in and see Rima. She will give you a Cadbury's, if you're lucky.'

'I've just had a mug of tea, thanks.'

They stood together, staring idly across the road.

'What do you think of the universe, Duane? Can it be explained?'

256

'Dunno. Never tried. It's not my thing.'

'Maybe it's a good job it can never be explained. People would only make political capital out of it.'

'Most likely.'

A brief crying fit came from the Williams baby in the Williams house. Duane grunted, possibly expressing his contempt for all weakling creatures.

'How's Kyle?' Sam asked.

'Okay.'

'Do you love her?'

Duane regarded Sam with curiosity. 'She's all right. Why?'

'Do you love her, Duane? Forgive me asking.'

'Yeah, like I say, she's all right. A good kiddie.'

'But do you love her?'

Duane sniggered. 'I'm shagging her, aren't I?'

'So you can't answer the question?'

'What's it to do with you any road?'

Sam wanted to say that he regarded the question of people loving each other as everybody's business. He felt it obscurely, but could not express his feelings in words. Nor was he up to trying to express it to Duane. Nor, indeed, as he had to admit to himself, was the relationship between Duane and Kyle something he should pry into.

He turned and went into the shop, leaving Duane to rock on his heels on the pavement, hands in pockets.

Rima was shuffling about in her tattered old satin dressing-gown. Sam had bought it for her in Brighton, as a birthday present – how many years ago? Her hair now had grey streaks in its thick mass. She held out a mug to Sam.

'Here's your Cadbury's, Sammy, *pyara*.'

They were leaning together against the sink, sipping the hot chocolate.

'Sam Junior back today.'

'Feast tonight! After the shop will be close.' She giggled with pleasure. 'To ask them up above or not? Zadanka and WW?'

'Nice. How about Duane and Kyle?'

Rima laughed. 'I know your jokes!'

The roar of an engine came from the street.

'Oh, there's Smith's van now.'

Sam set down his mug and hurried out to say hello to the black driver of the WH Smith's van.

'You're in the news all right, mate!' the driver said. He dumped the bundles of newspapers at Duane's feet and drove away in the direction of Nuneham Courtenay.

'What did he mean?'

'Here, look at this, Sam!' Duane exclaimed. 'Christ!'

On the front pages of both tabloids and broadsheets was a picture of a man with a strange donkey head and long ears, balancing naked on a five-barred gate. In tiny letters along the right hand side of the picture ran the legend: 'Photo Hetty Zhou.'

The headlines varied from 'OXEN IN OXON?' to 'FUNNY FOLK IN FERRERS'. The tabloids made the point that donkeys turning into men in the peaceful English countryside confirmed the judgement of townies that remote villages were places of strange dark rituals.

'Thank the living God these bastards never heard about Kakkabuk,' said Sam, as he helped Duane drag the bundles into the shop.

But that was to come later, when the Bishop of Oxford visited the Church of St Clement's in Hampden Ferrers and pontificated before reporters on what was now known as the Ferrers Tablet.

AD 2003

May, and the rain was holding off. The high street had been closed to traffic. The barriers were up at the west end, by the bridge over the brook, and at the east end, just past Professor Leppard's house. Rerouted traffic went via Cotes Road – from where, in consequence, many complaints had been launched, to be overcome one by one.

Sonia and the Jolliffe sons were showing people round the exterior of the church. The new buttress was much admired.

A banner stretched across the road, from Marion Barnes's house, number twelve, to the Pink House. It read 'ST CLEMENT'S CHURCH – TODAY 1500 YEAR OLD. WELCOME ALL!'

Indeed, many visitors had come to share in the pleasures of the day. ITV was there, doing interviews with prominent members of the community.

The entire street was decked with bunting. Bunting clung to trees, lampposts, open windows. Red, white and blue was everywhere. Even the members of the Celebrations Committee were astonished by the transformation.

Everywhere there were smiling faces. People found themselves overtaken by an inexplicable happiness.

Up in the gutters, and on some roofs, pigeons perched, looking down without interest on the vivacious scene, just waiting.

Stephen Boxbaum was one of the heroes of the hour. In his opening speech, he introduced Mr Huey Zhou, Hetty's millionaire father, and spoke of the local community.

'Human beings have always found it necessary to live together in communities. Most animals, like my cat Bingo, live solitary lives. We humans are the exception. At the same time, there are difficulties – difficulties with neighbours, difficulties with lodgers, difficulties even within marriage. Life's never free of problems. Ask our vicar about that.

'One form of community, perhaps the most exciting, is the city. Our neighbour, the city of Oxford, with all its resources of learning and the arts, is a benevolent example. But the village is another example of both the difficulty and the happiness – the sheer necessity – for us to be together. If our church has stood for one and a half millennia, then so has the village. The church has been our buttress. And today of all days we celebrate ourselves as a community. Today is the day when we love not only each other but the village of Hampden Ferrers. Long may it continue!'

Tables had been set up along half the length of the closed strip of road, with attendant chairs borrowed from schools and many houses. Most of the wives and a very few of the husbands had been baking or making sandwiches. The pâtisserie and Sam Aziz's Hill's Stores had contributed. As a result, the tables were laden with good things to eat.

Penelope Hopkins had provided three electric urns, borrowed from Brookes, which were now distributing tea to all and sundry. A trio sat on a platform outside the vicarage, currently playing 'All You Need is Love' and other old Beatles hits in the most soothing manner. As Jeremy Sumption said, 'As if the Beatles had been born in Ferrers instead of Liverpuddle.'

Stephen and Sharon Boxbaum were running a bring-and-buy stall, and doing good business. Those who had rid their houses of one lot of ornaments were eager to replace them with another.

Sam, Rima and Sammy Aziz Junior – the latter still limping slightly – were helping with the teas, as were WW and Doreen Aylet.

Earlier, donkey races had been run in an adjacent meadow. Four donkeys had been hired from a man who still did donkey rides on the sands of Great Yarmouth. Excited young village boys had ridden the beasts, only one winning, several falling off. John Greyling was in charge of this entertainment.

The Chinese contingent was seated rather grandly on chairs in the front garden of number twenty-two. The benefactor of this event, Mr Huey Zhou, was a plump man with dyed fair hair, immaculately dressed in a lounge suit. His long, hard face showed no sign of age – or, indeed, of pleasure, although he occasionally laughed at something said by his entourage of aunties, sisters and brothers, who had accompanied him from Hong Kong to witness this archaic event.

Penelope Hopkins was accompanying them, the heroine of the hour, with an express invitation to Hong Kong in the autumn to cruise on the Zhou yacht. She had not given up loving and yearning for Stephen, but she had given up hope.

261

Also of this entourage was Hetty Zhou, who had been expressly forbidden to marry Jeremy Sumption. 'Make with him once, take precautions, and then be finish,' said her father.

'Oh, we've done all that, Pop,' she said impatiently.

'My dear child, the day after tomorrow we fly to the United States. There you will forget all about this poor English writer and will no doubt meet a handsome young American millionaire who never writes a word.'

Hetty's sister, Judy, had wandered off into the woods with Rupert Boxbaum. There, to their embarrassment, they encountered Duane Ridley and Kyle Bayfield in a prone position.

Henry Wiverspoon was sitting in Professor Leppard's house with the old man, who was feeling unwell. They were listening to CDs of Wagner's *Götterdämmerung*, which the professor felt was appropriate to the day.

Rodney Williams had become reconciled with his sister Marion. They were looking after the Prettiest Baby Competition with Judith, and fully expecting that baby Nathaniel Williams would win. However, Cherie Aylet, Ishtar Squire and other infants were also competing. It was going to be a close-run thing. The judges, two of the Cotes men, were going to make a friend for life, as well as several enemies for life.

Bettina Squire was with Ishtar. Although she was smiling and chatting with friends, she had been disappointed in trying to persuade Father Robin to allow her to exhibit her paintings in the church.

Starman Barrie, together with his new friend, Dotty Ridley, was running an Aunt Sally in the grounds of the Carpenter's. Dotty's mother, Andrea, was running a cake stall; business was slack and Andrea was engaged in conversation with a striking-looking man who had just arrived in the village. 'Oh, you're French, are you?'

When he replied that his mother was French, Andrea immediately had a vision of a decent village in the Auvergne where one played *boules* and ate delectable *al fresco* meals with amusing local artists. In the background, a sardonic but kindly musician in a beret played an accordion. She sighed, feeling young again. 'We must see more of each other,' she said.

'Naturally,' he replied.

Among the many tents and booths set up along the street was one with Yvonne and her publicity lady in attendance. In Yvonne's tent piles of her book were exhibited for sale. It was newly published in a resplendent book jacket. The publishers had rechristened *Cockerels over Cotes* with the more catchy title *Happiness at Hampden Ferrers*.

The Ferrers Tablet was in the next booth with a translation and a copy of Tarquin Ferrers's letter, printed off from Marion's computer. Old Joe Cotes was guarding it, as he said, 'with his life' – and a newly sharpened reaping hook. Lingering outside the booth, occasionally strolling to and consequently fro, was Sergeant 'Other' Arsich, upholding the rule of law despite his resemblance to an ostrich.

St Clement's Church had rung its new peal of bells. Earlier, parishioners had been able to ascend the steep, winding new staircase to get to the top of the tower and photograph the proceedings below. The views from the tower were splendid. In one direction, it was possible to see the spire of the church in Nuneham Courtney, and in the other direction, the bare crest of Molesey Hills, sunny and calm in the warm sunshine.

Now all such spectators were banished. The church was required for the serious purpose of holy matrimony.

Most of the pews were filled. Violet and Wheelbarrow Bingham were there, dressed in their Sunday best. Witnesses to the marriage were Fred Martinson, accompanied by Nurse Ann Longbridge, the poet John Westall, and Maria's aunt, who was in charge of Maria's nine-year-old daughter.

The Reverend Robin Jolliffe was officiating, clad in his best surplice. A mouse-trap set in the lady chapel had caught a mouse. Robin kicked it out of sight as he went to the altar.

The lovely Contessa di Medina Mirtelli, Maria Caperalli, newly divorced, was being married to Frank Martinson. They stood side by side at the altar, hardly able to contain their happiness. The organ played, swelling to match their hearts.

Robin was asking Maria formally, 'Will you have this man, Frank Martinson, to be your lawful wedded husband, to live together after God's ordinance in the holy estate of matrimony? Will you love, honour and cleave to him in sickness and in health, forsaking all others, as long as you both shall live?'

'Oh, s`, s`,' cried Maria, 'Indeed I will, and gladly, gladly!'

'"I will" would be good enough for me,' said Robin, quietly.